DER
e
NT

church

S, INC.

This Dover edition, first published in 1987,
is an unabridged republication of the work as published by
Duffield & Company, New York, 1931
(first British edition by Collins, London, 1930).

Manufactured in the United States of America
Dover Publications, Inc., 31 East 2nd Street, Mineola, N.Y. 11501

Library of Congress Cataloging-in-Publication Data

Whitechurch, Victor L. (Victor Lorenzo), 1868–1933.
Murder at the pageant.

I. Title.
PR6045.H227M8   1987   823′.912   87-9015
ISBN 0-486-25528-X (pbk.)

1

"The sedan-chair used in this scene is the chair in which Queen Anne was carried on the occasion of her visit to Frimley Manor in 1705."

So ran the footnote on the programme of the pageant which was being held in the spacious grounds of Frimley Manor two hundred and twenty-four years after the above date; a pageant in aid of the funds of the local hospital at Chiltonbury, the neighboring market-town.

The scenario of the pageant had been written, and the various historical scenes in it produced, by Captain Roger Bristow, well known among his friends as a first-rate organiser of amateur theatricals, and down on the aforesaid programme as the "Master of the Pageant."

And so, once again, after the lapse of all those years, a bit of family tradition was being revived and the visit of that long-defunct sovereign was being enacted.

On the broad, grassy slopes of a rising bit of ground on the right front of the house sat, or stood, a large audience, drawn from the surrounding villages and from Chiltonbury. Before the spectators was a great sweep of lawn, intersected by the carriage drive which led from the high road to the manor, a drive which ended in a wide oval immediately in front of the house.

Some three hundred yards on its way from the house towards the road this carriage-drive crossed an ornamental bridge which spanned a stream running through the grounds. On either side were clumps of trees, forming, just then, the wings of the great scene. Behind one of these clumps, unseen by the audience, but in full view of the front of the house, a large marquee had been erected, forming dressing-rooms and a centre for the assemblings of the numerous properties.

1

Amid these sylvan surroundings Queen Anne came once again to Frimley Manor, in the traditional way in which she had come in 1705. For the story, handed down in the family, was that the Queen had alighted from her coach near the entrance gate, and had been carried up the drive in the sedan-chair belonging to the manor; carried by four stalwart serving-men wearing the livery of Sir Henry Lynwood, the Lord of the Manor.

So there it was, all over again, arranged accurately in detail by Captain Roger Bristow. From the terrace in front of the house came a little procession, led by the present Sir Henry Lynwood, all in the costume of the period, moving slowly towards the bridge, where a halt was made. Then a fanfare on the royal trumpets ushered another procession, which came into sight from behind a clump of trees, the procession of that amiable monarch, Queen Anne, with her attendant courtiers, ladies-in-waiting and soldiers.

Four lackeys arrayed in the historical livery of the Lynwoods— green and orange—bore the old sedan-chair, with Mrs. Cresswell, an old friend of the family, seated regally therein, wearing over her costume what Queen Anne certainly did *not* wear in 1705, her famous pearl necklace. Beside the chair walked Captain Bristow himself—it was the only scene in which he was taking a part—personating the celebrated Churchill, afterwards Duke of Marlborough, full wig and all.

On the bridge the bearers set down the chair, and Sir Harry Lynwood, hat in hand, bowing low, welcomed to his house a Queen—who extended her hand from the chair, through the open window, for him to kiss.

It was all very prettily done, and the spectators applauded accordingly. Perhaps, though, the sedan-chair drew as much of their attention as did its occupant. Some of them, friends of the Lynwoods, had often seen it as it stood in the hall of the manor, its long carrying-poles withdrawn from the side sockets and piled in the corner behind it. But the majority of the onlookers had never seen the sedan-chair before, though many had heard of it.

It was a very handsome old chair, lacquered in black and dark red and overlaid with brass filigree-work. The poles, also, were similarly ornamented. One of the bearers lifted the roof, which was hinged, slightly, and tilted it back, while another opened the side door. Queen Anne rose from her seat, stepped out, and graciously accepted the hand of her host. They led the way, followed by their respective retainers, to the entrance of the house, into which they disappeared. The historic scene came to an end.

The sedan-chair, having served its purpose, was carried by the liveried serving-men into the marquee behind the trees. People glanced at their programmes to see what was the next tableau.

It was late, but still daylight on the long summer day, when the pageant was over. The big audience had melted away. Players, drawn from all over the neighbourhood, were departing; many of them still wearing costumes which looked incongruous enough in car or on bicycle. At length only a little group, gathered beside the marquee, remained—the members of Sir Harry Lynwood's family and the house party invited for the occasion. All of them were in pageant costumes.

Sir Harry, a tall, upright man of about sixty, wore the garb of the reign of Queen Anne. Captain Bristow, of medium height and a little inclined to err on the side of stoutness, appeared as the Duke of Marlborough. Harry Lynwood, the eldest son, who had taken part in an earlier scene, was dressed in the trunk hose, puffed and slashed doublet, and flat cap of the Tudor period; his brother Charles, as a dandy of the Regency, wore white pantaloons strapped tightly at the feet, long blue coat, brocaded waistcoat. Anstice Lynwood looked perfectly charming in Early Victorian high-waisted gown and bonnet. She was talking to her great friend, Sonia Fullinger, an old schoolfellow, and about the same age as herself. Sonia had been taking the leading part in a scene which had been suggested by the Vicar, the founding of the Grammar School at Chiltonbury by the boy-king, Edward the Sixth, who had actually paid a visit to the town during his brief reign. And Sonia, in her puce-coloured velvet Tudor costume, made a charming little Edward, perhaps not exactly representative of that delicate and not very happy boy, for her laughing brown eyes, dark hair, and quick, agile movements rather belied what history has handed down as the appearance and demeanour of the weakly son of bluff King Harry.

Mrs. Cresswell posed still—very much posed—as Queen Anne. There was no doubt that she thoroughly enjoyed the impersonation, none the less because it gave the vain little woman the opportunity of flaunting her pearls.

Mr. Ashley-Smith, the Vicar of the parish, true to his cloth and calling, represented, at that moment, the Church of the Early Georgian period, being dressed in black gown, knee-breeches, silk stockings and buckled shoes, with white bands at his neck, and wearing a very dignified white, full wig.

Standing close by Sir Harry was a man wearing a Puritan dress, black velvet, with a cloak of the same material, broad-brimmed, high-crowned hat, with a silver band around it, and moustache and short chin-beard. Sir Harry was speaking to him.

"Very good of you to help us, Mr. Hurst. It's been a great success, don't you think?"

"Capital," replied the other, "and I've enjoyed taking part in it immensely. I hope you'll clear a good round sum for the hospital."

"I don't think there's much doubt about that. Yes?—" he turned half around—"what is it?"

A girl had come up to him from the direction of the house, dressed in plain black, and bareheaded.

"I was looking for Miss Fullinger, Sir Harry," she said. "She asked me, just now, to bring her something she wanted."

"Miss Fullinger?" replied Sir Harry, looking about him. "She was here a moment ago—Ah, there she is—coming out of the marquee."

The girl went up to her.

"I've brought you the clean handkerchief you asked for, miss," she said.

"Oh, thank you, Bates. I lost my other one, somehow."

The lady's-maid lingered for a moment.

"I'm putting out your apricot frock for dinner, miss. Will that be all right?"

"Oh, yes. If I want it. But I believe we're going to dine just as we are—anyhow, it's all right."

"Very good, miss."

The two men had turned instinctively, and were looking towards the entrance of the tent.

"By Jove!" exclaimed Sir Harry, "she makes a pretty boy, doesn't she?"

"Very," replied Hurst.

"Look here," went on Sir Harry, genially, "we're just going to have some sort of a meal. Everyone ought to be ready for it. Won't you come in and join us, Hurst?"

"Oh, really—thank you very much," said Hurst, still looking towards the two girls. "I don't know—" Then, as if suddenly making up his mind—"Yes, I'd like to—only,—these togs, you see?" and he laughed.

"That's all right," exclaimed the Baronet, and added, raising his voice for the benefit of the group around him, "Now then, you people! It's about time we fed, what? Come along in. We won't bother to change."

"How about the sedan-chair, daddy?" asked Anstice. "Hadn't we better bring it along?"

Sir Harry glanced into the big marquee, with its jumbled assortment of properties and discarded costumes.

"Oh, don't bother," he replied. "It isn't likely to rain and if it did, it wouldn't matter. It'll be all right in the tent with the rest of the stuff. You young folks will have to sort things out in the morning. Come along," he added to Hurst, who was still standing by him, looking at the vivacious Mrs. Cresswell, who was talking and laughing with two men of the house party. As he walked away with Sir Harry, he took the pageant programme from his pocket and glanced at it. Only the names of the leading characters were printed in each scene.

"I see," he remarked, "that Edward the Sixth—that pretty girl you were admiring just now—is Miss Sonia Fullinger. One of your house party, Sir Harry?"

"Yes. One of my daughter's friends."

"And Queen Anne?—She is staying with you, too?"

"Mrs. Cresswell? Oh, yes."

"You must have your house quite full."

Sir Harry laughed.

"We have. But they are all off tomorrow, except Bristow—he's got things to finish up before he leaves."

"Ah," replied Hurst nonchalantly, "so Her Majesty departs tomorrow—as an ordinary subject once more."

Sir Harry laughed again.

"Dear lady!" he exclaimed. "I think she thoroughly enjoyed playing her part. Well, I suppose all the women did. Love dressing-up, you know."

The others were following Sir Harry towards the manor, split up into little groups. Charlie was walking with Sonia Fullinger, in deep conversation with her. Anstice Lynwood, who, with her brother Harry, came after them, smiled. She had more than an inkling that Charlie and Sonia were getting extremely interested in one another, and the thought pleased her. Sonia was her very special friend—and the possibility of having her for a sister-in-law—

But, just then, Harry Lynwood, who was not living at home but had only run down for a few days to take his part, broke in on her thoughts.

"Who's the governor got hold of, sis? That fellow in the black cloak he's taking into the house? I've noticed him more than once.

Who is he?"

"Oh, that's Jasper Hurst. He's father's new tenant. He's taken The Gables, you know."

"When did he do that?"

"About a couple of months ago."

"Who is he?"

"Oh, I don't know. An old bachelor, I think. Anyhow, he lives by himself. Oh, he's all *right,* you know," she added. "Father called, and he's dined with us once. Rather a stuffy old bird—not much to say for himself. Charlie fixed him for this show."

"Looks rather like the villain of the piece, in that black rig-up."

Mrs. Cresswell's laugh rang out just then. Anstice glanced over her shoulder at her, and then said to her brother, in a low voice:

"Don't you think Mrs. Cresswell is a silly ass to sport those pearls of hers all over the place?"

"Why?"

"Well, they are frightfully valuable, you know. I think she's simply asking for trouble."

"Oh, you mean it's a temptation?"

"Well, you don't know who there might have been among the crowd we had in here today. I know one thing, and that is that her husband would be perfectly hectic about it if he knew she'd been wearing that necklace. He's most awfully particular about it—family heirloom, and all that sort of thing. They say he only lets her put the thing on when he's present, or at shows where detectives are engaged."

"Well, he isn't here today, anyway. And the thing's all over now. If any motor bandits were about they'd have had the bally pearls by this time."

"All the same," replied Anstice, "I shan't be sorry when she clears out tomorrow and takes them away. She only wanted to take the part of Queen Anne so that she could swank around with her beastly jewelry. You know, Roger hadn't really meant her to, but she had the cheek to ask for it, and he let her have it because he thought she'd sulk if he didn't."

By this time they had reached the house. The large entrance-hall quickly filled up with the assembling guests. Sir Harry raised his voice.

"Now, you good people, get ready as soon as you can—no changing, you know. I expect you are all precious hungry, what? Come along, Hurst," he added, beginning to lead the way upstairs.

At the end of a long corridor on the first floor was a large bathroom with a couple of lavatory basins. Here the men of the party assembled to make a hasty toilet, laughing and joking as they did so. Jasper Hurst washed his hands, glanced at his face in a mirror, adjusted his false moustache and beard, went out into the corridor, but, instead of making his way down again into the hall at once, stood, unobtrusively, at the extreme end of the corridor, apparently looking out of the window. Standing there, in his black suit, in the darkening shadows, he was scarcely noticeable. A shrewd observer, however, had there been one, would have remarked that he kept turning his head and glancing along the corridor, into which the doors from the bedrooms on either side opened.

One by one the men came out of the bathroom and went downstairs. Women appeared, also, coming out of their rooms. Mrs. Cresswell, followed by a girl in black, who was evidently her maid; then Sonia Fullinger, from a room exactly opposite. Presently Sonia's maid emerged. By this time Hurst had moved, and was slowly walking along the corridor to the stairs. He came down into the hall with one of the other men. There was a babel of conversation, and the butler announced that the meal was ready.

"In you go," cried Sir Harry. "No ceremony!"

"Oh," said one of the ladies, "but you *must* take Her Majesty in, Sir Harry. It's only proper. We'll all follow."

Sir Harry turned to "Queen Anne," who was still wearing the famous pearls, laid his hand on his heart, bowed low, and said:

"May it please Your Majesty graciously to permit me to escort you to the banquet?"

With a smile of appreciation, "Queen Anne," accepting his proffered hand, replied:

"We are delighted, Sir Harry."

Amid a burst of merriment Sir Harry and his regal companion led the way to the dining-room, the rest of the company following informally. Charles Lynwood, however, took care to have Sonia Fullinger close by him when the table was reached. Jasper Hurst slipped into a chair on the other side of Sonia, so that the girl sat between them.

It was more of a supper than a formal meal, and the excitement of the pageant and the actual wearing of the costumes produced hilarity fast and furious. Attempts were made to act parts over the supper-table. Hudson, the grave, white-haired old butler, was quite startled out of his dignified deportment by receiving such orders as:

"What ho, varlet! Wine in this goblet of mine. Dost hear, sirrah!"

"Queen Anne" enjoyed being constantly addressed as "Your Majesty," and quite felt the part. Sir Harry looked on, smiling, from the head of the table. He loved to see his guests in merry mood.

From time to time Jasper Hurst got in a few words with Sonia. Once he led the conversation to Mrs. Cresswell.

"She makes an excellent queen," he said. "Quite the right part for her."

"Isn't it? I don't know that I ever saw her looking so pleased with herself."

"Ah," he replied, "and you know her well, I suppose?"

"Oh, very well. She's a neighbour of ours. We both live at Hampstead, you see. Mr. Cresswell and my father are both on the Stock Exchange—and old friends."

She turned from him to answer some remark of Charlie's. Presently, however, he found an opportunity to talk to her again.

"I thought," he said, "that you and Mrs. Cresswell acted your parts splendidly in that earlier scene—the Norman one. Surely you must have had a lot of rehearsing—I mean more than we actually had here?"

"Oh, well, you see," she replied, "we both knew we were going to play in that scene—Captain Bristow fixed it up more than a month ago. So we *did* arrange a few details before we came down here. So glad you approved."

A burst of laughter arising from some joke at the other end of the table drowned conversation for a minute or two. Then Hurst said, casually:

"I hear this merry party breaks up tomorrow."

"Yes. Most of us are off."

"You go by train?"

"No. I ran down here in my car. As a matter of fact, I brought Mrs. Cresswell with me, and I'm taking her back. I've a ripping little two-seater," she went on, with all the car-owner's pride, "and I just love driving. What are you laughing at?"

"I was wondering how you managed to carry all your luggage," he said. "Mrs. Cresswell gives me the idea of the sort of woman who wouldn't be content with a dressing-case when she goes out to stay."

"You are observant," she replied. "She takes a small cargo with her. Much too much for my little run-about. So our respective maids take our goods and chattels by train. Saves a lot of bother."

"I suppose she doesn't send those pearls of hers with her maid?" asked Hurst, dryly.

Sonia shrugged her shoulders.

"Don't know," she replied lightly. "Never asked her. Anyhow, her maid's trustworthy. Been with her for years—Oh, Charlie," she went on, turning to him, "I want to ask you—"

Again a burst of laughter made conversation, for the time being, impossible. It was followed by one of those sudden silences which sometimes fall upon the most animated parties, a silence which was broken by someone saying, across the table:

"When was that sedan-chair of yours used last, Sir Harry? Or was it kept sacredly empty after the real Queen Anne had ridden in it?"

"No, no," he began. Then his face clouded a little. "I believe my family made use of it—until later Georgian times."

"And—the last occasion? Is there any record?"

It was the Vicar who asked the question. Harry Lynwood shot a quick glance at his brother, who frowned, slightly, and looked down on his plate. There was silence for a moment. Then Sir Harry said:

"It was a tragedy."

"A tragedy?" exclaimed Mrs. Cresswell, clapping her hands. "Oh, do tell us, Sir Harry!"

Sir Harry paused again; and then said:

"Very well. It's a bit of family history, and, perhaps, not quite creditable, what? But I'll tell you, if you like. That chair was last used by my great-grandfather, in 1814. And, as far as I know, no one has ever been carried in it since—till today."

A little murmur of expectation ran round the group. Sir Harry went on:

"My great-grandfather, Sir Charles Lynwood, was the second son. His brother, Harry, had died when quite a boy—we're always 'Harry' first, and then 'Charles,' we Lynwoods, you know. So Charles inherited the baronetcy and the estate. He was one of the old hard-drinking, stick-at-nothing in the hunting-field squires. Instead of coming to an untimely end with a broken neck, as most people thought he would, he developed gout, and had to give up hunting. But he didn't appear to give up his temper as well, which was as chronic and violent as his gout, it seems. And the hunt called him still, though he was a cripple and couldn't ride to hounds any longer. But, whenever there was a meet in front of the house here, he insisted on being carried outside in that sedan-chair, and the men who carried him had a deuce of a time of it, by all accounts. If they tilted the chair ever so little, or stopped when he wanted to go on, or went on when he wanted to stop, he let 'em have it—hot and strong.

"Well, one day, when the meet was outside, a restive horse began kicking up his heels close to the old man. The bearers made a move to get him out of danger, but one of them stumbled over a tussock of grass, and nearly fell. My testy ancestor was pitched forward, and his head broke the glass. Then he let out sulphur and brimstone, you know—and his face as hot as a coal, with a trickle of blood running over it. Suddenly he gurgled—and stopped—and—well—there was an end of Sir Charles."

"Apoplexy?"

The one word, spoken by the Vicar, broke the silence. Sir Harry nodded.

"Apoplexy," he echoed. "They brought him indoors—dead. And that's the last occasion until today, so far as I know, that anyone was carried in that sedan-chair. It has stood in the hall ever since."

Mrs. Cresswell shivered.

"And I—I—was the first—"

"Dear lady," broke in Sir Harry, smiling and turning towards her, "or may I say, 'Your Majesty'? Today your gracious presence within our old chair has broken any spell that may have attached itself to it. You have recalled the memories of all the dear, beautiful women who have sat in it. Never again can we associate it with a tragedy, what?"

"Oh, daddy!" exclaimed Anstice, "since when have you learned to pay such compliments?"

"Since I became one of Her gracious Majesty's courtiers, my dear," replied her father, placing his hand on his heart, and bowing to Mrs. Cresswell, gallantly.

"You play your part well, Sir Harry," said Captain Bristow. "I shall never attempt to coach you again."

Once more laughter and merriment broke out round the supper-table. Presently, the meal over, an adjournment was made to the hall. Cigars and cigarettes added incongruity to the various costumes.

Sonia Fullinger was the first to retire, on the plea of a headache; the other ladies followed. A move was made on the part of the men, to the smoking-room. The Vicar, who was a bachelor and kept late hours, was easily persuaded to stay for a little while. Hudson brought whisky, siphons and glasses.

The hour grew late. One by one the men slipped off. Sir Harry begged to be excused. He was tired, he said. Finally, only four remained in the smoking-room—Captain Bristow, Charles Lynwood, Jasper Hurst and the Vicar. The latter, like many of the clergy, was a reader of detective-stories and an amateur student of criminology. And, in the course of conversation, he discovered that Captain Bristow, in the last two years of the Great War, had been in the Secret Service. He tried to draw him; Bristow, at first, was reticent, but presently opened out a little—on general topics only, however. He ignored all innuendoes which might have led up to personal experiences. Charles Lynwood and Jasper Hurst for the most part were silent—but interested—listeners.

"Oh, well," the Captain said presently, in answer to a question put by the Vicar, "it isn't easy to answer. A *perfect* criminal! None of the criminals we know of were perfect. They wouldn't have been found out if they had been. If ever there was what you mean by a 'perfect' criminal, no one ever knew him as a criminal. Perfection, you see, in such a case, means absolute concealment. Doesn't it?"

"Well, yes, I suppose it does," agreed the Vicar. "What do you think, Hurst?" he went on.

Jasper Hurst took his cigar from his mouth, flicked the ash from it with his little finger into one of the trays on the table, and said, thoughtfully:

"Absolute concealment, yes—as far as the criminal himself is aware. But there may have been those—and no doubt there were— who imagined themselves to be perfect criminals, as you call them, but whose secrets were known by someone else, all the time."

"Someone who never let it out, you mean?" asked Charlie.

"Exactly."

"Someone who himself kept the secret from motives of self-preservation?" hazarded Charles.

"Not necessarily," replied Hurst. "One might keep the secret of another's crime out of purely altruistic motives."

"But, surely," broke in the Vicar, "that would be extremely immoral, wouldn't it?"

It was a little difficult, on account of his false moustache and beard, to see if Hurst was smiling slightly, as he answered:

"That depends upon how one interprets moral action—or, in the case we are considering, inaction."

"Well," said the Vicar, "to go back to what we were saying about the perfect criminal. Reverse the question. Is there such a thing as a perfect detective?"

"Can't be—unless he's the Pope," replied Bristow, with a smile.

"The Pope?" asked Charlie.

"The Vicar understands—don't you, Vicar?" said Bristow.

"Infallibility?" suggested the cleric.

"Exactly. The perfect detective must be infallible in method, deduction—and even instinct."

"Which latter," observed the Vicar, "is much more, by its nature, inclined to infallibility than method or deduction. But," he added, "that brings us from the realms of criminology into an even more extensive area, in which I, for one, haven't time to wander tonight—I mean psychology. Oh," he went on, glancing at his watch, "I'd no idea it was so late."

He got up. So did the others. Charlie, acting as host, pointed to the decanter.

"Another—?" he began.

"No, thanks," said the Vicar. "I limit myself now and then to a small one. And I've had it."

"Hurst?"

Jasper Hurst, also, refused.

"Well," went on the young man, "a cigarette—to start with—" and he produced and opened his case. "Oh! da— I beg your pardon, Vicar! Hang it all!"

"What's the matter?" asked Bristow.

"Empty," replied Charlie, showing his case. "Fact is, I took my last box with me to the dressing-tent. Thought they'd be useful there."

"I've got plenty," said Bristow.

"Thanks, but I'm used to my own peculiarly vicious brand. I'll run over to the tent and get the box."

The four men walked to the hall. The Vicar found there the old-fashioned, three-cornered hat belonging to his costume, and put it on.

"The back gates are not locked, are they?" he asked Charlie.

"No. They're all right."

"That's my nearest way. A bit further round for you, Hurst?"

"Yes," replied Hurst, putting on his big, black, broad-brimmed hat. "I'll go down the drive."

Charlie opened the front door.

"Don't wait up for me, old man," he said to Bristow. "I'll lock up when I get back."

"All right," replied Bristow. "I'm going up to bed. Good night."

He stepped outside, however, on to the terrace. The moon, well on in her last quarter, had risen, but behind clouds. There was just light enough to see dimly. He watched the three men as they left the house—and separated. The Vicar turned to the left, to make his way through the stable-yard to the back entrance; the sombre figure of Jasper Hurst took the carriage-drive towards the bridge and the main entrance; while Charles Lynwood walked across the lawn to the marquee. He was the most distinct of the three, on account of the white trousers he was wearing.

Then Roger Bristow came in, shut the door quietly, and slowly went up the stairs from the hall. Half-way up, in a niche, stood a grandfather-clock. As he passed it it struck—once. He glanced at the dial. Half-past one.

2

Roger Bristow was tired. The pageant had given him much work, both of brain and body, and, that day, he had been on the go since an early hour in the morning. He was not sorry to get to his room, and confessed to himself that the prospect of bed was an inviting one.

His room was one of several in the front of the house, opening into the long corridor on the first floor. When he entered it, heavy curtains were drawn across the window, and the room was in darkness. He turned on the electric light and began to divest himself of his garments. Off came the long jack-boots, the voluminous, full-skirted coat and full wig. He gave a sigh of relief, filled and lighted his pipe, and sat down in a comfortable arm-chair for a final whiff. He was in one of those tired, lethargic moods when one knows the sooner one is between the sheets the better, and yet dawdles in the preparations for getting there.

Presently, however, he knocked the ashes out of his pipe and lazily proceeded to take off the rest of his clothes and get into pyjamas. He wound up his watch, placing it on a small table beside his bed, and laid by it a little pocket electric torch. He liked to know what time it was if he woke in the night.

Turning off the light, he found his way to the window, drew aside the curtains, and opened one of the casements, lingering for a moment or two to breathe the cool, fresh air. It was a very still night outside; the moon was obscured by slowly-moving clouds, but there was just light enough to discern the larger objects, the trees, the broad sweep of the carriage-drive, the bridge with its low stone parapets, and, especially, the big white mass of the marquee, standing solidly against its background of trees, a white mass broken by a dark square shape in its centre, the opening into the tent.

He was just about to move away from the window and get into bed when he hesitated: a blur appeared against the white of the marquee—someone was coming out of the opening—Oh, Charles, of course, he thought. What a time he had been, though! No—it was very strange—against that white background something else appeared—a crude, big mass of a thing, followed, as it moved slowly, by another figure. Just then the clouds partly cleared for a moment from the moon, the dim light strengthened. There could be no mistake about it.

It was the sedan-chair, being carried by two men out of the marquee. Charlie!—no, neither of them could be Charlie—he was wearing white trousers. And the two moving figures were as dark and black as the trees.

Astonishment at so weird an occurrence in the middle of the night gave way to a smile. What a cumbersome thing to steal, and how could it be disposed of afterwards? For that was the first thought that entered his mind. It had become known that a valuable antique had been left in the marquee for the night, and thieves were calmly carrying it away. But they should not get far with it, anyhow. He would see to that. He was wide-awake once more, now.

Without turning on the light he slipped into a jacket, put on a pair of shoes, took the little electric torch, and opened the door very quietly, turning on his torch as he stepped into the corridor. He went swiftly down the stairs: the hall, which had a single electric light burning in it when he had gone up to his room, was now in darkness. Of course. Charlie had turned off the light when he had come in. By the door in the hall was a stand full of umbrellas and walking-sticks. Taking one of the latter, a good, heavy one, he prepared to unfasten the door.

But it proved to be unlocked and unbolted, and he had only to turn the handle to open it. "Queer!" he thought. "Charlie must have forgotten to lock up."

He had extinguished his torch before going outside. He had no wish for a light to be seen. Outside he stood still for just a moment on the terrace. He could just discern the two men, still carrying the chair. They were taking it away from the house, along the drive, and had almost reached the bridge.

Stepping lightly over the gravelled oval of the drive, Bristow made for the lawn, and sprinted silently over the grass. But he forgot, in his haste, that a gravelled path, leading from the drive, crossed the lawn about half-way to the bridge. As he raced across it, "scrunch-scrunch" rang out his two footsteps in the quiet night.

"Damn!" he ejaculated beneath his breath. For he knew that he had given the alarm.

Then he saw, in the shrouded moonlight, the bearers set down the chair and start running down the drive. He gave chase, passing the chair, which was now standing on the bridge. The two men had a start, but Bristow, in spite of his inclination to stoutness, was a quick runner, and hoped condition would tell.

But the instant he had rounded the slight curve beyond the bridge, he caught sight of something which had been, up to this time, completely hidden by intervening trees—a small, open four-seater motor-car, with its head pointing down the drive. Already his quarry had scrambled into her, and he heard the "Whir-r-r-chug-chug" of the engine as the electric starter was pressed. She began to move off, slowly, on first gear, but without her light showing. He sprinted, desperately, to overtake her, if he could, but there was a grinding noise as a hasty change of gear was made, she gathered speed—and he knew the chase was up.

But he did not lose his presence of mind. The lights on the car were still extinguished, so that the rear number-plate was indiscernible. He flashed on his torch, however, just in time to read and memorize the registration number:

"QV 5277."

Then he stopped to recover his breath. Even then he laughed to himself. It all seemed so absurd. How could a clumsy sedan-chair be carried away in that little car? Was it, after all, only a practical joke?

He stood for a minute or so, listening. He could hear the car, as she ran down the drive—no longer in sight, though. Then came silence. She had stopped. Ah, probably while one of the inmates got out to open the gate leading into the high-road outside the Manor grounds. Yes, that must have been it—for he heard her starting again. Well, he had missed the bit of fun he had anticipated—but, anyhow, the beggars hadn't got away with that chair!

He began to walk back to the house leisurely, being still a little out of breath. As he rounded the curve the sedan-chair came into view, a dim mass, standing on the bridge, just faintly outlined by the cloud-hidden moon, which was directly in front of him. Sir Harry's grim story flashed into his mind, and he pictured the irascible old baronet being carried for the last time in that historic chair. As he came up to it he slackened his pace. The interior of the chair, facing him, was naturally in deep shadow, the moon being behind. Bristow still held his little torch in his hand, and, acting on a chance impulse, flashed it upon the old chair—then stopped short.

There was someone inside. The first idea that came to him, following naturally upon the train of thought suggested by Sir Harry's story, was that Charles Lynwood—but no! Charlie had evidently come back to the house and turned out the hall light, though he seemed to have forgotten to lock the front door.

The next moment he was peering through the open side window of the chair, the beam of light from his torch illuminating the inside. And there, seated, was Jasper Hurst in his black velvet cloak, the false moustache and beard torn off his face, and a dark dribble of blood trickling down one cheek from what appeared to be a wound on his temple.

Captain Bristow was one of those men who rarely lose their self-possession in an emergency. The first thing he did was to take the limp, dangling hand of Jasper Hurst and feel his pulse. He thought there was just a faint beating, and the thought was justified when he saw—as he held the torch towards his face—the eyelids of the man quiver, very slightly. The head was resting back in a corner, motionless.

Then Jasper Hurst's lips moved. He was trying to say something— Bristow bent his head down to catch it—just a whisper—almost inaudible; in fact, he only caught two words:

"the . . . line . . ."

Then Hurst's mouth opened—the lower jaw fell—there was a deep sigh . . . Bristow tore aside the heavy cloak and thrust his hand under his clothing . . . there was no response. Jasper Hurst's heart had ceased to beat now. He was dead!

Captain Bristow, eminently alive to the importance of immediate action, and eminently cool in carrying out such action, did not pause to consider the strangeness of the circumstances. Jasper Hurst was dead. Bristow had seen too many men die to doubt this, and felt that there was nothing more he could do for him, though he realised it was imperative to get a doctor as swiftly as possible. He was not only dead, though, but apparently, murdered. And the murderers had had a start. The hunt was up. The hounds must follow quickly.

Thank goodness he had taken the number of that car! As he hurried back to the house, he found himself repeating it—"QV 5277"—at least he was certain of *that*.

He let himself in, ran upstairs, tapped at the door of Sir Harry's room, entered it before the suddenly-awakened Baronet could collect his dazed ideas, and turned on the light by the switch beside the door.

"Eh—what the deuce—?" began the astonished Sir Harry, sitting up in bed. "Bristow! What's the matter?"

Hastily Bristow told him. And seemed to take command of the situation.

"I'll telephone to the police at Chiltonbury, while you get some things on, Sir Harry," he said, "if you'll give me the number. And is there a doctor in the village?"

"Chiltonbury Nine is the number of the police. The telephone's in the hall. Yes—Dr. Forbes lives in the village," replied Sir Harry, who was out of bed now. "I'll call Harry, and ask him to go for Forbes. You might rouse Charlie, if you would. Good God, Bristow—this is a terrible thing. I——"

But Bristow was already out of the room, speeding along the corridor. Half-way along, he stopped, at Charles Lynwood's room—a room that looked out at the back of the house. Charlie was in bed. Bristow explained.

"All right," said Charlie, his head still on the pillow. "I'll be down in half a shake. *Dead*, you say?"

"Yes—best not rouse the guests," replied Bristow, leaving the room—and leaving Charlie still in bed.

A sergeant on night duty at Chiltonbury Police Station, three miles away, answered the call.

"Right, sir," he said, when he had taken in the grim message. "I'll have the Superintendent up at once, and we'll run out in a car. We'll bring the police surgeon with us."

"Sir Harry is sending for the local doctor at once."

"I see. But we'll have our man out all the same. Please repeat the number of that car, sir."

"QV 5277."

"You didn't see which direction it took when it got out on the main road?"

"No. Too far off. And they hadn't lit up."

He rang off. Sir Harry, half-dressed, came down the stairs, followed by his eldest son.

"No need to disturb the whole household," he said, in a low voice. "You've rung up the police, Bristow?"

"Yes. They'll be here directly."

"Good. You go and fetch Forbes," he went on, turning to his son.

"Right," said Harry. "I'll run the two-seater up the village. I can get out the back way without making a row. If Jarvis is about, I'll bring him along, too."

"Who is Jarvis?" Bristow asked the Baronet as Harry went out.

"Our village policeman. Sharp fellow. Ah—here's Charlie."

Charlie came down into the hall. He appeared to have slipped on those Regency white trousers, as the first thing that came to hand. And a golf jacket, tightly buttoned, with the collar turned up and a muffler round his neck. Sir Harry said:

"Bristow, we'd better go outside—and see to things. Coming, Charlie?"

"I—I think I'll stay here, dad,—in case anyone gets alarmed, and——"

Bristow, about to go out with Sir Harry, turned abruptly, and broke in:

"Didn't you lock the front door when you came in from getting your cigarettes, Charlie?"

"Did I?—no—yes—no—hanged if I remember. I was awfully tired and sleepy."

"You didn't see anything—outside?"

"This beastly business?—Hurst, you mean?"

"Yes."

"Nothing."

Sir Harry and Bristow were in the act of stepping outside when another voice made them stop and turn. Hudson had come into the hall, his dress-coat over his pyjamas, a poker in his hand.

"Is anything the matter, Sir Harry? I thought I heard——"

"Hush! We don't want to wake everyone. Yes. There's been an accident. You might ask James to dress and come down—but don't make a noise about it. Come along, Bristow."

The two men hurried to the bridge. Bristow flashed his torch on the face of the dead man. Sir Harry exclaimed:

"Poor chap! It's ghastly, what? To think he was with us at supper tonight. A tenant of mine, you know, Bristow," he added.

"Yes?"

"And that's about all I know concerning him. He's only been in my house, The Gables, a couple of months. Quiet, decent fellow."

He leaned forward, putting his hand against the chair.

"Better not do that, Sir Harry," remarked Bristow. "Finger-prints, you know. Not that there's much to be got out of them, for plenty of folks have touched that chair in the last few hours. But it's best to leave everything alone—for the police."

Sir Harry turned to him.

"I forgot, Bristow," he said. "Bit of policeman yourself, aren't you? Secret Service, and all that. What?"

Captain Bristow shrugged his shoulders, slightly.

"I'm out of that now," he replied, "and even if I wasn't—this isn't my business. Ah!" he went on, "Harry's back, I think."

For they heard a car coming into the stable-yard beside the house. In a moment or two three dark figures came quickly across the lawn. Harry, Dr. Forbes, and a man in police uniform.

"He's found Jarvis," said Sir Harry.

Dr. Forbes was a little man, with a round face, and small bristly moustache. He spoke in a quick, staccato manner.

"Terrible business, I hear, Sir Harry. Can't do much, from what your son tells me. Let's have a look, though. Ha!—flash that torch a bit nearer, sir," to Bristow. "That'll do. Good. Umph! Don't take long to diagnose this. The poor chap's dead, right enough. Nasty-looking wound that, too!"

"Broke his skull, what?" asked the Baronet.

"Can't say, Sir Harry,—not without a further examination. That'll come. Burton, from Chiltonbury, will have to take things in hand. Yes. Quite!"

"The police surgeon?" asked Bristow.

"Exactly. I can't do any more at the moment. Unprofessional. Harry tells me he's on the way here now. Good!"

The policeman stepped forward, addressing Bristow.

"Are you the gentleman who found the body, sir?"

"Yes."

"Mr. Harry Lynwood tells me there was a car driven off by two men, and that you had noted the number."

"Quite right. I've already 'phoned it to the police-station at Chiltonbury."

"What was it, sir?"

"QV 5277."

Jarvis, if the light had been sufficient, would have been seen to raise his eyebrows.

"You're certain, sir?"

"Quite."

"That's very queer, then."

"Why?"

"QV 5277 is the number of the Vicar's car. I know it well."

"The *Vicar's* car?" exclaimed Sir Harry.

"Yes, Sir Harry. A four-seater Morris—open tourer. Was that it, sir?" he added, to Bristow.

"Four-seater. Yes. I couldn't swear to the make. I only caught sight of the back of it, you see."

"Oh, that's the Vicar's car, right enough, sir. Funny thing!"

"Queer business, queer business!" ejaculated the little doctor. "Man knocked on the head and carried off in sedan-chair. Murderers make their getaway in the padre's car. Queer business," he repeated.

"Here comes one who can solve it, if anyone can, I reckon," said Jarvis, just a vestige of pride in his voice as being connected with the solver to whom he alluded. "Here's the Superintendent."

A glaring beam of light shot out towards them, coming round the curve of the drive. The chair, with its silent, still inmate, was illuminated brilliantly, as was the little group of men standing beside it. The driver was the first to get out when the car stopped. Turning, for a moment, as he came forward, to say a word to one of its other occupants, his face was lighted up in the glare of the headlights; a clean-shaven, cultured face, rather long, with pointed chin, large nose, and dark, penetrating eyes.

Then he turned once more.

"Ah, Jarvis," he said, before addressing anyone else. "Glad you are here. Go straight to the Vicarage and get hold of Mr. Ashley-Smith. Find out if his car is in the garage there, and, if so, if the radiator is warm. But don't touch it, or let anyone else do so. Find out all you can about that car, where it was tonight. The Vicarage is on the telephone, so you can 'phone your report straight through to the Station before you come back here. And tell the Vicar I shall want to see him,—later on. You needn't bring him back."

Jarvis, first casting a look on the assembled company which plainly said, "I told you so," was off like a shot. Superintendent Kinch went on, speaking to the police surgeon, who had got out of the car:

"You will do what is necessary to begin with, Doctor. . . . Now . . ." he summed up the little group, swiftly, eliminating the Baronet and his two sons, and Dr. Forbes.

"Who telephoned to us?" he asked, looking straight at Bristow, as if he knew already.

"I did," replied Bristow.

"Ah! And you found the body?"

Bristow nodded.

"He was not dead when I found him."

"Yes, I understand that. Your name, sir?"

"Bristow—Captain Roger Bristow."

The Superintendent shot a keen glance at him. But, if he knew him by repute, he said nothing.

"Staying at the Manor?"

"Yes."

"I'll get you to tell me, presently, the whole sequence of events. Ah, Doctor," he went on, "you've finished?"

"All I can do now," said the police surgeon. "The Coroner is pretty well sure to order an autopsy. I——"

"Oh, surely," broke in Sir Harry, "the cause of death is pretty plain? A blow on the forehead, what?"

Dr. Burton shook his head, in a non-committal way.

"Externally it looks like it, certainly," he replied. "All the same, ——" and he arched his eyebrows questioningly, at his fellow-professional.

"Quite so, quite so," ejaculated Dr. Forbes, "I thought you'd say so, Burton."

"Well," said Sir Harry, "we can't leave the poor chap here, eh?"

"Where does he live?" asked the Superintendent.

"At The Gables. Best part of a mile away."

"Would it be possible—at all events for the time being—to take him into the Manor House?" asked Kinch. "If you wouldn't mind, Sir Harry?"

"No," said Sir Harry; "I think we might manage that, er——"

"How about the gun-room, dad?" asked Harry Lynwood.

"Ah—that would do. I'll go back and make arrangements."

"If you will," said the Superintendent. Then he turned to the other man, who had come with him and the police surgeon from Chiltonbury, a big, good humored-looking fellow with a broad, open face, clean-shaven, and fair hair; a man who was dressed in civilian clothes and who, up to this moment, had not opened his mouth.

"You'll stay here, Mentmore? You'll know what to do?"

Mentmore nodded.

"I'll come back presently—and run home. See you before I go."

Again Mentmore only nodded. He seemed to be a man of few words. Then the Superintendent turned to Bristow. The two doctors, deep in conversation, were following Sir Harry and his son towards the house.

"Now, sir," said Kinch, "I'd like you to tell me exactly what happened tonight, if you will."

He listened to Bristow's concise, clear account of events, occasionally asking a question, but, for the most part, letting the other run on without interruption. He evidently realised that Bristow had the knack of putting things into a succinct form. When the latter had finished, however, he did ask a few questions.

"You noted the time?"

"The clock struck the half-hour—half-past one—as I went up to bed. It would be about twenty minutes later, more or less, that I looked out of my bedroom window and saw the chair being carried out of the tent."

"I see. And these three people who went out of the house. Let me get that clear. Hurst came along this drive. The Vicar went out at the side gate, and Mr. Charles Lynwood towards the tent?"

"That is so."

"You didn't see Mr. Charles come back?"

"No."

"Yet, when you went downstairs again you told me the front door was still unlocked?"

"Yes. But the hall light was out. And I asked Charles about the door. He forgot to lock it, apparently."

"And he said he saw nothing of this affair?"

"Quite so."

"I suppose he *did* go into the tent?"

Bristow shrugged his shoulders.

"Presumably," he said. "I haven't asked him that. As a matter of fact, I've only had a moment or two with him since."

"Ah, well. Perhaps he may help us later. About this tent. I'd like to have a look at it now. You've got your torch?"

"Come along, Superintendent."

He led the way, along the drive and then across the lawn, to the big marquee, flashing his torch into it when they reached the opening. There was light enough for the Superintendent to see that the interior was divided into three parts, the larger portion, into which the opening led, in the centre, and two others, one on either side, screened by canvas.

"They were our dressing-rooms, so to speak," explained Bristow. Kinch nodded.

"And this chair," he said, "can you remember whereabouts it was left?"

"In this middle division—not very far inside."

The Superintendent glanced round the tent. In it were lying in confusion paraphernalia which had been used in the pageant—odd costumes, hats, tin helmets, spears, swords—many made of wood covered with silver paper—a couple of trumpets—used in the fanfare announcing the arrival of Queen Anne—banners, scarves, a Maypole with its ribbons—in all a very *olla podrida*.

The Superintendent shrugged his shoulders.

"Writers of detective fiction would have plenty of choice of clues here," he said, dryly. "The trouble is, of course, that if there happens to be anything worth noting, how in the world can one pick it out from the others?"

He stood for a moment, thinking. Then he said:

"It's part of our business to comb things out, though. Look here, Captain Bristow—I understand you produced this pageant?"

"Yes, I did."

"Well, is there a property-list?"

"There is. Miss Lynwood drew one up—a very careful one."

"And these costumes?"

"Most of them hired—and all of them only worn by people living in or staying in the house. The other players provided their own dresses—and took them away or wore them home."

"So you would be able to check these?"

"I think Miss Lynwood might. She was extraordinarily careful in making lists—and, of course, the firm we hired the things from sent their own list with them."

"Good! I won't have anything touched here till the morning. I'll put Jarvis on guard outside the house. Then I shall have to ask Miss Lynwood to check all that is here— One moment, sir, please."

He took the torch from Bristow's hand, and advanced into the tent, flashing it in every direction. Bristow stood, just inside the tent, watching him. A detailed search in that realm of costumes and properties with only a small torch to help was an impossibility.

Presently Kinch came back to Bristow.

"Found anything?" asked the latter.

As a matter of fact, the Superintendent had not. But he was non-committal. His business, just then, was to ask for information—not to give it. He made no reply to Bristow's question. A little smile twitched on the lips of the questioner, but he said nothing.

The Superintendent gave back the torch to Bristow.

"Thanks," he said. "I'd like to go to the house for a few minutes and see Mr. Charles Lynwood—if he hasn't gone to bed again. Then I'll run back to Chiltonbury with Dr. Burton. I'm leaving a good man in charge here," he went on, as the two started walking across the lawn back to the house. "Mentmore—Detective-Sergeant Mentmore. You can rely on him. I shall be out again about eight o'clock. Of course I shall want to interview everybody in the house—as a matter of routine—and I don't want any of them to leave before I come. I shan't

disturb them now. But I'd like you to have a list of all the people who
are in the house—including the servants,—please, ready for me when I
come out."

"I'll see to that. But it is clearly an outside job, don't you think,
Superintendent?"

"Looks uncommonly like it, certainly. I suppose you can't give me
any details about these two men who made off with the car? Didn't
notice anything about them?"

"I'm sorry I can't. I didn't get near enough. And it was too dark to
make out anything."

"Ah! I was afraid so. Curious thing about that car, though," he
added.

"I suppose you are taking steps—" began Bristow.

But the Superintendent broke in, with a keen glance at his
companion—they were entering the hall now, and the light shone on
Bristow's face—

"What do you think, sir? Within five minutes of getting your
message we had all stations warned to look out for QV 5277. They
hadn't time to get far before you gave the alarm. I don't think for a
moment Jarvis will find that car in the Vicar's garage, but what I do
think is that—"

Sir Harry, who was waiting in the hall, came forward.

"Ah, there you are, Superintendent," he said. "A telephone
message has just come through from your police-station at Chiltonbury. I took it down—here it is."

And he handed the Superintendent a penciled slip of paper.

"Constable Chalmers has just 'phoned from Drifford. He reports a
Morris Oxford four-seater in a ditch on the main London road, seems
to have run into a telegraph-pole. Both number-plates are missing."

The Superintendent handed the paper to Bristow, a little smile on
his face as he did so. Then, with just a word to Sir Harry, asking
permission, he took up the telephone-receiver.

"Four-two Drifford, please. . . . Hullo. . . . Yes. . . . Superintendent Kinch speaking. . . . Just got your message sent on
from Chiltonbury. . . . Yes. . . . Constable Chalmers found the car.
. . . I know. . . . I want you to start a search for those number-
plates. . . . Yes—along the ditches—hedges—and so on—taking the
breakdown as the centre. . . . Yes, report straight to my office,
please. . . . All right."

He turned to Sir Harry and Captain Bristow, a smile on his face.

"You can remove number-plates with a spanner in three minutes," he said, "but you don't carry the things about with you afterwards—if you are trying to make a getaway. Ah—here's Jarvis. Car in the Vicarage garage, Jarvis?"

"No, sir. I——"

"All right. That's all I want to know just now. The rest can wait. You've 'phoned your report to Chiltonbury?"

"Yes, sir."

"Very well. Go outside the house and keep an eye on that big tent. Don't let anyone go in till I'm back."

"One word," said Bristow. "How far is Drifford from here?"

"Twenty miles or so the other side of Chiltonbury—on the main London road," answered the Superintendent. "I know what you're thinking, sir. Some speed, eh?"

"Oh, well," replied Bristow, "one can always run to a fair speed in the small hours of the morning. After all, there's nothing in that."

The Superintendent looked at him, curiously.

"Do you think they saw you flash your light on the car as they made off?"

"One of 'em did—not the driver—t'other fellow turned his head. I could just see that. You're sharp, Superintendent. You have guessed what I was thinking of, evidently."

"I return the compliment, sir," replied Kinch, suavely. "That is, if I guessed correctly."

"A waste of time?" hazarded Bristow.

"Exactly," retorted the Superintendent. "And now," he went on to Sir Harry, "if I might have just a word with your son—Mr. Charles——"

Sir Harry quietly led the way to the smoking-room, explaining as he did so that the body of Jasper Hurst had been conveyed into the house. In the smoking-room were Harry and Charles Lynwood, and Dr. Burton, the police surgeon. Hudson had made them some coffee. The Superintendent accepted a cup.

"May I ask you one or two questions, sir?" he began, speaking to Charles Lynwood. The latter, who was smoking a cigarette, nodded.

"Captain Bristow tells me you went out of the house with the Vicar and Hurst just before half-past one."

"Yes. That is so."

"The Vicar left by the side gate—and Hurst started going down the drive?"

"He did."

"He didn't give you the appearance of a man who was expecting to meet someone?"

"Not at all. He made a casual remark about the pageant—and said good night. Nothing more."

"And you went on to the marquee—to get a box of cigarettes you had left there?"

"Yes."

"Well, sir, would you mind telling me exactly what happened there?"

Charles arched his eyebrows—as in surprise at such a question.

"What happened?" he echoed. "Why—nothing, you see. I found my cigarettes—"

"At once?" asked Kinch, sharply.

"Oh, well, I had to rummage about a bit first—to see where they were."

"And there was no one in the tent?"

"Not that I know of, Superintendent."

"And then?"

"I came back to the house—and went to bed."

"Without locking the door?"

"I suppose I must have forgotten—you say you found the door unlocked when you went out, Roger?" he asked, turning to Bristow.

The latter, who had taken a cigarette from a box on the table, was smoking thoughtfully. He was looking down on the floor—near Charles' feet. He raised his head.

"Yes," he said.

Kinch, who had been jotting down pencilings in his notebook, got up.

"That doesn't help us very much. Come along, Doctor. I'll run you back. I'll be out again about eight o'clock," he went on to Sir Harry. "We shall have to find out all about this poor chap, Hurst."

"There I fear I can be of no use," said the Baronet. "I know very little about him—now," he added, "we'd all better get a little sleep, what? There's nothing to be done for the moment."

They all went into the hall, the Superintendent going out of the house with the police surgeon. Bristow was standing by the front door as they left. Just for a moment Kinch stopped and turned, and the two men found themselves looking at one another. A faint, enigmatical smile broke over the Superintendent's pleasant face.

"We shall meet again in a few hours," he said, as he went out. Sir Harry closed and locked the door, and then, with the others, crept up to bed again very quietly. Apparently no other members of the household or any of the guests had been disturbed. On a sofa in the gun-room lay the corpse of Jasper Hurst. Frimley Manor was enshrouded in stillness once more—the only sound in the neighbourhood being the "chug-chug" of the Superintendent's car. Detective-Sergeant Mentmore was conversing, in whispers, with Constable Jarvis, just outside the marquee.

The moonlight was a little brighter now, the clouds having partially cleared. The moon itself, too, had risen higher in the heavens.

"What's that?" suddenly exclaimed Jarvis, raising his voice slightly.

"What?"

"I thought I saw a window on the side of the house there flash in the moonlight as if it moved."

"Let's go and see," said the Detective-Sergeant.

They crossed the lawn and made for the side of the house. The stone terrace continued round the side, and facing it were four French windows, two belonging to the dining-room and two to the library—windows which opened outwards. Jarvis produced his lantern, and the two policemen tested each window. They were all fastened on the inside, and heavy curtains were drawn across them, screening the two rooms.

"Must have been your fancy," grunted Mentmore.

3

Superintendent Kinch sat in the library at Frimley Manor, that room having been placed at his disposal for the time being, his open notebook on the table in front of him. He glanced at the clock on the mantelpiece—twenty minutes past eight. Then he lighted a cigarette and leaned back in his chair, mentally reviewing the events of the night.

He had only snatched two or three hours' rest after his return to Chiltonbury, in the very early hours of that morning, for there had been much to be done of that meticulous routine work which is so little known to the general public and bears such a minute part in modern detective fiction.

In the first place, he had devoted no little time to the question of that derelict car that had been found in the ditch a little way out of the village of Drifford. He had begun, when he first received the message about it at Frimley Manor, to attach great importance to the finding of this car. Naturally, for, at first sight, everything seemed to fit in so exactly. The car had been found about twenty-three miles from the scene of the tragedy, just about the distance that a good driver would have reached, having, as Captain Bristow had pointed out, a practically totally clear road in that hour of the night. Moreover, it was the London road, the very route that nine out of ten escaping criminals were most likely to take. Again, in answer to further enquiries, he had ascertained that no one had turned up either at hotel or garage in the neighbourhood of Drifford, with the story of a breakdown of his or her car, as would have happened to the ordinary, innocent driver. This car was absolutely abandoned, as it was likely to be by a fugitive escaping from justice. Furthermore, the car was of the same make as that which was missing from the Vicar's garage.

And then, there was the removal of the number-plates, which was very significant. It was not only significant, however. There was a snag in it, raising a doubt. Bristow had seen this. If the driver knew that the number had been taken before he had time to get out of the range of light of that torch, why did he waste even the few precious minutes it would have taken him to unscrew the fastening nuts with a spanner and remove the plates? There was only one answer to this question, and that was that the criminals, whoever they were, had bungled, as criminals always do bungle.

So he was taking no risks. His men, and men of adjoining counties, were still on the look-out for a four-seater car numbered QV 5277, color dark blue, left rear mudguard bent and dented, paint very much scrubbed on the bonnet (the astute Jarvis had obtained these details from the owner); they were also on the look-out for two unknown men who were wanted for the crime of murder. Moreover, assuming that the car might be abandoned in the neighbourhood, and that its inmates might possibly be planning to make off by train, he had issued instructions for a number of railway stations to be watched, from such time as the first trains of the day began to run.

As to the derelict car at Drifford, even if it was not the one he wanted—and very soon he would satisfy himself on that score—it was not negligible. A car the registration number of which has been removed cannot be negligible in the eyes of the police. True, it was quite possible that it had nothing to do with this particular case at all, but no good Superintendent of Police centers so much on one particular case that he neglects others. There was something wrong about that car, anyhow.

Just before he left Chiltonbury a message, in reply to his instructions, had come through from Drifford that the car had been got out of the ditch, that though the engine was hopelessly out of gear the wheels and steering-gear were intact, and he had given orders to have it towed direct to Frimley, so that he might confront the Vicar with it without bothering that worthy cleric to make a journey. Besides, it was probably as quick a method as any other. And the car might arrive at any moment now.

Early as it was, he had already interviewed, briefly, one member of the household whom he had not seen on his previous visit, and that was Anstice Lynwood. Anstice was fond of a canter before breakfast, and, in spite of the fatigues of the day before, had come down a little after half-past seven. It was Hudson, who was, in his way, as much a friend of the family as a butler, who had told her of the tragedy, but then he knew "Miss Anstice" well, and was quite aware that beneath the vagaries of buoyant youthfulness, hers was one of those strong characters which can face an emergency calmly.

Superintendent Kinch, now wearing his uniform, had come just as Hudson had finished his gruesome story, and the girl had turned to him, a little pale, it is true, but otherwise quite collected.

"Hudson has just told me," she said. "But this is too terrible. Is there anything I can do?"

And Kinch, a quiet, but keen, observer of human nature, had summed her up quickly. He liked those steady grey eyes of hers—and the firm little mouth. And he made an ally of her at once.

"You can help me considerably, Miss Lynwood," he said. "Captain Bristow tells me that you have a list of all your hired costumes, and of the properties in the tent. I want you to check this list very carefully and, if you find anything—no matter how insignificant—in that marquee which is not on your list, I want you to keep it back for me. Can you do this?"

"I'll do my best—of course I will. I'll go over to the tent at once and overhaul all I can before breakfast."

"Plenty of time," said Kinch, with a smile. "Here—one minute, Miss Lynwood," and he tore a sheet from his pocketbook and scribbled something on it. "Give that to Jarvis—he's outside, by the tent—and then he'll let you go in."

She smiled back in return.

"We are all under orders, I see!"

"For the present, yes. But you mustn't mind that, Miss Lynwood."

And now he was sitting in the library, quietly smoking a cigarette, but knowing that the work of a very busy day was beginning. And he was planning it out.

The door opened, and in came Charles Lynwood.

"Ah—they told me you were here, Superintendent. Look here, it's coming it rather strong that we're being treated as suspects or prisoners."

The Superintendent arched his eyebrows.

"Yes?" he asked.

"I was simply going to our garage to tell our man to get out the two-seater, when that fellow of yours outside asked me where I was going, and said you'd given orders that none of us were to leave our own house till you'd seen us."

"Quite so," replied Kinch, urbanely. "I'm very sorry, Mr.

Lynwood, but in a case like this I have to take ordinary precautions. It isn't a matter of suspicion, only I must interview everyone. It is only usual."

"Well, you've interviewed me already," replied Charlie. "Is there any reason why you want me any longer?"

"Why?" asked the Superintendent.

"Because, as it happens, I want to catch the eight-forty-five train at Chiltonbury. I have an engagement in London."

"Oh!" said the Superintendent, drumming on the table with his finger-tips. "I see. Are you returning tonight?"

"Possibly."

"Because I'm fixing the inquest for tomorrow. And it is very necessary that you should be there."

Charlie thought for a moment or two. Then he said:

"Are you going to have all the people staying in this house at that inquest? Because, if you are——"

"Certainly not, sir. But I shall want Sir Harry and you and the Vicar and Captain Bristow, at all events. I can't tell about all the others till I've seen them, but, as far as I know, with the exception of your brother, they knew nothing of what was taking place."

"Because," went on Charlie, still in rather a bullying tone, "most of our guests had arranged to leave today."

"Very well," said Kinch, quietly. "I don't suppose I shall find any reason to prevent them from doing so. But I must see them first."

"Well," said the young man, glancing at his wrist-watch, and speaking sarcastically, "have I your permission to catch that train?"

"Let's see—you've told me all you know, I think?"

"Of course I've told you all I know."

"Quite so. Very well, then. Your chauffeur is driving you in, I suppose?" and he, also, glanced at the time. "You'll do it quite easily, sir. But don't forget the inquest, please—tomorrow afternoon at two."

"All right. I'll be there," and he went out of the room.

The Superintendent sat quite still for a moment or two, a little smile playing around his lips.

"Not much use asking him any more questions while he's in that mood," he said to himself. "Daresay there's nothing in it, but I'm taking no chances."

And he went into the hall and rang up the police-station.

"Hullo—yes—Superintendent Kinch speaking." He lowered his voice, looking swiftly around the empty hall, and said, "Is Stevens there? . . . Yes, tell him I want to speak to him. . . . Ah, Stevens, are you in plain clothes? . . . Good. You know young Mr. Charles Lynwood by sight? Very well. He's going up to London by the 8:45—now. I want you to go too, and shadow him. He'll probably come back tonight. If not, I'll leave it to you to get further help up there. Right!"

As he replaced the receiver, Captain Bristow, dressed in a brown plus-four suit, came down the stairs and said good morning. At the same moment came a ring at the front door.

"They'll be coming along to breakfast now," he said, jerking his head towards the stairs. "You'll let them have that first, I suppose?"

"Oh, certainly, I——"

James, the footman, had crossed the hall and opened the door. In came the Vicar, and went straight up to Kinch.

"Oh," he exclaimed, "I thought I might find you here instead of going into Chiltonbury. And, naturally, I didn't want to use the telephone. Jarvis is outside, and I was so relieved to hear from him that you were here, though I've come on a very painful errand. Ah—good morning, Captain Bristow. What a terrible affair! Now," and he turned once more to the other, "I want to have a word or two with you. A terrible affair—a terrific affair!"

"It is, indeed, sir. And it must be distressful to you to have your car mixed up in it. I hope we shall find it for you——"

"Oh, it isn't that, it isn't that!" broke in the Vicar, and his voice trembled. "It is something else that worries me exceedingly. Something you ought to know. . . ."

"Come into the library, won't you, Vicar?" asked the Superintendent, soothingly.

"Yes, yes," said the Vicar. "Bristow, I wish you'd come too,—as a friend I know I can trust."

Bristow arched his eyebrows enquiringly at the Superintendent. The latter nodded assent. The three men retired to the library.

The Vicar seated himself in a chair, drew his handkerchief from his pocket, and passed it over his face. He was making an effort to control himself. The Superintendent waited patiently for a few moments; then the Vicar began:

"You see, it was only half-an-hour ago that I realised . . . that . . . it's a very painful matter, but I felt it was my duty to see you at once."

Kinch's interest was awakened. A sudden thought struck him. The Vicar had, perhaps, seen something when he went out in the night.

"May I ask you one or two questions first?" he suggested. "I was

going to do so later on. I understand you left the house just about
half-past one, with Mr. Charles Lynwood and Hurst."

"Yes, yes," said the Vicar.

"And you went out by the side gate?"

"That is so."

"Now—did you see anyone?—did you——"

"It isn't that at all," broke in the Vicar. "Perhaps it will be best for
me to tell my story in my own way,"—he had begun to recover
himself—"it is more difficult than I can say to have to do so at all, and
I sincerely trust my fears are groundless. I assure you the dictates of
conscience are hard to obey, but I know it is my duty to put you in
possession of certain facts."

Kinch nodded, silently. The Vicar went on:

"You will understand, Superintendent, that I was absent from my
Vicarage from a little before two o'clock yesterday until I returned
very early this morning—quite twelve hours in all. I took part in the
afternoon and evening performances of the pageant, and stayed here to
dinner afterwards. I met no one on my way home, and when I reached
the Vicarage, of course my domestics—a housekeeper and a maid—
had gone to bed.

"I let myself in very quietly and went straight up to my room. As a
matter of fact, I don't think I went to sleep. Anyhow, I was awake
when I heard steps outside—I always have my window open—and I
got out of bed and looked out. It was your man, Jarvis. I recognised
him in his uniform in the half-moonlight. He said he wanted to see
me, so I slipped on some clothes and went down. Then he told me
about the murder and my car, and we went to the garage—which was
empty.

"What I want you to see is that neither my housekeeper nor my
maid were aroused, and it wasn't until I came down this morning that
I saw either of them. I felt it was no use disturbing them about the car
in the middle of the night. So it was only just now that my
housekeeper told me what—well—what I'm afraid you ought to
know."

"Yes?" asked the Superintendent.

"It is not a matter that I care to talk about—even to my intimate
friends. But I have a relative, Superintendent,—a nephew,—who has
caused me much anxiety and, I may say, no little expense. He is my
sister's son. His father died when he was quite young, and my sister
also died a few years ago. I am his nearest relative, and—er—well,
being an orphan, how could I refuse to acknowledge him?"

"If I may suggest it—a ne'er-do-well?" asked the Superintendent. The Vicar shook his head, sadly.

"I'm afraid it's a true description," he replied. "Over and over again he has promised—well, a good many things. And over and over again I have set him on his feet. But—bad companions and a weak nature . . . well, to make a long story short, my housekeeper told me just now that he called at the Vicarage soon after eight last evening—and asked for me. I may say I haven't seen him for many months. In fact, I had to tell him plainly I would not receive him again till he showed palpable signs of amendment."

"Did your housekeeper know this?" asked Kinch.

"No. I don't discuss my private affairs with her. But she knew *him*, of course. She told him where I was, and that I should be home after the pageant was over. She did not know I was remaining here to dinner."

"And then?"

"He said he would wait. She served him with a meal, and after that he appears to have sat in my study, smoking. About ten o'clock she went in to him and asked if she had not better prepare a room for him. He replied that he could not stay the night, but that she could go to bed if she wanted to."

"And did she?"

"Yes. And now comes the painful part of my story. Her room overlooks the yard into which the garage opens. I don't keep the door of the garage locked. She says it may have been about half-past ten, or perhaps nearer eleven, when she heard the front door bang. In a minute or two there were steps in the yard. She looked out. He was there. He opened the garage door, went in, started the car, and drove it out."

"And she said nothing?"

"It never occurred to her that anything was wrong. When he had stayed with me before he had several times taken the car out for a run. And she thought that, tired of waiting, he was coming here to find me."

Superintendent Kinch looked grave.

"Your nephew left no message—in writing or otherwise?" he asked.

"None whatever."

"Have you any idea why he came to see you last night?"

The Vicar shook his head.

"I'm afraid," he answered, "from past experience that there could be only one reason. He probably came—well—er—to ask me for money."

"I see. Now, tell me, Mr. Ashley-Smith. Let us, for the moment, assume that he came for this purpose. Have you any idea where he would come from—where his home is?"

"I fear I can't tell you."

"When did you see him last?"

"Before Christmas—yes—it was about the beginning of December."

"He came here?"

"Yes. It was then that I told him I could help him no further, unless he gave me proof of having turned over a new leaf. Since then I have heard nothing of him."

"Did he know anyone in the neighbourhood—Hurst, for example?" asked the Superintendent.

"I don't think so. He occasionally stayed with me for a few days, but, except casually meeting any friends in my house, he knew no one. As for poor Hurst—certainly not. Hurst has only been living at The Gables for a couple of months or so."

Superintendent Kinch reflected for a few moments, and then said very sympathetically:

"I quite understand how painful it is for you to come and tell me this, Mr. Ashley-Smith, and I am grateful for the fine sense of duty which prompted you. You must realise that it is very serious?"

"I do, indeed."

"And I'm sure you will understand," Kinch went on, "that I have a duty to perform. I am making no accusation—there are not sufficient facts to go upon. But it is of paramount importance that we should find your nephew as quickly as possible."

"I realise that, Superintendent. But, as I have told you, I have no idea where to look for him."

"For your sake I should be glad of that, I suppose," said Kinch, "for it releases you from an exceedingly unpleasant situation. All the same, I must ask you for some further information."

And he took up notebook and pencil.

"Your nephew's name?" he asked.

"Curtis—Leonard Ashley Curtis. Ashley is a family name," he explained, "but he does not hyphenate it as I do. In his case it is baptismal."

"I see. His age?"

"Twenty-nine."

"His description?"

With the help of a few leading questions Kinch was able to get a fairly adequate description. Then he said:

"You mentioned, sir, that he had fallen in with bad companions."

The Vicar nodded.

"You don't happen to know who any of them are?"

"No."

"Or any of his friends?"

The Vicar thought for a moment.

"I did hear him mention, sometimes, the name of some man who, he said, was a chum of his."

"Yes?"

"Let me see—yes—'Bob' he generally called him—Bob Gilbert— that was it."

"Mention him in any connection?"

"Well—er—I think he did, once. Yes. He said they were members of the same club."

"Oh, come!" said the Superintendent, "that's something to go upon. A London club?"

"Yes."

"Which?"

The Vicar shook his head and smiled, wanly.

"Not the sort of club I should approve of. A night-club. But he did not tell me the name of it."

"I see. . . . Well, sir, I don't think I want to ask you any more, at present."

"You'll—you'll let me know—?" began the Vicar, "I shall, naturally, be anxious, and——"

"Oh, I'll let you know, sir, if we find out anything about your nephew—that is, as far as I can. We can't always, in the interests of justice, you see, tell even our friends all we know about a case. Thank you very much for coming to see me at once, sir."

Captain Bristow, who had lighted a cigarette, had been a silent listener as the Vicar told his story. A frown had gathered on his face and he appeared to be lost in thought. The Vicar was just about to get up to go when Bristow turned to him.

"I'm heartily sorry for you, Vicar," he said; "it's a beastly worry for you—first you lose your car, and then this nephew of yours crops up in connection with it. Used to take it out when he stayed with you sometimes, you told us. With your permission, of course?"

The Superintendent had leaned back in his chair, and was watching

Bristow intently, his eyes half-closed—but alert, all the same. The Vicar smiled.

"You don't know my nephew, Bristow," he said, "or you wouldn't have asked that question. He took my car when he thought he would: and as for asking my permission—well, the younger generation of today," he went on, in true parsonic style, and, therefore, sententiously, "the younger generation appear to me to have lost their good manners with their lack of respect for their elders. They only think of themselves."

"Precious careless sort of chap, eh?" put in Bristow, the Superintendent still watching him narrowly.

"Absolutely. On the last occasion he was here I wanted my car to run into Chiltonbury—but it was not in the garage. I had to go in by 'bus, and the first thing I saw there—in the market square—quite unattended, was my Morris Oxford. He had run in to see the pictures— But he didn't come out in the car," he added, grimly. "*I* saw to that!"

Bristow laughed.

"What did he say for himself afterwards?"

"Laughed at me to my face and told me no one would ever think of stealing a five-year old Morris. My car may be a trifle aged as the lives of cars go," the Vicar went on, a humorous twinkle in his eye now, "but the care of the aged is a Christian duty, and——"

"Ah!" ejaculated the Superintendent, for there was a tap at the door. "Yes? Come in."

Jarvis entered.

"They've just brought that car from Drifford, sir," he announced. "Towed it. It's in the stable-yard."

"Oh, come along then," said the Superintendent. "Shan't keep you a minute, sir," he explained to the Vicar, "but this is a car which was found abandoned about an hour after the murder had taken place, and I want you to tell me if it is yours."

In the stable-yard stood a blue Morris Oxford, open two-seater, the radiator and bonnet crumpled up, the wind-screen smashed to splinters, one of the wings wrenched off, and otherwise damaged. But, directly he saw it, the Vicar exclaimed:

"Oh, no. That's not mine—that's one of the later models."

The policeman from Drifford, who had been steering the car as it was towed, came up. The Superintendent asked him:

"Found the missing registration-plate?"

"No, sir. They are searching still."

"Umph! No matter. We'll have the number of the engine."

The Drifford policeman went on:

"I didn't think you'd find this was the car you were after, sir. When we looked into her a little more closely, we found she couldn't have been going from Chiltonbury to London. You see, sir," he went on, "she must have skidded to begin with; then she struck a telegraph-post on the side of the road, and went off into the ditch. But the way she struck that post showed she was coming from London."

Captain Bristow, who had been silently regarding the car, turned to the policeman.

"Let me see," he said. "You found this car near Drifford, didn't you? Small village, isn't it? I seem to remember seeing it stuck up at a station."

"That's right, sir. Drifford is on the main line. The car was found about a mile out of the village."

Captain Bristow went on:

"I suppose," he said, "you haven't any idea as to the time when the smash took place, have you?"

"No, sir,—not the exact time. But, anyhow, it must have been after half-past eleven. I know that, because I was along the road myself at that time—I had a point at Farley Crossroads," he went on, addressing the Superintendent, "and I know the car was not in the ditch then."

The Superintendent nodded. But he was not looking at his subordinate. Once again his eyes were directed towards Bristow, a slightly expectant expression in them. But if he expected Bristow to make any further remarks, he was disappointed. Bristow merely frowned, and shrugged his shoulders slightly.

"Better tow the car into Chiltonbury," said the Superintendent, to his man. "We'll have to make enquiries, of course. But it doesn't seem to have anything to do with the matter here. Well—good morning, sir," he added, to the Vicar; "as soon as we get a line on your Morris, I'll let you know."

The Vicar went out by the gate beyond the stable-yard, Kinch retraced his steps towards the house, Bristow walking with him. And the Superintendent said:

"I'm glad of the opportunity of a word or two with you, sir,"— Bristow glanced at him quickly, but if he thought this genial policeman was going to share any confidence with him, he was mistaken. "There's a lot to be done, you see, and you might help me, if you would. I'd like to see all the people who were in the house last night—directly breakfast is over. Perhaps you'll be good enough to let me leave out that list?"—Bristow nodded. "I'm having the body taken to The Gables directly—the Coroner has ordered an autopsy, and the doctor will run out there for it. And, besides, it isn't fair on Sir Harry to keep the corpse in his house any longer. My sergeant—Mentmore—is at The Gables, getting information about Hurst, and I hope to have him back with his report soon—then we may have something more to go upon. I shall run round there myself as soon as I can, but after I've interviewed the people here I want to look over the list of costumes in the tent—Miss Lynwood has already promised to see to that. Then, of course, there are the arrangements for the inquest. I rang up the Coroner before I came out. He's fixed tomorrow afternoon. I thought of asking Sir Harry if it might take place here. Mr. Charles Lynwood," he broke off abruptly, "has gone to London for the day."

"Gone to London?"

There was a note of genuine surprise in Bristow's voice.

"Yes."

And Kinch looked sharply at his companion. But he only got a monosyllable to crown his own.

"Oh!"

They reached the house and Bristow opened the door. In the hall were Sir Harry and his eldest son, Sonia Fullinger, two other guests, Mrs. Cresswell's maid, and Mrs. Cresswell herself. In fact, they were all standing round Mrs. Cresswell—a very excited Mrs. Cresswell she was, too. There was a babel of confusion. Then Mrs. Cresswell caught sight of the uniformed Police Superintendent coming into the hall, broke away from the little group, rushed excitedly towards him, and cried:

"The police! Oh, I'm so glad you've come, Sergeant—or whatever you are! Did you know? Have you found them?"

"Found what, madam?" asked the somewhat bewildered Kinch.

"My pearls," almost shrieked Mrs. Cresswell, "my pearl necklace! It's gone. It's been stolen! I thought you'd come to tell me you'd got the thief. What are you going to do about it? I tell you, they're frightfully valuable. You *must* get them back for me. Haven't you a clue, or something? Oh, why don't you say something?"

"My dear madam," replied Kinch, very suavely and soothingly, "I assure you this is all news to me. I know nothing about your pearls."

"Then why are you here? I thought—Oh, *surely*——"

"Suppose you tell me all about it?" he went on, in his calmest manner. "Anyhow, I *am* here, you see, madam, and if you will just let me know what has happened it's my business to help you. Shall we go—?" and he looked at Sir Harry.

"Yes," said Sir Harry. "Come along, Mrs. Cresswell—into the library. And then you can tell the Superintendent all about it."

"Oh, my darling pearls!" she went on, as she followed Sir Harry. "I wouldn't have had this happen for the world. There's a thief in your house, Sir Harry. Everyone must be searched, and——"

Her voice died away as the much harassed Baronet led her out of the hall, followed by the Superintendent.

Harry Lynwood turned to Bristow.

"By Jove, Roger! *More* complications, eh?"

"Possibly simplifications," replied Bristow, dryly. "I've been wondering all along where the motive was. This may be it."

4

"Now," said Kinch, when he had succeeded in reducing Mrs. Cresswell to a state of comparative calmness, "you just try to tell me exactly what has happened. I'll ask any questions afterwards."

"When I had finished dressing this morning——"

"No, no," interrupted the Superintendent, gently. "Better begin before that. When you were last wearing your necklace, let us say."

"I was wearing it yesterday. I was playing the part of Queen Anne in the pageant, you see"—even in the midst of her calamity her inherent vanity asserted itself—"I wore the pearls at both performances. After the pageant was over none of us changed for dinner. I was still wearing them then, and, of course, I had them on when I went up to my room."

"Just a moment," said Kinch. "What time was that?"

"Oh, rather late. Did you notice, Sir Harry?"

"Just after eleven, I think it was," said the Baronet.

Kinch nodded.

"Go on," he said.

"I put the pearls in their case when I took them off. It was the first thing I did when I got into my room. I'm always *most* particular. Then I locked them up safely in my small leather dressing-case. I know they were there when I went to bed. And no one else knew—not even my maid. I had put them away before I rang for her. I always do. Well, that's all that happened last night, and then, this morning——"

"Excuse me," Kinch broke in, "you didn't leave your room after you had locked up the necklace—I mean last night?"

"Why, yes, I did—but only for a minute. I recollected I wanted to ask Miss Fullinger something—she was to drive me to London this

41

morning, you see. So I went out to the corridor and tapped at her door. But she didn't answer. I suppose she was asleep."

"She must have undressed very quickly, Mrs. Cresswell?"

"Oh, no, not necessarily. She went up early, didn't she, Sir Harry?"

"Yes, quite," said Sir Harry. "She was tired and had a slight headache. Also I remember she said something about getting her maid to help her pack some of her things last night, didn't she?"

"Yes, she did," said Mrs. Cresswell.

"Then you were actually out of your room for a short time?" asked the Superintendent.

"Only a few moments. Besides, I should have noticed anyone going into my room from the corridor. And—oh, yes—the necklace was there when I got back."

"How do you know?"

"I opened the dressing-case again, to put a bracelet in, I'm quite sure. Well, as I was saying, when I had finished dressing this morning I wanted something out of the case, and unlocked it. Then I missed the pearls. They were gone. I looked everywhere. Oh—you *will* get them back for me, *won't* you?"

"You may be sure we shall do our best," replied Kinch, soothingly. "And now, let me ask you a few questions. You say you were wearing your pearls all yesterday afternoon and evening?"

"Yes."

"So everybody had an opportunity of seeing them?"

"Why, of course. Quite a lot of people told me how much they admired them."

Kinch smiled, and went on:

"What sort of a case did you keep them in?"

"Oh, an ordinary jewel-case, you know. Oval in shape; flat. Dark-red leather outside."

"Was it locked?"

"It *has* a lock. But I mislaid the key some time ago. No, it wasn't locked."

"But the dressing-case was?"

"Of course. I told you I locked it."

"And the key?"

"It was one of a bunch."

"I see. And where did you put that bunch after you had locked the dressing-case?"

"In the left-hand little drawer of the chest of drawers," replied Mrs. Cresswell promptly.

"Ah!" said the Superintendent, noting her quick answer. "Does that mean you are in the habit of keeping your keys there?"

"I am very methodical. Yes; when I am not carrying my keys about with me, I always keep them in the left-hand drawer."

"Not always a good thing to be methodical, where valuables are concerned," commented the Superintendent. "Other people get to know one's habits, you see. But, tell me, were the keys still there this morning?"

"Yes."

"Exactly where you had put them?"

"Yes—certainly."

"These dressing-cases frequently have duplicate keys, and——"

"I know what you are thinking of. Yes, there *are* two keys. But, as it happens, both of them are on the ring—of the bunch."

"Have you that bunch?"

"I left it upstairs—in my room."

"All right. I'll have a look at it presently. Now, you say your *maid* did not see you put the pearls away. Tell me about her, Mrs. Cresswell."

"She is quite out of the question, if you imagine she had anything to do with it. Your suspicion——"

"My dear madam," interrupted Kinch, "I don't ask you from that point of view. I am hazarding no theories at present. But I must—if only for her sake—have some information about her."

"Well, Ellen Crane has been in my service for seven years or more. She is thoroughly trustworthy. If she had ever wanted to steal those pearls, she has had scores of opportunities."

Kinch nodded—and asked no further questions about her. He turned to Sir Harry.

"There was no one in the house—no outsiders, I mean,—after dinner last evening, except the Vicar and Hurst, I understand, Sir Harry?" he asked.

The Baronet shook his head.

"Not that I know of," he said. Then he added, as if it had suddenly occurred to him, "You haven't forgotten that my son forgot to lock the door when he came in from the marquee, Superintendent?"

"No," replied Kinch, thoughtfully. "I understand what you mean. I'd already made a note of it." He turned once more to Mrs. Cresswell. "There was a guest at dinner here last night," he said, "a Mr. Hurst. Did you notice him at all?"

"In Puritan dress," explained Sir Harry, remarking the puzzled expression on Mrs. Cresswell's face.

"Oh, yes—I remember him. But I don't think I spoke to him."

"I think I ought to tell you," went on Kinch, gravely, still speaking to Mrs. Cresswell, "that a more serious thing has happened than even the theft of your pearls. That is really why I am here. This Mr. Hurst was found dead near the house, very early this morning, and everything points to the face that he was murdered."

The Superintendent made the announcement very quietly. Nor did he expect that the grim news would upset Mrs. Cresswell nearly as much as the loss of her necklace. He had summed her up carefully, and felt it was only the sense of what was really personal that affected her strongly. Nor was he mistaken. She gave a little shudder of horror— but remained quite calm.

"How perfectly terrible!" she exclaimed, turning to Sir Harry, who nodded, silently. The Superintendent went on, still very quietly:

"I am, naturally, inclined to connect both crimes, Mrs. Cresswell, and not to treat them as coincidences—"

But Mrs. Cresswell interrupted him.

"You think, then, this Mr. Hurst had something to do with my necklace—that it was he who took it, perhaps? And that they murdered him because— Yes, I see! The murderer has got my pearls. Oh, you *must* catch him—"

Kinch smiled, in spite of himself. It was plain that the murder of Jasper Hurst was quite a minor point in comparison with the pearls— so far as Mrs. Cresswell was concerned. He held up his hand.

"I have to look at the case from every point of view before I can theorise," he said. "But I agree with you that we must, if possible, trace the person or persons who committed both crimes. That is only our duty. And that we shall probably find that both crimes are closely connected. And now," he went on, "I'd like to have a look at your room, please, Mrs. Cresswell—before any of the maids begin to tidy it. Will you come, too, Sir Harry, please?"

As they were going, the Superintendent asked Sir Harry:

"By the way, Sir Harry, when Hurst was in your house last night, did he, by any chance, go upstairs?"

"Not after Mrs. Cresswell went to bed—if that is what you mean. He did go up before dinner, with some of the other men, to the bathroom."

"Not afterwards?"

"Not that I know of."

"Ah, well, Captain Bristow and your two sons will be able to tell us if he did. I'll ask them. . . . Is this the room? One moment, please; I'd like to go in first, if I may."

Kinch produced no magnifying-glass or measuring tape, after the manner of the approved detective of fiction, when he went into Mrs. Cresswell's room. He was pretty observant, all the same. He looked well at the carpet, but if he thought he might find traces of dusty footprints there, he was mistaken. The room was in the front of the house, and had two windows. He looked out. The wall outside was quite bare, no creeper of any kind. The cleverest cat-burglar could hardly have scaled it. He gazed upwards. There was no storey above— no windows—and the roof projected with sharply-sloping eaves. It was quite unlikely that anyone had reached the window from above.

Obviously, then, if Mrs. Cresswell had given a correct description of matters, the thief must have come in by the door. Kinch went back to the door, and closed it—by the handle. The key was on the inside. Lying on the floor by the door was a tiny, shining shred of something. Kinch picked it up and examined it. It appeared to be a minute bit of gold braid—torn. He dropped it into an envelope and put the envelope back in his pocket. He turned to the door again, and examined the handle plate, carefully. Then he opened the door again and invited Mrs. Cresswell and Sir Harry to come in.

"Show me exactly where you kept your keys, will you, please, Mrs. Cresswell?"

"In here." She opened the left-hand top drawer of a chest of drawers standing near the window; "in this corner—underneath my spare handkerchiefs."

"Where were they before you came to bed? Did you carry them about with you?"

"Oh, no, I'd left nothing of value in my dressing-case. They were here—from the time I dressed for the pageant till I came up after dinner."

"So that anyone could have got at them all the time?"

"I suppose they could. But I don't see why—if anyone did. My pearls were not stolen then, you know."

"Quite so; but a first-hand knowledge of the scene of an intended crime beforehand is a very useful thing, Mrs. Cresswell."

"I daresay it is. But how could it have helped in this case? No one *knew* that I was going to lock up the pearls in that dressing-case."

And she pointed to the case itself, which stood open on a chair not very far from the door, the bunch of keys hanging from the lock. The Superintendent glanced at it—at the chest of drawers—and back at the door.

"If you make a habit of locking up the necklace when you are staying away from home—as you do?"—she nodded;—"well, you

know, habits become known. It was probably known you were
bringing the necklace here, for my impression is that this is a carefully
thought-out job—as regards your habits—and then a clever taking
advantage of the opportunity. You see," he went on, "to anyone who
knew, it would hardly take a minute to come into the room—step
across to the chest of drawers—get the bunch of keys—open the case
and take out the pearls—put the keys back—and, well, there you are!
Quite simple to anyone who knew the ropes beforehand. By the way,
you didn't lock your door, I suppose?"

"No. I never do that."

"Quite so. And—when you were asleep, were those windows
draped?"

"Not both. I drew up the blind and opened this one," she pointed it
out, "before I got into bed."

"Ah! Plenty of light—it was dim moonlight outside. You sleep
soundly?"

"Very—as a rule."

"Probably they knew *that*, too," said Kinch, with a grim little
smile. "And now let's have a look at those keys."

"Finger-prints, what?" said Sir Harry, who was a very interested
spectator.

Kinch shook his head.

"Not very much chance of that with keys, Sir Harry," he replied.
"No—I want to make sure of something else."

He took the key from the lock of the dressing-case and, keeping it
separate, spread out the rest of the keys which were on the ring
fan-wise on the palm of his hand. There were about a dozen of them,
of various sizes. He examined each one of them narrowly, and a little
smile broke out on his face. Then he said to Mrs. Cresswell:

"You told me there were duplicate keys of this dressing-case?"

"Yes—there are."

"And that both were on this ring?"

"Why, of course."

He shook his head.

"There's only one of them here now, at any rate," he said.

"My God!" ejaculated Sir Harry. "That's queer!"

"Oh, do you think so?" replied the Superintendent, dryly. "Well, it
doesn't exactly surprise me. This affair has got some clever brains
behind it, and was carefully planned. You see, it would be much easier
to have the key in one's possession beforehand. The thief knew he had
to come into this room and do the job while Mrs. Cresswell was here.
It was a risk anyhow, and a greater risk still to open that drawer and

get the keys first. But, by securing the duplicate key beforehand, he not only took the minimum of risk, but he saved more than half the time in doing it. Now, Mrs. Cresswell, do you think you can tell me with certainty the last occasion when you *knew* both keys were on the bunch?"

"Yes, I can," she replied. "I've just remembered. It was yesterday afternoon—directly after the first performance of the pageant."

"How do you know?"

"Because I came up here. You see, the spring of a bracelet I was wearing broke, and I wanted to put it away in my dressing-case. I took the keys out of the drawer—I was in a great hurry. The first one wouldn't fit—there was a bit of fluff in it, or something. Anyhow, I *know* I used the second. I suppose I ought to have told you all this before, only, in the confusion of discovering the loss of the pearls it escaped my mind, and——"

"Oh, it doesn't matter. The point is that we are now certain that someone took the duplicate key after—what time shall we say, Sir Harry?"

"The afternoon performance was over about half-past five."

"After that hour, then. Who would be in the house, Sir Harry?"

Sir Harry laughed.

"A good many people," he said. "All the house-party came in to tea—and a number of my personal friends in the neighbourhood as well. There were the servants, of course, though I sincerely hope——"

"No, no," broke in Kinch, "we must try to have a perfectly open mind. It isn't a question of suspecting or not suspecting any particular individual—yet. And then," he went on, "after tea—during the evening performance?"

"The servants were here—most of them. But people were going in and out of the house. Some of my guests—and I myself and my sons—changed our costumes here, in our rooms, between the scenes."

"Ah—yes,"—he thought for a moment. "And you said Hurst came upstairs?"

"Yes—er—but——"

"What, Sir Harry?"

"You must, in fairness, Superintendent, remember that *he* wouldn't have come into the house at all if I hadn't invited him to dinner—at the last moment."

"Um!" ejaculated Kinch, thoughtfully. "Yes—that's true. Well, we've got to find out all about this poor fellow, Hurst, Sir Harry. My sergeant, Mentmore, is at The Gables now, making enquiries, and is coming to me here presently, to report. Well, madam," he went on to

Mrs. Cresswell, "I won't trouble you any further just now—and I'm sure you both want your breakfast. After that——"

"Oh," broke in Mrs. Cresswell, "you *will* find my pearls for me, won't you?"

"I shall do my best, you may be sure, and——"

"But haven't you any idea? What are you going to *do?*"

Kinch smiled.

"A great deal, Mrs. Cresswell. There is any amount of machinery to put in motion. We are losing no time—but this promises to be a very complicated affair—this double crime,—and you must have patience.— One moment,"—he turned to a sofa upon which an array of gorgeous clothes were lying. "Is this the costume that you wore yesterday?"

"Yes."

Superintendent Kinch solemnly took up each garment, held it, and turned it over.

"Very pretty," was his comment. "You only wore this one costume?"

"That is all. Why do you ask?"

"Your dress must have suited you admirably, madam," gravely replied Kinch, as he laid down the skirt on the sofa. "And now I think we'll go down."

They were all three leaving the room, when Mrs. Cresswell suddenly exclaimed, with a shudder:

"It's terrible losing my necklace; but, oh, suppose I had woke up when the thief came into the room, and screamed—I *know* I should have screamed—he'd probably have murdered me. Ugh!"

"Not necessarily, Mrs. Cresswell," said Kinch, blandly. "I can't say, of course, but it's just possible you might not have screamed, you see. You might not, even, have been surprised."

"Eh?—what's that?" asked Sir Harry. "I don't understand."

But the Superintendent made no reply to this. All he said was that, after breakfast, he would like to interview all the inmates of the house in the library.

In the hall was standing a tall, distinguished-looking man, with a decided military bearing, dressed in a grey suit, the cut of which suggested Savile Row, a man with iron-grey hair, small moustache, and aristocratic face.

"Ah, good morning, Major," said Sir Harry.

"Good morning, Sir Harry. I'm not going to bother you now—they tell me you haven't had breakfast yet. But I came—of course. Beastly business. I'm sorry. You go and feed, and I'll have a word with you afterwards. I want to see Kinch now."

"Have you breakfasted, Major?" asked Sir Harry, with hospitable interest.

"Long ago. That's all right."

"Well, shall I send you a cup of coffee in the library?"

"Thanks. I won't say no. Now—Kinch."

Major Bainbridge, Chief Constable of the County, was essentially, so he said himself, a military man. He would tell his friends that he was not, for all his title suggested it, a policeman, least of all a sleuth. That it was his business to organise the men who dealt with crime rather than to handle crime itself. He told the Standing Committee this, more than once. The Standing Committee never regretted having appointed him, however, for although he might not have been a policeman, he had the rare gift of knowing men and of being able to put the right man in the right place, and the Standing Committee knew that, in the five years he had been in office, he had brought the police of the county to a high state of efficiency.

Among the police themselves there were just two predominant opinions about Major Bainbridge. In the first place, every man, rank or file, felt that he was personally known by the Chief Constable. He never failed to call every constable by his right name, and the homely little questions he asked them about their domestic affairs made them feel he took a personal interest in them. The second opinion was held by those of the more exalted rank, such as Superintendent Kinch, and was the fruit of more confidential intercourse. They knew very well that although the Major professed to be "no policeman," he had a pretty shrewd intellect and that whenever he chose, in his diffident way, to "offer a suggestion," in some knotty problem, that suggestion was by no means to be despised.

"Well, Kinch," he said, as he sat down in a chair in the library, and lighted a cigarette, "this is a big job we're up against, it seems. Now I don't want to barge in and burden you, for I know you've got your hands full, but I would like—just a brief summary of the case, so far."

This was characteristic of the Chief Constable. He always gave the officer with whom he was discussing a case the impression that *he*, the officer, had it in hand, and that the last thing he wished to do was to rob him of any credit. Kinch told him, in as few words as possible, all that had happened up to date.

"Um," said the Major. "Not much doubt that the two crimes were connected, eh?"

"Looks like it, sir."

"Who was this poor chap, Hurst? Know anything about him?"

"Not much, sir. I've put Mentmore on that job. He'll report here presently."

"Good. And this nephew of the Vicar's. He's got to be found."

"Yes, sir. I've 'phoned through to the station. Fellowes has gone up to London. He'll call at Scotland Yard. Question of enquiries about night-clubs."

"Yes—I see. Why have you had young Lynwood shadowed?"

"Because I've an inkling he knows more than he says. And it was queer he wanted to run up to town on the spur of the moment. Of course there may be nothing in it, but I'm taking no chances."

The Major nodded.

"Queer thing carrying off the body in that sedan-chair," he mused.

"But he wasn't dead then, sir."

"Well?"

"Question of getting him out of the way—in the car, wasn't it, sir? They couldn't have brought the car nearer—because of the noise. After all, it was the handiest way of carrying him."

The Chief Constable, who had been meditatively gazing at the end of his cigarette, which he held in his hand, suddenly looked up.

"You don't think they meant to kill him, then?"

"No—I don't," said Kinch.

The two men looked at one another.

"Oh!" said the Chief Constable. Then he went on: "You don't want Scotland Yard called in ?"

"I hope not," replied Kinch, briskly and confidently.

"Good," sighed the Major, almost beneath his breath.

Kinch understood.

"Thank you, sir," he said.

Major Bainbridge lighted a fresh cigarette, smoked in silence for a few seconds, and then said, nonchalantly:

"Captain Bristow is still here, I suppose?"

"Yes, sir. None of the guests have left yet. And I understand Captain Bristow is staying on for a few days."

"Oh! You may or you may not know, Kinch, that Captain Bristow was, for some years, in the Secret Service?"

"Yes, sir. So I've heard."

"Good record, Kinch, good record. I happen to know that he was looked upon as one of their smartest men. He hasn't volunteered any theory, I suppose?"

"Not to me, sir."

"He wouldn't. It's not his job, of course, and he wouldn't interfere. But, all the same, I expect he's got a few notions. A reticent fellow, Kinch, from what I've heard of him. I—er—presume you hadn't thought of taking him into your confidence at all?"

"I rather prefer to work on my own, sir,—and with my own men."

"Oh, quite so, quite so."

"But—"

"Well?"

"I knew something about him, sir,—so I'm—well, in a way, interested. And I'm noticing any remarks he makes without letting him know."

"As, for example,—?"

"Well, he's asked a few questions—of the Vicar, and others. I've got them jotted down," and he tapped his notebook, which lay on the table beside him.

"I think you are wise, Kinch," remarked the Chief Constable. "Any opinion of his—if he offers it—would be worth considering. And he wouldn't ask questions without a motive. Keep your eye on him, anyhow, even if you don't deal with him directly."

Kinch half hesitated—then began:

"He seemed rather keen on that derelict car we found at Drifford, but I couldn't see the point he was driving at."

"What did he say?"

"Wanted to know if there was a station at Drifford—and the exact time the car was wrecked. That must have been after half-past eleven."

"Oh!" the Chief Constable's eyes twinkled. "Well, I'm fond of crossword puzzles—if the clues are well hidden and call for a little thought."

He half-closed his eyes. The Superintendent glanced at his watch, then entered a few notes in his book. It was nearly time that Mentmore should come to report about his visit to The Gables. And then there were all these people to interview. He glanced at the list he had now received—the members of the family—guests, servants. He began ticking them off in the order in which he would have them in the library. He half forgot Major Bainbridge's presence.

Lazily, the Chief Constable reached for a Bradshaw which was lying, with other books of reference, on a writing-table; turned over the leaves, studied it for a moment or two, put it down, and said:

"Kinch, may I offer a suggestion?"

"Yes, sir!"

The Superintendent was alert now. He had had previous experience of these "suggestions" of his superior officer.

"I'm rather curious to test Captain Bristow's train of thought. You say they haven't found those registration number-plates anywhere near the place the car broke down. I suggest you might arrange to have them looked for by the side of the line between Drifford and Chiltonbury—the down side, and probably nearer Drifford than Chiltonbury. Possibly platelayers—but there, it's only a suggestion."

"How on earth—" began Kinch, but the other waved his hand to silence him.

"All right—you try. There may be something in it."

A tap at the door stopped further conversation. Anstice Lynwood appeared.

"May I come in—if I'm not disturbing you?"

The Chief Constable sprang to his feet.

"Good morning, Miss Lynwood. Yes—come in, by all means."

"I'm frightfully hungry," said the girl, "and I want my breakfast too badly to worry you for long. But I've checked all those costumes and properties," she went on, speaking to the Superintendent, "and I've found two things in the tent that had nothing to do with the pageant—at least, I don't think so. Here they are."

She laid on the table, first of all, a navy-and-white muffler.

"This certainly doesn't belong to us or to any of the hired costumes, and I don't remember anyone having it on yesterday, though, of course, someone might have been wearing it in the ordinary way. And the other thing—well, here it is, but I can't make it out at all."

"*I* can," said Major Bainbridge; "it's what we call a knuckle-duster,—that's what this funny-looking bit of brass is, eh, Kinch?"

"That's right, sir."

"A knuckle-duster?" echoed Anstice.

"A sort of metal boxing-glove," explained the Major. "You just slip your fingers in those holes, and let out at a fellow. And when he gets it in the face—well, it's a knock-out in the first round, generally. Where did you find it, Miss Lynwood?"

"Half hidden in the grass—on the floor of the tent. . . . Then, you think—?" she asked.

"I don't think there is much doubt about this being the weapon with which Hurst was killed, Miss Lynwood," said the Superintendent, gravely. "You see, sir?" and he arched his eyebrows as he turned to the Chief Constable.

Major Bainbridge nodded. There was a dark brown stain on the outside of the formidable little brass weapon.

5

By no means the least important phase in a criminal case is that which embraces the routine work of the police, work that is often at once elaborate, detailed, exceedingly dull in parts, but invariably painstaking. To write the real, complete story of any crime, however interesting in itself, its detection, and its result, would be to weary the reader intensely.

Better, therefore, in this story, only to give hints of the movements which, emanating from the police-station at Chiltonbury, spread far and wide throughout the country, like the ripples emanating from the splash of a stone falling in the midst of a pond. By means of the telephone at Frimley Manor, and by police messengers who dashed in and out from Chiltonbury, Superintendent Kinch constantly set the machinery in motion, in the hope that some little movement of it, somewhere, would lead to the results he had in view.

Descriptions of the Vicar's nephew, of Mrs. Cresswell's necklace and of the Vicar's car, had been broadcast. Search was being made, in relation to frequenters of night-clubs in London, for traces of Bob Gilbert, the man the Vicar had mentioned as being one of his nephew's friends. "Fences" were being kept under observation, and even Charles Lynwood, in blissful ignorance, was being tracked to his London club—to which he directed his steps after arriving at the terminus.

And all this before Sir Harry's house-party had finished their breakfast and Kinch had had time to interview them. But, all the time, he felt he had no real knowledge of the central figure of the tragedy, the man who lay, cold and stiff, in his house, The Gables. And he waited, a little impatiently, for Mentmore's report.

As a matter of fact, Mentmore came back from The Gables in time to have a close and confidential interview with the Superintendent before the latter tackled the delicate task of interviewing personally the inmates of Frimley Manor. The Superintendent welcomed the burly, good-tempered-looking Detective-Sergeant, as the latter came into the library. He did not at all resemble a ferret, but Kinch knew that this heavy, lethargic-looking man had all the ferret's character-istics in finding the scent and in sticking closely to the trail. He also knew, from long experience, that the report which Mentmore would present to him would be a plain, straightforward statement of facts, unvarnished, and nothing redundant about it. Mentmore invariably stuck, like a bull-dog, to the point.

"Ah, Sergeant," he said, "glad to see you. We may be able to get a bit forrader now. By the way—there's another crime——"

"The lady's pearls. I know. The chauffeur told me as I came through the yard. Anything doing, sir?"

"Humph! A good deal may depend upon what you've found out at The Gables. Let's have it, Sergeant."

Mentmore produced and opened his pocket-book.

"And that isn't much, sir. Up against a blank wall, mostly."

"Go on."

And Mentmore, his eyes steadily fixed on his notebook, made his report.

"There's a married couple in the house, Barnes by name, and a girl. Jobbing gardener comes in three times a week. I've seen them all. The girl belongs to the village—a bit of a fool. No information worth having from her. And the gardener's much the same.

"Barnes is an ex-sergeant of the Downshires. Intelligent man. Since his discharge accepted several posts as butler and valet. His wife does the housekeeping and cooking. Superior, reliable people, both of 'em. They've only been with Hurst two months—since he came here. Answered an advertisement in the *Morning Post* for a married couple to live in; address, Office of the paper. Hurst replied, writing from the Queen's Hotel, Leeds. Barnes kept the letter. Here it is, sir."

And he handed it to Kinch, who read:

"James Barnes,

I am in receipt of your answer to my advertisement. I shall be in London on Thursday next and would like to interview you. I am lunching at the Savoy Restaurant. Kindly call there at 2 o'clock and ask the Commissionaire at the door for me. I will leave word for him. Bring testimonials.

Yours faithfully,
JASPER HURST."

"Well?" said the Superintendent. Mentmore went on:

"Barnes kept the appointment. Hurst was satisfied and engaged him and his wife. Said he had just taken a house at Frimley, near Chiltonbury, and wanted Barnes and his wife to go there to get ready for him. Explained all arrangements. They came here on May the eleventh, same day as the furniture arrived——"

"Where from?"

"Felter's—Tottenham Court Road. All new. They got it in. Hurst came three days later—sending a wire first. Came in his car. New car, too. One of the conditions was that Barnes was to act as chauffeur when required. And that's all Barnes knows about him, sir."

"But—he's been here two months. Surely——"

"I asked that, naturally. Occasional visitors—to lunch. Never stayed night. Two gentlemen—Barnes met the London train and ran them out. One came twice, the other once. He didn't know their names. Sir Harry Lynwood called—and the Vicar, locally. That seems about all."

"Couldn't tell you of any relatives?"

"No. Hurst never mentioned any."

"How about correspondence?"

"Well," replied Mentmore, "I shouldn't say Barnes or his wife are the kind to read other people's letters. I asked, of course. Very little actual correspondence, I gathered. And *they* knew nothing about it."

"They told you what sort of a man he was—habits and so on?"

"Yes, sir. Here's the summary. A gentleman. Knew what's what, Barnes put it. Quiet and retiring. Read a fair amount. Evidently in good circumstances. Went to London occasionally. Fond of walking, but, apparently, not a sports-man. Methodical, in the house—you know what a woman like Mrs. Barnes would say—'gave no trouble.' And that's about all."

The Superintendent nodded.

"Find anything?" he asked, curtly.

"Nothing much. Searched his writing-desk, and so on, of course. Seems to have destroyed all letters—if he had any. Not even an envelope with a postmark lying about. Only tradesmen's bills, circulars, and what-not. Here's his cheque-book. London and Western Bank, Fleet Street branch. Enquiries to be made there. And this may be of use—though there isn't much in it."

"This" was a small address-book, evidently new, lettered alphabetically at the edges. The Superintendent consulted it with interest and began turning over the leaves. "A" was blank. "B" had the addresses of a baker and a butcher in Chiltonbury. "C" produced a local chemist, and underneath the word "Carnations" was evidently a florist's address.

"Ha!" exclaimed Kinch, as he turned to "D." "This may be worth looking up."

What was written on the "D" page was "Doctor. P. H. Sefton, M.D., 58ᵃ Harley Street."

"E" was blank. "F" detained the Superintendent for a moment. It contained this entry:

"F. Wisteria, 71 Hampden Road, St. John's Wood, N.W.8."

"Well," he said, "*that*'ll have to be noted. First private address, apparently, I've seen."

"And the only one," said Mentmore; "all the rest are tradesmen or the like. And this may only turn out to be something of the kind. 'Faith-healer'—'Fortune-teller'—'Face massage'—Most likely a frost," he added, with a grin.

"Well," said Kinch, "we must find out how he took the house—references, and so on. I haven't had time to ask Sir Harry yet."

"I have. Saw him just now as I came in. He'd put The Gables in the hands of Aston & Newman, 113 Piccadilly—auctioneers and house agents, and advertised it in the *Times*. Hurst saw the advertisement, called on the agents. They arranged the let. He gave them his bankers as a reference, and they thought it good enough."

"I see. Now then, photos?" he asked, tersely.

"Yes, sir. Here's one. Recently taken, Barnes thinks."

"Good! The Press will be swarming about here in no time. Get it published—they'll be glad to have it. And a full description, of course. That may bring something. I've got to interview these folks now. But, look here, Mentmore—ring up that Harley Street doctor—there's a London telephone directory in the hall. Got the address? Right. Ask him to tell you anything he knows of Hurst. And then, I want you to go to the Vicarage. There may be nothing in it, but take this scarf with you. The Vicar's been round with a story. His nephew took that car of his last night——"

"Good Lord, sir!" That's some news!"

"I hope so. He'll give you details. Interview his housekeeper. See if she knows anything about the scarf. Careful, mind. Don't thrust it at her. You'll understand."

"Right, sir."

"Come back here and report. Then I shall want to run in to Chiltonbury."

Kinch thereupon settled down to the task of inverviewing. Sir

Harry came in first. His contribution consisted mainly of brief notes concerning the guests and servants.

"I'm afraid we shall have a lot of trouble," the Superintendent confided, "in finding out about Hurst. At present he's a dark horse."

"Do you think," asked the Baronet, "that he—well—that *he* took Mrs. Cresswell's pearls? Slipped back into the house after my son had gone into the tent?"

"Candidly, I don't know *what* to think about that yet, Sir Harry. That he was mixed up with the theft is pretty obvious. But *how* he was mixed up is a puzzle at present. And now, please, I'll see your eldest son—and then Miss Lynwood."

Harry Lynwood's visit to the library was a brief one. He had nothing to add to what Kinch knew already. His sister followed him.

"You have saved me a lot of trouble, Miss Lynwood," began Kinch, "by checking those costumes. They were hired, I suppose?"

"Most of them were."

"Well, I want to see them all before they go back. Are they still in the tent?"

"Yes. We have a few in the house. Do you want to see them as well?"

"Please. Also hired?"

"Not all. We made some."

"Well, let me have a look at them, too. Now, tell me. You didn't hear anything in the night?"

"Not a sound. You see, I was fast asleep."

"Your room opens on the main corridor?"

"Yes, but I might have been anywhere. I was frightfully tired, and went to sleep at once."

"I see. Tell me about Mrs. Cresswell. I suppose you arranged for her to come here long before the pageant took place?"

"Of course. And Sonia Fullinger too. They live near one another in London."

"Yes. And—er—well, I suppose Mrs. Cresswell rather enjoyed showing off that necklace? If I may say so, she seems that sort, eh?"

Anstice smiled.

"She did: very much. I was only saying yesterday I thought it rather silly of her, with all those people about."

"She was likely to talk about it beforehand?"

"Beforehand?"

"Before she came here, I mean."

"I expect she was. I don't want to be nasty, Superintendent, but we all know how Mrs. Cresswell loves the opportunity of parading her jewelry. Poor thing! she's in rather a state about it now—I don't mean only losing her pearls, but her husband will be so frightfully angry. She's telephoned to him—and he's coming down today."

"Well," said Kinch, "we must try to find them for her. Thank you very much. I'll see Mr. Singleton now,"—he glanced at his list. "A barrister, isn't he?"

"Yes. I'll ask him to come in."

There entered one of the guests, a tall, middle-aged man, his profession clearly stamped on his clear-cut, intellectual face.

"Good morning, Mr. Singleton. I'll get to the point at once. Can you throw any light on this case?"

"I wish I could, Superintendent," replied Singleton. "My particular line happens to be criminology, so I'm intensely interested. But I know nothing. I slept soundly, and it was only when I came down to breakfast that I heard what had happened."

"Well, let's go back a bit before that, sir. Sir Harry tells me that this poor devil Hurst went upstairs with some of you gentlemen before dinner. Were you one?"

"Certainly. He and young Underwood and I went into one of the bathrooms for a wash and brush-up."

"Yes, I see. Now, if you can remember, tell me what happened."

Singleton looked at him, keenly.

"Let me see," he said. "Yes—I can do that. Hurst washed his hands and brushed his hair. I was talking to him at the time. Then he went out—into the corridor. Underwood and I must have remained in the bathroom for four or five minutes. But when I came out Hurst had not gone downstairs. He was still in the corridor."

"Oh!" The Superintendent leaned forward. "What was he doing?"

"Looking out of the window—at the end of the corridor."

"And he'd been there several minutes?"

"Must have been."

The Superintendent was thinking quickly. This would have given Hurst plenty of time to slip into Mrs. Cresswell's bedroom and get the duplicate key off the bunch. The weak link in the chain of reasoning was, of course, the fact that Sir Harry had told him that Hurst was only invited to the house at the last moment.

"Thanks," he said. "I think that's all, Mr. Singleton."

"You won't want me any more? I had arranged to take a morning train back to London—I'm rather busy."

"Oh, that's all right, sir. You won't object to Inspector Hughes—

he ought to be here now—in plain clothes—taking a look at your things before you go? I've got, as a matter of form, to have a search. It's a job I hate, though."

"Certainly," laughed Singleton, "though I don't think you'll find that necklace in the house."

"Sure I shan't. Will you ask Mr. Underwood to come in?"

Frank Underwood, a young Cambridge undergraduate, had nothing of importance to tell Kinch. He, too, had slept soundly through the night. He had not noticed Hurst when he came out of the bathroom. He, too, was returning that day, and, as there was no reason for detaining him, the Superintendent told him he might do so.

The next on the list was Mrs. Cresswell, but as Kinch had already seen her, and as Anstice Lynwood had told him that she was remaining in the house—at all events till her husband came—he passed her over and asked for Sonia Fullinger.

He looked up as she came into the room. A pretty, vivacious girl, with dark shingled hair and brown eyes, quick in her movements. He also noticed her firm chin and rather compressed lips. To him these meant more than her piquant beauty, for they were an indication of a decided character.

He had, of course, asked Singleton and Underwood what were their respective addresses, and he began in the same manner with Sonia Fullinger.

"Ah! Miss Fullinger, I believe. Do sit down. And will you, please, give me your home address?"

"Why?" she asked, her eyes rounding a little.

"Well, you see," he said, urbanely, "I'm asking all the guests to let me know where they live—it's a matter of routine."

"Oh—very well, then. St. John's Wood. . . ." He looked, enquiringly, "Hampden Road, St. John's Wood," she completed it.

"Yes—and the number?" he asked, with pencil poised over his notebook.

"Seventy-one."

There was the slightest flicker in his eyes, otherwise he betrayed no particular interest. Kinch was a master of outward expression. Apparently quite casually he reached for the other notebook which was lying on the table, the address-book Mentmore had brought from The Gables, opened it nonchalantly at the letter "F."

"Ah, yes," he said, smiling. "Is there any particular name to the house—besides the number?"

"Wisteria."

Kinch closed the address-book and put it back on the table. Not by a single gesture or facial expression did he betray his intense interest. On the contrary, the bland, encouraging smile broadened on his refined, pleasant-looking face. He looked innocent and fatherly.

"You live there with your parents?" he asked.

"Of course."

"And your father? May I ask what is his profession?"

"My father? Oh, he's on the Stock Exchange."

A rapid succession of thoughts flashed through the keen brain of the Superintendent. This address in Hurst's little book might mean no more than that Mr. Fullinger was his broker—it harmonized with all the other addresses in the book. And yet, one does not generally enter the private address of one's broker in lists of this kind. His next question, seemingly quite casual, was a clever one.

"Oh, yes. Thank you. Jobber or broker?"

The girl's eyes rounded in surprise.

"I don't see why you want to know all this," she replied; "but he's a jobber."

That rather settled it. The public do not deal direct with jobbers on the Stock Exchange. At the same time, he was aware that he had aroused a feeling of antagonism in the girl with these seemingly irrelevant questions. He would have to proceed warily. And his instinct and experience told him that blunt, direct methods would be out of place. Besides, he was anxious not to arouse the slightest suspicion in her mind.

"This is a very serious crime, Miss Fullinger," he said; "a double crime. And I am trying to get all the information I can about it. Of course I want to know about this unfortunate Mr. Hurst, and I thought, perhaps, you could give me some information."

"I!" she exclaimed. "Oh, but why should you ask me that?"

"Well, I gathered that you knew him."

"I never saw him before yesterday," she replied.

"Oh? Nor knew anything of him?"

"Of course not. I'm frightfully sorry for what has happened, but I can't help you."

"He never came to your house, I suppose?"

"To our house? Certainly not."

There was a gathering resentment in her tone of voice. And Kinch knew that a defiant witness is of little use.

"Well, now, tell me—you saw him yesterday, didn't you? And he dined here, I understand."

"Yes. I was sitting next to him."

"Oh! And he talked to you, naturally. Was there anything in his conversation—"

"Not at all," she broke in. "He only spoke to me two or three times—about the pageant, and so on."

"Mention Mrs. Cresswell's pearls?"

"Did he?—er—yes, as a matter of fact, he did. But it was nothing particular."

"Still," said the Superintendent, blandly, "sometimes a chance word helps. What did he say about the pearls?"

"Let me see"—she paused a little. "Oh, yes, I think I remember. I was telling him I was going to run Mrs. Cresswell to London this morning in my two-seater, and he wanted to know how we managed about her luggage. I told him our maids took that—by train. And then he asked if Mrs. Cresswell would take her pearls with her, or send them by her maid. And I said I really didn't know."

"Oh!"

He was trying to piece things together. If what she was telling him was true, there could be no doubt that Jasper Hurst had been showing rather an inquisitive interest in those pearls. On the other hand, there was that marked coincidence in her home address being entered in Hurst's book—and under the letter "F" Fullinger. He had a half a mind to ask her what it meant—but his intuitive caution got the better of him. If she had lied about the matter of knowing Hurst she would equally prevaricate on the question of the address. And there were other methods.

"Nothing more?" he asked.

She shook her head.

"Well, let me ask you something else." He looked at his notebook. "Sir Harry tells me you went up to your room last night rather earlier than the others. And Mrs. Cresswell says she tapped at your door later on—before she retired for the night."

"Did she?" asked the girl. "I didn't hear her, then."

"I see. I suppose you must have been asleep. And you heard nothing in the night?"

"No—nothing at all."

"Umph! Well—I think that's all. Thank you very much, Miss Fullinger. Are you leaving today?"

Sonia shot a glance at him—half-mischievous.

"If I may be allowed to do so," she said.

"Certainly. I shan't want you at the inquest. By the way, I must see your maid. You have one, I understand?"

"Yes."

"Been with you long?"

Unconsciously he had relapsed into an official attitude, and was rapping out his questions. That gleam of defiance came once more into Sonia's eyes.

"I'll tell you all about her, Superintendent," she retorted, "without troubling you to cross-examine me. Her name is Bates. I fancy her Christian names are Phyllis Aurelia—but I call her Bates. She has been with me for about a month—straight from her last place, which was with Lady Challington, to whom she was lady's-maid for four years or more. Excellent testimonials. Height about five feet two, clear complexion—when it's natural, which it often isn't—fair hair, grey eyes. And she doesn't squint, and she hasn't, so far as I know, got a strawberry-mark on her left shoulder. Will that do?"

Superintendent Kinch replied with perfect gravity, and with just the vestige of a twinkle in his eyes:

"An excellent description, Miss Fullinger. Thank you very much. And now, please, I will see Phyllis Aurelia Bates, if you will very kindly send her to me."

Sonia Fullinger nodded, got up and walked out of the room, Kinch looking after her, a puzzled expression on his face. In a minute or two the maid, Bates, came in. She was a young woman of about twenty-three years of age, wearing a plain black frock, very neat; almost prim in the severity of her appearance. A good-looking young woman, but with rather a "baby" type of countenance, marked by the slightly open mouth and a half-wondering look in her grey eyes. Pretty fair hair, bobbed and very carefully brushed. And her mistress was right as to her complexion; she had powdered her nose rather apparently, and her cheeks were tinted by art in exclusion to nature.

"Ah," said the Superintendent, "Miss Fullinger tells me you have only been a short time in her service."

"Yes, sir. Just about four weeks. My late mistress was leaving for India, and I didn't want to go abroad."

"Lady Challington?"

"Yes, sir. I've got the testimonial she gave me, here, if you'd like to see it."

Kinch took and read it. It was quite an ordinary testimonial. Bates had been with Lady Challington for four years—was perfectly honest and of good moral character—understood her duties thoroughly—a good needlewoman. . . . Lady Challington could confidently recommend her as an efficient lady's-maid.

"Very well," said Kinch. "And you heard or saw nothing last night?"

"No, sir. Nothing. I sleep soundly, and my room was in another wing of the house—at the back."

"I see. And what do you know about Mr. Hurst—the gentleman who was murdered?" He shot the question at her, suddenly.

"Mr. Hurst, sir? I'd never heard of him before."

"Never heard Miss Fullinger—or any of her people—mention him?"

"No, sir. Not till this morning."

"I see. Now, tell me, please. I suppose you went into your mistress's room last night—when she went to bed?"

"Why, of course I did, sir. It's part of my duties. I always go and—"

"Yes, yes, I know. She went to bed early, didn't she?"

"She—she went up to her room early, sir."

"Eh?" He looked up from his notebook sharply. "I mean—well—she was *in* bed early?"

The girl shook her head.

"I couldn't say, sir," she replied. "You see, she hadn't gone to bed when I left her room."

Kinch was interested.

"What time was that?"

"I didn't notice, sir."

"Come, try to remember. Was it, for example, before or after eleven?"

Bates puckered her forehead.

"I can't be certain, sir. But I think it must have been after eleven though it might have been a few minutes before."

"Tell me exactly what happened—when you went up to her room. She rang for you, I suppose?"

"Yes, sir, and I went straight up."

"And she?"

"She was sitting down, sir,—smoking a cigarette."

"You're sure she wasn't in bed?"

"Of course she wasn't sir. She hadn't begun to undress. She was still wearing her acting clothes."

"I see. Well, and what then?"

"I packed her large suitcase, sir,—ready for going away this morning. And then she told me I might go. That was all."

The Superintendent leaned back in his chair and looked at Bates, thoughtfully. He was puzzled. If Sonia Fullinger was still up and dressed about eleven o'clock, why, then, she must have been pretty quick in undressing, getting into bed, and falling asleep before Mrs. Cresswell tapped at her door. But *was* there anything in it? He knew quite well that, in a case of this kind, an open mind had to be kept, and he knew, also, that it was fatal to centre suspicions on a particular person from slender reasons. Rapidly he debated in his mind whether he should see Sonia Fullinger again before she left, ask her to explain why she was so long undressing, and whether she was really asleep when Mrs. Cresswell tapped at her door. Immediately, however, he saw the futility of such a question. Whether there was anything in it or not, her reply was sure to be that, whatever time Mrs. Cresswell knocked, she had not heard it. There was no real evidence of anything that mattered.

"Well," he said, after a pause, "I think that's all. You are returning to town with your mistress, I suppose?"

"Yes, sir. I was to have gone by train, but now Mrs. Cresswell isn't coming, Miss Fullinger is going to take me and the luggage in her car."

"Very well. I want to see Mrs. Cresswell's maid now. You can tell her, please."

Mrs. Cresswell's maid, Crane by name, was a self-possessed young woman of about thirty, her rather plain face giving the impression of sound common-sense. She looked shrewd and capable. The Superintendent summed her up quickly.

"Well," he said, "there are a few questions I want to ask you, please. You went up to Mrs. Cresswell's room last night?"

"Yes."

"Did you see the necklace then?"

"No, sir. My mistress had locked it up in her dressing-case before she rang for me, I suppose. At any rate, she was not wearing it."

Kinch nodded. This tallied with Mrs. Cresswell's story.

"There was nothing out of the way?"

"No, sir."

"You knew Mrs. Cresswell kept the key of the dressing-case in that left-hand drawer?"

The woman smiled.

"Yes, sir, I knew that very well. It was her fixed habit. I've taken those keys out of her drawer hundreds of times—to unlock something for her. I sometimes thought it wasn't quite wise always to keep them in the same place."

"I suppose others knew as well?"

Crane shook her head.

"Not as far as *I'm* concerned," she replied. "I mean, I never told any of the other servants."

"Quite sensible of you. But—well, say Mrs. Cresswell's friends. Do you think any of them knew where she kept those keys?"

"I should think they must have done—some of them. You see, sir, ladies often take their friends up to their rooms to show them their dresses, and so on."

Kinch smiled. Being a married man, he was well aware of this.

"Yes, I see," he said; "her *intimate* friends, of course,—such as Miss Lynwood here—or Miss Fullinger?"

"Oh, yes. Miss Fullinger is often in our house. She lives quite near."

The Superintendent followed it up.

"I suppose," he said with a laugh, "Mrs. Cresswell tried on that Queen Anne costume she was wearing yesterday, and showed it to her friends, didn't she?"

The maid laughed in return.

"That's a fact," she replied. "Before dinner here—the evening before last. The ladies were all going into each other's rooms."

"And she'd show then the pearls as well?"

Again she laughed.

"I can't imagine her *not* doing so," she said, dryly.

"Well," went on Kinch, as though he had been digressing, "I mustn't waste time talking about the ladies showing off their dresses. Let's get back to the point. Everybody except Captain Bristow and Mr. Charles seems to have slept very soundly last night. Did you?"

"I did, sir. It had been a busy day, and I was late going to bed. I—"

"How late?"

"Nearly twelve o'clock, sir."

"Oh. And you heard nothing?"

"Nothing at all. I didn't know anything had happened till I came down into the servants' hall this morning. The butler told me, then, about the murder—and a few minutes later my mistress rang for me and I found her distracted over the loss of her pearls."

He asked her a few more questions, and then dismissed her. Methodically, but as briefly as possible, he proceeded to interview the house servants, but not one scrap of information could he get from them. He closed his notebook and looked at his watch. It was time to get back to Chiltonbury, but he had to wait until Mentmore returned from the Vicarage before he started.

He left the library and went into the hall. Its only occupant was

Captain Bristow, who was sitting in an arm-chair, pipe in mouth, quietly reading the morning paper. He looked up.

"Finished your interviews, Superintendent?"

"I've seen everyone who was in the house last night, yes, sir."

"Ah!" replied Bristow, tersely.

The two men looked at one another for a moment or two.

"Of course there's you, sir," said Kinch. "I didn't ask you to come into the library. But you've told me all you know, I suppose?"

"Yes. I think I've told you every fact, Superintendent."

"Queer case, sir."

"Very."

It may have been that each man was wondering, not about facts, but about any theories the other might have. But, if this was so, neither of them asked a question or volunteered a remark. And, just then, Mentmore came in.

The detective-sergeant was just about to speak to his superior officer when he caught sight of Captain Bristow—and hesitated. But Kinch said, with a quick glance at Bristow first:

"All right, Mentmore. You've been to the Vicarage?"

"Yes, sir."

Kinch turned to Captain Bristow.

"We found a scarf in the marquee," he said, "which didn't belong to any of the costumes—Ah—that's it," for Mentmore had taken the scarf out of his pocket. "Well," he went on to the detective-sergeant, "how about it?"

Bristow laid down his paper and eyed Mentmore with interest.

"I saw the Vicar's housekeeper, sir. She told me all about the visit of young Mr. Curtis last night. I produced this scarf, and she recognised it before I'd time to ask her any questions about it. She says Mr. Curtis was wearing it when he called at the Vicarage. It was hanging up in the hall with his light overcoat all the time he was in the house."

"By George!" exclaimed the Superintendent. "No getting away from *that,* Captain Bristow."

"May I ask your sergeant a question?" was Bristow's reply.

"By all means."

Bristow turned to Mentmore.

"When the Vicar told us about his nephew a little while ago, he said his housekeeper was not quite sure of the time when Mr. Curtis took the car out of the garage; she thought it may have been about half-past ten or nearer eleven. You didn't happen to find out the exact time he started the car, by any chance?"

"Yes, I did, sir. The maid knew. She didn't *see* the car, but she heard it drive off. And she struck a match and looked at her alarm clock. The housekeeper was a bit out—it was five minutes past eleven."

"Oh! Thank you."

He took a little notebook from his pocket, looked up a page of it, replaced it, and started filling his pipe. For the first time, the Superintendent's curiosity got the better of his taciturnity.

"What do you think of it, sir?" he blurted out.

Bristow had struck a match and was lighting his pipe.

"I think"—puff-puff—"that the padre's nephew"—puff-puff—"must have been in a deuce of a hurry. And, on his uncle's showing, he's a careless young man, you know."

The Superintendent looked at him, but forbore asking further questions.

"I'm running back to Chiltonbury in my car now," he went on, to the sergeant. "Just a word with you first," and he walked towards the front door, inviting Mentmore, with a gesture, to follow him.

"Oh, I say," said Bristow, "do you mind running me in with you? I want some tobacco—and a walk as well. I'll walk out."

"Certainly, sir—in two minutes. My car's outside."

In a couple of minutes Bristow strolled out. Kinch was seated in the car, ready. Mentmore was making towards the marquee. And what the Superintendent had said to the sergeant in those two minutes was:

"Look here, I found this shred of gold lace on the floor of Mrs. Cresswell's room, close to the door—torn, you see. And the metal finger-plate of the door, inside, was a bit loose and had a sharp corner—must have caught it. Also, there wasn't any gold lace on Mrs. Cresswell's costume. I want you to go through all those costumes in the tent—and there's some in the house as well—Miss Lynwood will show you—and see if it came off any of them. Understand?"

The detective-sergeant nodded.

"Not bad, that, sir," he remarked.

6

Twenty miles or so distant from Frimley was a lonely spot beneath the downs known as Hawley Vale. At least, so it was marked in the ordnance map, but in local parlance it was usually spoken of as "Yew Tree Bottom." It was a large, horseshoe-shaped valley lying between the spurs jutting out from the downs, and backed by the downs themselves.

The only access to it for vehicles was at the open mouth of the valley, reached by a by-road, or rather a lane, which branched off from the main road, and ended on the turf itself at the mouth of the valley. But then it was seldom that any vehicles found their way into Yew Tree Bottom, unless a picnic-party had a mind to drive their car right away from the haunts of men for their meal.

Yew Tree Bottom was quite destitute of human habitation. It was rather an eerie place. Dark juniper bushes grew on the slopes of the downs, and in the very centre of the secluded valley was a group of giant and venerable yew-trees. Tradition said that they had once found a Druidical grove in which mysterious rites were celebrated. Certain it was that there was something awe-inspiring in the place. Beneath the cluster of yew-trees one found oneself in a sort of cathedral, formed by nature: gnarled trunks for pillars, and overhead a thick roof of dark, intertwined foliage.

It was doubtful, however, whether the man who came slowly down the slope of the hills into the valley was troubled with any feelings inspiring awe, though, evidently, he was a cautious man. Every now and again his dark, piercing eyes gazed around the great sweep of country very watchfully. Every now and then, too, he stooped down, and when he rose again he had something in his hand, pegs of wood and a noose of fine string—sometimes something more substantial, in the shape of a rabbit—once, and he chuckled as he took it from the snare, a very respectably-sized hare. This, and the rabbits, were disposed of in the capacious pockets of an old, loose coat he was wearing.

The man himself was worthy of notice, tall and dark, swarthy of complexion, long, hatchet-shaped face, clean-shaven except for small, black side-whiskers, eyes rather close together on either side of a thin nose, humorous curl at the corners of his mouth. Anyone in the neighbourhood—the village policeman, especially—would have told you that he was Joe Cyster, that his particular bent of sport was perfectly well known, but that it was an exceedingly hard matter either to catch him in the act or to find, on searching him, that he carried any proof of his nefarious occupation, in the way of snares or spoils. Joe Cyster was a very astute man—and he knew it.

It was about eight o'clock in the morning that he reached the bottom of the valley. He had been out most of the night, and had a keen appetite for breakfast. Nor was he going to wait for that meal until he reached his cottage—two miles away, in the nearest village. Before he made for home he meant to dispose of the contents of his pockets—a hare, and four rabbits. The poacher has his "fence" as well as the burglar, and the "fence," in this particular instance, was Bill Alder, a mixture of village publican, market-gardener and dealer, who made a journey three times a week with his old pony-cart into the market town, and knew how to dispose of sundry birds and rabbits where no questions would be asked.

But Joe Cyster was not worrying about his breakfast. For the simple reason that it was close at hand, where he had deposited it on starting his rounds. Making his way into the recesses of the grove of yews, he came to his hiding-place, and took, from the hollow trunk of one of the trees, first a workman's basket, then the square top of an old biscuit-tin, and, finally, a tin can.

And a very good breakfast he had, too: collecting dried sticks, he soon had a fire, boiled water in the tin can, throwing in—from a screw of paper—some tea, put the biscuit-tin lid on the fire embers, produced a dab of butter and a couple of rashers of bacon from his basket, and fried them carefully in that old square of tin. A hunch of bread completed the meal—followed by that most delightful of all smokes—the after-breakfast pipe.

He sat, his back against the old tree-trunk, if not exactly at peace with the world—so far as it contained men in blue and gamekeepers—

at all events quite at peace with himself. And yet all the time, he was on the alert. His ear was quick to detect the slightest sound.

One such sound drew his attention. He heard the soft fluttering of a bird's wings—then silence—then the cooing of a wild pigeon. He turned his head slightly, peering in the direction of the sound, through the foliage. Pigeons had attractions for him, but he had left at home a certain handy little rook and rabbit rifle which could be detached into two parts and put into one of his deep pockets. As he looked, his gaze strayed lower, through the undergrowth.

Here and there the rays of the ascending sun penetrated gaps in the foliage, and he saw something very bright and shining through the masses of green. At once he got up and made his way to the spot, to find, in a moment or two, that the light shone reflected from nickel silver plating on the radiator of a motor-car.

The car stood in a small, open clearing in the midst of the grove of yews. And stood quite by itself. There was no sign of anyone there.

Joe Cyster, knew, perfectly well, that occasionally cars made their way into Yew Tree Bottom for picnic purposes, but he had never known one there at such an early hour in the morning. And he was curious.

Detective-Sergeant Mentmore, had he been present, would have been interested, from a professional point of view, in the poacher's movements. Joe Cyster laid his hand on the car's bonnet. It was cold. Then he noted its tracks—how it had been driven in under the trees from the open sward outside—he could see the marks of the wheels on the turf—driven straight in and left there.

The poacher, by virtue of his calling, might now have given points to Mentmore. He was an expert in all matters relating to the open. It did not take him long to find that whoever had driven the car there had walked away from it through the wood. Rank grass, trodden, and brushed in one direction, a freshly-broken bramble-branch showed him this. He followed the track unerringly to the edge of the grove. Dew had fallen in the night, and, outside, the grass was still damp— especially where it was in the shade.

A single set of footsteps on the grass—going away from the wood. Out in the open, where the sun had dried the dew, he could trace them no further. Hastily he skirted the wood, where the dew was still lying, on either side of the outgoing tracks. But there were no returning footsteps.

Whoever he was who had left his tracks on the grass, he had not returned to the car. Moreover, he was not in sight. And, further, when he had come down the hill a short time ago, he knew full well that no one was in that valley—or on the slopes of the downs around it.

It was not idle curiosity which prompted Joe Cyster to take these observations and then to make his way back to the deserted car. Joe Cyster's ideas of "meum and tuum" were fairly lax—when opportunity served. He had no thoughts of running off with the car itself— he couldn't have driven it to save his life and he wouldn't have known what to have done with it if he *could* have driven it—but a previous experience, when he had come across a car standing on the roadside, its occupants engaged in picking bluebells in a neighbouring wood, had taught him that sometimes people leave in a car portable property that is worth having.

In this particular case, however, there was not very much to be found. A couple of rugs lay on the back seat, but they were old and worn and not worth taking. He looked on the front seat. On the extreme left of it, half hidden, for it had worked its way between the edge of the cushion and the side of the car, was a patch of white. A small pocket-handkerchief. He promptly annexed this—small value, but it would come in handy for his wife.

Then he found the receptacle for tools—and examined the tools. Ah—that hammer would be useful—and the two screwdrivers—also the screw spanner. He pocketed them. The jack and the rest of the tools he left. A couple of sparking-plugs he took. He knew what they were for, and he might sell them for the price of a few pints of beer to young Willie Penfold, who had a motor-bike. But it wasn't much of a haul.

On the two front doors were pockets. He felt in them. Three or four maps, an "A.A." handbook, some rags, and—what was this?

A flat, oval case covered with dark red leather. He opened it. Lined with blue velvet, but empty. He gave an exclamation of disgust, snapped the case shut again, and pitched it away, with a vicious gesture. It went hurtling through leaves and branches, and he heard it fall somewhere in the underwood.

Having collected and pocketed all the portable property that he considered worth having, Joe Cyster made his preparations for the homeward tramp. The biscuit-tin top, the tea tin, and a choice collection of snares he put in the cache in the old tree-trunk. He stamped out the still smouldering embers of the fire and kicked the ashes, scattering them about. Then he took a final look at the car. Among other things he read the registration number, casually enough. The thing was no longer any concern of his, and he certainly was not likely to talk to anyone about it.

Along the grass, as he walked away, he could trace the tracks of the car, till the turf merged into the by-road. Even then there were impressions, where dust lay. Finally, he reached the tarred high-road, where all distinctive marks soon ceased.

A small public-house stood by the roadside a couple of hundred yards or so outside the village, in strategic position to catch the thirsty wayfarer or motorist before he came to a larger and more attractive inn a little further on, in the village. It bore the sign of the "Blue Lion." Before he came to it, Joe Cyster stopped, looked carefully around, climbed a gate by the side of the road, and, hidden behind the hedge, emptied his capacious pockets of the four rabbits and the hare, putting them in an old, broken culvert.

When he passed the "Blue Lion," Bill Alder, the landlord, was standing at the door in his shirt-sleeves, hands in pockets, pipe in mouth. He nodded to the poacher.

"Mornin', Joe," he ejaculated, without moving, and with no apparent interest.

"Mornin'," replied Joe, tersely, passing on without stopping, but jerking his thumb over his shoulder in the direction whence he had just come. Whereupon Bill Alder winked, and, subsequently, strolled along to that gate with an empty sack on his arm.

Meanwhile, Joe Cyster went on, reached his cottage, exchanged a brief sentence or two with his wife, went straight to the bedroom, took the tools, the sparking-plugs and the handkerchief out of various pockets, and put them in a drawer; divested himself of coat, waistcoat, boots and trousers, and incontinently got into bed and was asleep in a few minutes. Be it remembered that he had been up all night, and that dishonest toil earns repose quite as much as honest work does.

Because of the variety of Joe Cyster's hours of work, the times of the meals in his cottage varied also, and were not regular as other men's. The breakfast he had eaten in Yew Tree Bottom was the equivalent of "supper"; the meal to which he came downstairs later on, about five o'clock, was a nondescript one. It was an excellent meal, too—a nice juicy rump-steak with well-cooked vegetables, followed by an appetising pudding and bread and cheese. Mrs. Cyster was a good cook, and, often, they could afford to live better than many of their neighbours whose work was of a more honest variety.

The meal, however, was incomplete, and Joe glanced with interest at the clock. It wanted malt liquor to wash it down, and malt liquor, owing to the stern law of the realm, was not to be bought before the happy hour of six. Like many working-men—for Joe Cyster *did* work, after all—he preferred drinking his beer as a separate course, and drinking it in the companionship of his fellow-men in the place which was designed for the drinking of it—the "Blue Lion." Thitherward, therefore, he bent his steps, a few minutes before the clock struck the hour.

Destiny, however, was not going to permit Joe Cyster to order his pint of beer at one minute after six that evening. He had scarcely stepped outside his cottage when he met Price, the village policeman; and the policeman stopped him.

"Hullo, Joe," he said; "I was just coming to see you."

"What for?" asked Joe, with an air of injured innocence. "I ain't done nothin'."

"Not so sure of that," retorted Price, with a broad grin. "You were out all night, weren't you?"

"Can't a man take a stroll to get a breath o' fresh air without you pokin' your nose into his business?"

"Fresh *air*," replied Price, "the sort of *air* you were after had an 'h' in front of it, I reckon! But I don't want to know anything about that—this time. I want to ask you a question about something else, Joe."

"Well?"

"The parson over at Frimley, near Chiltonbury, has had his motor-car stolen in the night. There's a warning been issued to all of us to make enquiries. Now, you didn't happen to see a car anywhere—before it was light this morning?"

Joe Cyster thought swiftly.

"This here parson offering a reward, then?" he asked.

"Pretty certain to give the fellow who traces his car something for his trouble," replied the policeman. As yet he knew nothing about the murder. His orders were simply to look out for a car, number QV 5277, belonging to the Vicar of Frimley, containing two men, and to detain anyone he might find with it.

"What sort of a car?" asked the wary Joe.

"Morris Oxford. Four-seater. Dark blue. Number QV 5277," he replied, refreshing his memory from his notebook.

"QV," repeated Joe. "I forget the rest. But I reckon I do know where a car is wi' those letters, a blue 'un, too. Look here, if I tells you, will you see as I gets the credit of it—and no questions asked as to how I come to be where it is?"

"You've *got* to tell me, anyway, now, Joe," said Price, sharply. "All right," he went on, with a grin, "you needn't get the wind up about yourself. I won't ask you any questions about that. Where did you see the car? In which direction was it going?"

"It wasn't goin' nowhere," replied Joe Cyster; "leastways, not when I saw it last—'bout half-past nine this mornin'. 'Twas standin' still in the middle o' the old wood down at Yew Tree Bottom."

"Anyone with it?"

"Didn't see no one."

"And you left it there?"

"Well, it warn't mine, was it? O' course I left it there."

"Then I'll get my bike out and go and have a look. I'll 'phone first to Chiltonbury, though. I wish you'd spotted who was in her, Joe."

"He'd made off, seemin'ly."

"He?" repeated the policeman. "How do you know there weren't more?"

Joe Cyster laughed, a short little laugh, and looked pityingly at the policeman.

"How do I know there was only one of 'em? Why, I got eyes, ain't I? I saw the tracks he made a-goin' out o' the wood. And there was only one set of 'em."

"In which direction?"

"He was headin' straight for Bow Hill when he left the wood. But there warn't no tracks as soon as he got on the dry grass, and the Lord knows if he kep' on in the same direction."

"If he did—Bow Hill, you say? Why, that would take him into Linderton."

"Ah, that's right—if he kept straight on. Well, that's all I knows about it, and I wants to get a glass at the Blue Lion now. You won't forget to tell this parson as how I found the car—if 'tis his?"

"That'll be all right," said Price, turning on his heel and heading for the village Post Office, where he rang up the police-station at Chiltonbury. The reply, from the sergeant in charge, was terse, but to the point.

"Very well, Price. Get your bicycle and run out to that car, sharp. And stay there till we send someone. Don't touch it, and if anyone comes along, keep 'em away from it. Linderton, you say? I'll ring up the station there. Off you go!"

In about an hour Detective-Sergeant Mentmore arrived at Yew Tree Bottom in the police-car, a man with a camera seated beside him. They found Price on guard, a little tired of his lonely vigil. But when

Mentmore told him there was something more in the case than a stolen and abandoned car, he became keen enough.

The photographer carefully dusted, with a light powder, the steering-wheel, handles of brake and clutch lever, door-handles, starting-crank, and bonnet. Only on the latter, however, were there any finger-prints, and he proceeded to photograph them. Meanwhile, the detective-sergeant asked Price:

"This poacher chap who found the car—he didn't take anything out of her?"

"Not that I know of."

"Didn't you ask him?"

"Well—sergeant—I didn't think of it."

"You should have. But I'll see him myself. Now let's have a look."

Very carefully he examined the interior of the car, going over every part. But found nothing of interest. He turned to Price again.

"You say this poacher—what's his name?"

"Cyster."

"Cyster. Yes. He told you he found tracks going out of the wood in the direction of Bow Hill. Let's see if we can find 'em."

Sharp-eyed as he was, he found it none too easy to mark the tracks which Cyster, with his knowledge of woodcraft, had seen so plainly. By this time, of course, outside the wood the turf was quite dry. There were one or two heel-marks. That was all.

"You're sure Cyster said only one person seemed to have gone out of the wood?"

"That's right, sergeant."

"It's queer, too. There were *two* men in the car when she started from Frimley Manor."

Price essayed to show his sagacity.

"Seems to me," he said, "one of 'em must have got out before the other ran the car in here."

"Regular Sherlock Holmes, aren't you?" bantered Mentmore. "You'll be one of the Big Five at Scotland Yard one day, Price. Now, look here. They—or he—would leave Frimley shortly before two. Give him an hour—or an hour and a half to get here—say half-past three. You know the country better than I do. Tell me what you think?"

Price tilted his helmet back on his head.

"Well, sergeant, I should think *he* knew the country about here, too,—or he'd never have driven in here."

"Brilliant!" snapped Mentmore. "Absolutely brilliant! But go on."

"In that case, sergeant, if he was making for Linderton, he'd go straight across yonder, and up the side of Bow Hill. Half-way up there's a grass track that winds over the hill and down the other side till it joins the road from Heathdean to Linderton. Take him, at a fair rate, a matter of an hour and a quarter, or more."

"That's better," said Mentmore. "Getting daylight by then. Well, I hope Linderton may get a line on the beggar. It's a chance. Now, before we go, we'll have a thorough look round the car: you take that side, Price—I'll try this."

It was Price who found the jewel-case. Mentmore examined it.

"Answers to the description," he said. "Well, that clinches the connection of the two crimes. Empty, of course. It would be! Shows we're on the right track. Finished with those photos?"

"There's only one—the prints on the bonnet," said the man with the camera. "Yes, I've done now."

"That's probably Joe Cyster's hand," said Price. "He said he felt the bonnet to see if it was warm."

"Damn!" exclaimed Mentmore. "All the trouble for nothing, I expect. I'll take his prints and compare them. Now," he went on to the photographer, "you get away back to Chiltonbury in our car and make your report to the Super. Take that jewel-case. I'll drive the Morris to Frimley Vicarage and settle the question of identification with the Vicar—then I'll get into Chiltonbury as soon as I can—by 'bus, if there's no one to run me in. Now, Price, hoist that bicycle of yours into the back of the Morris and I'll drive you home. I want a word with Cyster."

Joe Cyster was engaged, in the innocent occupation of gardening, in front of his cottage. Mentmore proceeded to put him through a catechism. But he never wavered. He had come across that car—accidentally. Had he touched it? Yes—as he had told Price, he had felt it to see if it was warm. It wasn't. Nothing else? Of course not. Not taken anything out of it? Certainly not. He was an honest man, he hoped.

Price, who was standing by, chortled. Mentmore said sharply:

"Very well. Now I want to take your finger-prints, my man."

Cyster shot a furtive glance at the detective-sergeant out of those dark eyes of his.

"What the . . . what for, guv'nor?"

"Oh, you needn't get the wind up. I only want to make sure it was your marks we found on the bonnet."

Cyster submitted, sullenly, to the operation. He was not fond of over-close dealings with the police. In the back of his mind he had a hazy suspicion that the possession of those finger-prints of his might be used as evidence against him some time or other. He even suggested something of the kind.

Mentmore laughed.

"Oh, we know *you*, my friend—without any need of records. So long as you keep your hands off non-perishable goods, *this* won't make any difference."

"Look here," said Cyster, as Mentmore prepared to depart, "ain't I go get nothin' out o' this job? This here parson——"

"All right, all right. You've been a bit useful to us, I admit, and I'll let the parson know you found his car. Anything else is a matter between you and him, but the best reward he could give you would be a sermon on keeping the Tenth Commandment. It goes something like this—'Thou shalt not covet thy neighbor's hares, nor his rabbits, nor his pheasants.' Good evening, Cyster. I daresay we may meet again!"

Mentmore ran the Morris back to Frimley and saw the Vicar, who recognised his car at once. His satisfaction in getting it back, however, was marred by his anxiety about his nephew.

"You say you found the case in which Mrs. Cresswell kept the pearls?" he asked the detective-sergeant. "Close by?"

"We did, sir."

The Vicar shook his head.

"I *can't* think my nephew could have had anything to do with it."

Mentmore shrugged his shoulders.

"Well, sir," he said, "I can venture no opinion. But we've got to try and find him."

"I suppose so," replied the Vicar sadly. "But, on thinking it over, an idea has come into my head. Don't you think my nephew may have been kidnapped—or that he was stopped, and the car taken away from him?"

The sergeant smiled.

"That is an idea, sir," he said, in a non-committal tone of voice. "Well, we shall see. Anyhow, we've got your Morris—and none the worse for being run away with, I hope. And now I must get into Chiltonbury. Here's the name and address of the man who found your car."

Detective-Sergeant Mentmore was very tired and very sleepy when he reported to the Superintendent that evening, but, before doing so, he satisfied himself by comparing Cyster's finger-prints with a recently-developed photograph of the prints on the bonnet of the car, that they were the same. No clue there!

The Superintendent was also tired. Both men had had a long day.

But they conferred together at some length, nevertheless. Kinch wanted to know the result of the examination of the costumes.

"Nothing, sir. Two of 'em had gold lace on 'em—but untorn."

"And those in the house?"

"Same result, sir. Only there's one costume I didn't see."

"Whose?"

The sergeant had his open notebook in his hand.

"Miss Fullinger's."

"Ah!"

"A man's clothes, sir. She was acting as King Edward the Sixth in the pageant. She brought the costume with her, and, you see, I didn't know anything about it at first."

"And she's taken it back?"

"Yes, sir. Before I could get hold of it."

"That's a pity."

"It's quite all right, sir. Miss Lynwood told me she'd hired it from Sparkson's—the theatrical people. I 'phoned them. I thought that was the best thing to do. They'll keep it back for us to have a look when Miss Fullinger returns it—without unpacking it."

"Good. Now, there's another queer thing come to light. We carried out the Major's suggestion—I told you, you know?"

Mentmore nodded.

"Well, he was right. Both number-plates of that derelict car at Drifford have come in. They were found on the railway embankment, by the down-track, about a mile this side of Drifford. SB 1852 was the number."

"You've enquired, sir?"

"Naturally. But it doesn't help us. SB 1852 is owned by a doctor in Chichester."

"Missing?"

"Not a bit of it. The car—a Hillman—was in the doctor's garage when they made enquiries there. That's what the Chichester Super 'phoned me."

"Faked number, of course," said Mentmore. "And not so much of a coincidence as it looks. If you take a two-letter four-figure registration, you'll as likely as not hit on the identical combination of somebody else's car. It's already being said there won't be enough combinations to go round with increasing output. But, of course, it shows——?" And he raised his eyebrows.

"Exactly," and Kinch tapped a Bradshaw on his desk. "There's only one down-train from Drifford to Chiltonbury after eleven-thirty—stops at Drifford at 12:54 and gets here at 1:13. They must have been thrown out of that train. The snag is that if the beggar had anything to do with the case, he couldn't have walked out to Frimley in time. And I know he didn't hire a car. I've seen to that."

"And the station?"

"I went there myself. When the 1:13 came in there was only one porter on duty, and the ticket-collector. Neither of them noticed anything. The ticket-collector says about a dozen people came out of the station, but he was very vague about them. There was something else I found out at the station."

"What was that, sir?"

"Captain Bristow was nosing around there this morning—after I'd run him in."

Mentmore whistled.

"Did *he* want to know about the passengers of that last down-train, sir?"

"He did *not*. He was asking about the last train up—the 11:23 from here."

"What did he ask?"

"If the train ran to time—and how many minutes before its arrival it was signalled from the previous block."

Mentmore laughed, shortly.

"A dark horse, sir . . . in more ways than one, maybe," he added, slowly.

"How do you make that out?"

"Well, sir, we've only got his word for the way he discovered things last night. It isn't corroborated in any way. How do we know he went to his room when Mr. Charles Lynwood and the other two left the house?"

"Oh—I don't know, Mentmore. There—I can't say. But I do think he's worth observing, especially if he's trying to ferret out things on his own."

And then Mentmore, who had been smoking his pipe thoughtfully for a few seconds, suddenly said:

"You say this fellow—whoever he was—who might have got off the train here at 1:13 this morning hadn't time to get out to Frimley— but suppose the Vicar's nephew had run in here and taken him out in his uncle's car, sir?"

"I know," replied Kinch, nodding his head, slowly. "I'd thought of that. But, again, there's a snag. How could Mr. Curtis, the Vicar's nephew, tell the other had broken down in his car?"

"Telephone?"

"No. I've made enquiries at the Exchange. No one was put through to Frimley Vicarage last night."

"Good Lord, sir—my head's getting in a maze. I'll be off and turn in."

"One moment," said Kinch. "You're going out to Frimley tomorrow?"

"Not quite sure yet."

"Well, anyway,—see if the Vicar sets his speedometer when he garages his car. We might find out how far that Morris ran last night, and whether the mileage tallies with the distance to Yew Tree Bottom—and your run back. Good night."

7

The dinner at Frimley Manor that evening was rather a contrast to the hilarious meal of the night before. Murder and robbery had cast a gloom over the depleted household. Mrs. Cresswell was much subdued. Her husband, who was staying the night at the Manor, had arrived in the afternoon, and had evidently talked to his wife seriously. He looked as if he was able to do this. He was a massive, slow-moving man, with iron-grey hair and small moustache, keen, rather hard, grey eyes, and determined-looking mouth, one of those men who can be exceedingly masterful in a quiet, deliberate way.

The Lynwoods knew perfectly well that he had always taken exception to his wife's rather careless methods where valuable jewelry was concerned, and that he would not have sanctioned her flaunting those pearls at the pageant. In fact, she had told them she was glad her husband had not been present, as he would probably have made a fuss about it. The necklace had, originally, belonged to his mother, and although he had given it to his wife, he was very particular about the occasions when she wore it.

Exactly what he had said to Mrs. Cresswell none of the Lynwood family knew. If he had delivered a lecture, he had done so in privacy. But, anyhow, Mrs. Cresswell had lost that gay, sprightly manner of the evening before. No wonder. The theft of her pearls, followed by what her husband had to say about it, was enough to damp any woman's vivacity.

Not that, at dinner, Mr. Cresswell had anything to say about the necklace. He, for the most part, talked politics and finance with Sir Harry. In fact, very little allusion was made, at the meal, either to the robbery or the murder. By tacit consent, these subjects were avoided.

Charles Lynwood had come back from London, arriving only just in time to change for dinner. A gloom seemed to have settled upon him, as well as upon Mrs. Cresswell, for he hardly spoke, and, when he did so, it was only to answer others in a few brief sentences. More than once Bristow glanced at him, keenly, across the table.

After Anstice Lynwood and Mrs. Cresswell had left the room, the men lingered for a short time over port and coffee. Mr. Cresswell moved up to his host, and continued their discussion over the political situation and its effects on finance—Mr. Cresswell was a prominent City man, and talked with authority. Harry Lynwood came round the table to be near Bristow, and golf formed the staple subject of their conversation. Charles sat, silent for the most part, fidgeting with his wine-glass and smoking a cigarette.

Presently a move was made, and the five men strolled into the hall. It was still daylight, a warm, still evening. The hall door stood wide open and the women's voices could be heard outside. Anstice, who was seated on the terrace just in front of the door, looked over her shoulder.

"We're out here, daddy. There are plenty of chairs—it's much too stuffy indoors."

"Come along, then," said Sir Harry to Mr. Cresswell and Bristow. "We'll go outside."

As they moved out Bristow glanced at the sedan-chair. It had been replaced in its old position in a corner of the hall, its carrying-poles withdrawn, and leaning against the wall. To Bristow's mind the beautiful antique had become sinister. Two men had given up their lives, seated in that old chair. And there was a mystery over the second of the two. If the chair could only give evidence——!

The sinister appearance of the sedan-chair must have struck Charles Lynwood as well. He, too, looked at it as he made his way to the door, frowned slightly, and shrugged his shoulders.

Outside, garden chairs were on the stone terrace. One by one the men seated themselves. Sir Harry moved a chair close to Mrs. Cresswell, and began talking to her. Anstice motioned Charles to come near her. Mr. Cresswell stood, cigar in mouth, apparently admiring the view. Captain Bristow strolled a little way along the terrace, and took a chair slightly apart from the rest. As soon as he had done so Mr. Cresswell promptly joined him, bringing a chair close to his.

"I wanted a word with you," he began, coming straight to the point at once. "Sir Harry has told me about you, I hear it was owing to you that the murder was discovered last night?"

"By mere chance—yes, it was."

"And I also hear that you are a professional, Captain Bristow."

"A professional?"

"Sir Harry told me you had made a reputation in the Secret Service."

"Very flattering of him. Oh, but my bit of work there was done some years ago."

"Quite so. But I don't suppose you have lost your interest—well, in criminology?"

"Well, I don't suppose I have. But you must get rid of the notion that I'm a professional any longer."

Mr. Cresswell laughed.

"It isn't likely," he said, "that a man of your experience would get into touch with a crime like this—even by chance—without his interest being excited. And I've no doubt you've got some theories— from your own observation. I should be interested to know what they are, if I may?"

Bristow paused for a moment, then replied:

"If you think I can suggest any clue to the recovery of your wife's jewels, Mr. Cresswell, I'm afraid you will be disappointed. One tries to think things out, naturally, but this affair is in the hands of the police: not mine. You ought to consult them."

"I shall, of course. But I was wondering if you could give me any hints."

Bristow lighted his pipe, and turned a little in his chair towards Mr. Cresswell.

"I take it," he said, "that you are mostly interested in the recovery of the necklace?"

"Naturally. Those pearls are of extreme value—not only intrinsically, but as a family heirloom. What are your views on the chances of getting them back?"

"I wish I could tell you. There's so little to go upon, as yet. The police have not taken me into their confidence—and, of course, there is no reason why they should."

"What sort of a man is this Superintendent who has charge of the case?"

"A first-rate man, Mr. Cresswell. I happen to have heard something about him. You may rest assured that the case couldn't be in better hands—even if Scotland Yard were called in. Superintendent Kinch had a good record before he came to Chiltonbury. The Chief Constable of the County, Major Bainbridge, has the knack of getting hold of good men—and Kinch is one."

"Humph! I suppose he will be all the more keen to recover my wife's property because the theft is mixed up with the murder?"

"Of course."

"Oh, well," replied Mr. Cresswell, "one must hope for the best, I suppose. I can't see there is any more that I can do."

"You can offer a reward for the recovery of the necklace. It's often a very strong incentive, you know. It sometimes means recovery of valuables quite apart from the efforts of the police."

Mr. Cresswell puffed thoughtfully at his pipe.

"Of course I'd thought of that," he replied, after a short pause, "though I much dislike the idea. It always seems to me to be condoning blackmail. A fellow steals your goods, and you pay him to get them back."

"Oh, well," said Bristow, with a laugh, "it's a question of value, isn't it? I should have thought it would pay you to offer a few hundreds for what is worth thousands to you."

"A few hundreds!" He frowned. "I don't want to throw away— Oh, confound it!"

"But it wouldn't be throwing it away if you got the necklace back, would it?"

"I suppose not," replied Mr. Cresswell, shortly. There was a pause. Neither man seemed inclined to pursue the subject. Captain Bristow puffed, lazily, at his pipe. Then he said:

"I'm so sorry for Mrs. Cresswell. It's frightfully rough on her."

"She ought to have been more careful," replied Mr. Cresswell, frowning slightly.

"Wasn't she?"

"Never. Unfortunately. I've warned her over and over again about taking ordinary care of that necklace."

"And you couldn't do anything?"

Mr. Cresswell glanced at him sharply. But Bristow was lounging lazily, his eyes half closed.

"How could I? You know what women are. My wife's one of the best, but I never could get her to appreciate the risks she ran."

Bristow laughed.

"So you gave it up?"

"I gave it up."

"I'm afraid this will be a severe lesson to her."

"It *will!*"

And there was almost a gleam of humour in his eyes—the satisfaction that comes, even in exasperating circumstances, of saying, "I told you so."

"Hullo!" exclaimed Harry Lynwood at that moment, raising his voice. "Here's the Vicar. Anything fresh happened, I wonder."

The Vicar came walking across the lawn, greeting the little group on the terrace.

"I thought I must come round to let you know," he began. "My car has been found. The police brought it back to me this evening."

"Oh, where did they find it?"

"Sit down, Vicar, and tell us all about it."

"Was anyone with it? "

"How did they find it?"

The chorus of excited questions died down. They gathered round the Vicar while he told them the story.

"They found your jewel-case, too, Mrs. Cresswell," he added, "lying under the trees close to the car. It was empty, unfortunately."

"Nothing else?"

"No. Nothing. The sergeant who drove the car back to me told me they searched it carefully, but there was nothing to go upon except the jewel-case. That proves, of course, that the jewels were taken away in the car."

"You must be glad to get it back," said Anstice.

"I am, of course. But—" and he shook his head. "It hasn't relieved my chief anxiety—about my nephew."

"What is that?" asked Charles Lynwood.

"Oh, I forgot," said Sir Harry, "you'd left this morning before the Vicar came—and—" he paused.

"It's common property," said the Vicar, sadly. "One can't stop servants gossiping, and it's all over the village by this time that my nephew was out in my car last night. I *can't* make it out."

"Your nephew, Vicar?—what, Curtis?" asked Charles.

The Vicar told him.

"You remember him, of course," he went on, speaking still to Charles Lynwood. "He was with me for a week last summer, and came with us to that picnic at Camley Towers."

"Oh, yes, I remember," said Anstice. "Sonia was staying with us, you know, Charlie. And they were absolutely mad; they would climb up that rackety old ruin."

Charlie frowned.

"Yes," he said, to his sister, then turned again to the Vicar.

"And Leonard Curtis was *here*—last night?"

"I'm afraid so," said the Vicar. "I can't make it out at all."

Charlie did not reply. He lighted a cigarette and began smoking— fast. The Vicar went on talking about his car.

"I must send the man who found it a small reward," he remarked. "The police tell me he's a poacher and was probably engaged in his lawless pursuits at the time. I own I feel inclined to condone with him. For he's done me a good turn."

"The car wasn't damaged in any way?" asked Bristow.

"Not a bit. The only thing is that some of the tools are missing, and I fancy a couple of new sparking-plugs should have been there—but they were not."

"What tools?" asked Bristow.

"A hammer, two screwdrivers and a screw-spanner—a useful tool I valued."

"Oh!" replied Bristow, thoughtfully. "Did you tell the detective-sergeant?"

"No. It was after he had gone that I found out. He did say that he'd asked Cyster—the poacher fellow—if he had taken anything out of the car. But the man declared he hadn't. Well, I must be going. We shall meet at the inquest tomorrow, Sir Harry. Good night."

Captain Bristow got up from his chair, but, instead of saying good night to the Vicar, began walking with him away from the house, across the lawn.

"You've roused my interest, Vicar," he said. "I wonder whether you'll mind my suggesting something?"

"Why, of course not."

"You said you were going to give this man Cyster a reward?"

"Yes. I—er—suppose two or three pounds would be enough?"

"Oh—ample. I'd rather like to see him—and this place, Yew Tree Bottom. If I can borrow a car here directly after breakfast tomorrow, I'll run over—you say it's only twenty miles. And, if you like, I'd take your gift to Cyster. Save you the trouble of sending it."

"That's very kind of you. But why not have my car, Bristow? I shan't be using it tomorrow morning."

"Thanks very much. I'll take it, then—about nine. Good night, Vicar."

"Good night."

When Bristow returned to the terrace, the others were just preparing to go indoors. The little party broke up. Anstice went with Mrs. Cresswell into the drawing-room, while the latter's husband was taken off by Harry Lynwood to the billiard-room. Sir Harry said he had letters to write, and went into the library. Bristow and Charles Lynwood sought the smoking-room.

For the first few minutes Charlie, who appeared to be a little ill-at-ease, skipped from one subject of conversation to another—

cricket scores in the evening paper—his London club—the matinée, a revue, he had been to see that day—the chances of birds in the autumn—anything, Bristow noticed, except the pageant, the murder, and the theft of Mrs. Cresswell's jewels. Nor did Bristow help him out at all in giving a lead, but sat quietly smoking, leaning back in his chair with half-closed eyes.

But, as time went on, and the younger man made no attempt to leave him, he felt sure that, sooner or later, Charlie would blurt out something he wanted to say all the time. He had followed Bristow to the smoking-room—it was his own choice.

Bristow waited patiently. After a somewhat lengthy silence, Charlie suddenly fired a question at him.

"Look here, Roger, I suppose you're helping the police over this beastly business?"

"Now, what makes you say that?" asked Bristow, very quietly.

"Well, you're more or less a policeman yourself."

"I *was*—in a way," assented Bristow.

"Well, of course they know that, and I suppose they've been pretty thick with you—trying to use your brains, and all that sort of thing."

"As a matter of fact, Charlie, you're quite wrong. They haven't taken me into their confidence, in the least, or told me more than they've told the others here. I shouldn't even wonder if Kinch is inclined to look upon me as a possibly suspicious person."

"*You!*" exclaimed Charlie, leaning forward. "What on earth makes you think that?"

"Oh, it's quite reasonable," replied Bristow, with a laugh. "They've only my own word for what I told them took place, to begin with, and they have to keep an open mind. Come to think of it, Charlie, I might easily have done it."

"How?"

Bristow shrugged his shoulders.

"Well, I'll tell you. I had every opportunity of slipping into Mrs. Cresswell's room and taking the key off the ring—you've heard about that? And then, when you went out last night, I could have got the pearls and, after your return, taken them out to that nephew of the Vicar's—with whom I had previously made an arrangement."

"Yes—but the murder?"

"Quite simple. Hurst might have seen young Curtis lurking about outside, and stayed to watch him—seen me come out, and interfered, thinking something fishy was taking place. Then one of us knocks him on the head and we stage that bit about finding him in the sedan-chair—to make more of a mystery of it. Off goes young Curtis with the necklace, and I go back to the house and give the alarm to deceive the police. The very fact that I said *two* men went off in the car would only heighten suspicion—only *one* man got out of her, so this poacher fellow says."

"Good Lord!" cried Charlie. "Why, at that rate, any of us might come under suspicion?"

"Quite true," replied Bristow, calmly, "and probably have done so."

"Even I?"

"Oh—certainly *you*," retorted Bristow, with a laugh.

"Why?"

Captain Bristow turned in his chair and looked at Charlie.

"Do you want me to tell you?"

"Oh—I don't know—yes—if you like."

And he looked a little uncomfortable.

"All right, I will. Well, *you* were the last person—except the Vicar—seen with Hurst, and the Vicar went out at the side gate, leaving you two in the grounds. You might have met young Curtis—by appointment—and knocked Hurst on the head, between you. Then you might have slipped back into the house and got the pearls—there was plenty of time before I came down—and taken them out to Curtis. And you may be sure that Kinch has noted the fact that you left the front door unlocked—your explanation was a bit clumsy, you know—and he might easily conjecture that you came back into the house after I had gone out—and left the door unlocked because you'd seen me and knew I should come in again. And this morning you suddenly run away to London. We all know you had no intention of doing so last night. Don't you think Kinch noted *that?* I wouldn't mind betting you a fiver he had you shadowed."

"Oh!" exclaimed Charlie, his face paling a little. "Anything else?"

"Yes. Something I don't think Kinch knows; but *I* do. You hadn't undressed when I came into your room after the murder."

"What do you mean?—I was in bed."

"I know you were. But you took good care not to get out of it while I was in the room. And when you came downstairs a few seconds later, you'd got those white trousers strapped round your shoes. You couldn't have put them on and done that in the time."

There was silence for a few moments. Charlie was staring at Bristow. At last he said:

"After all, there was no harm in not taking off my clothes directly I got in."

"Of course not. But the queer thing about it is that you didn't want me to know you hadn't done so."

Then Charlie said:

"Are you going to tell the police this?"

"I didn't say I should, did I? But, you see, they know enough already to make them keep their eye on you—the unlocked door, and the running up to London, suddenly."

Charlie laid down his half-finished cigarette in an ash-tray. He was still looking hard at Bristow.

"You don't mean you think *I* had anything to do with the damned affair?"

Bristow looked at him sharply, shrugged his shoulders slightly, and said:

"I'll tell you what I do think, Charlie."

"What?"

"That you know a dashed sight more about it than you've told the police—or anyone else."

Charlie was playing nervously with a fresh cigarette he had taken from his case.

"I'd nothing to do with it," he growled, after a slight pause.

"I didn't say you had, but I can't help noticing things—it's a habit born of experience. Of course, I've no right to ask you any questions, but I can jolly well see you're precious uncomfortable about something or other."

"I'm—well, I'm a bit bothered," admitted Charlie.

Bristow waited. There was another short silence. Then Charlie said:

"I suppose if I told you you'd only say I ought to see the police about it."

"Even if I did," answered Bristow, "that might be better by a long shot than for them to find out—well, whatever it is, and to know that you had been keeping it from them; better for you, very likely, and certainly for any innocent person mixed up in it."

"That's just it," Charlie blurted out. "And I'm perfectly certain——"

He stopped short. Captain Bristow waited.

"Look here, Roger. Can I trust you?"

"I hope I'm your friend."

"You won't tell this damned Superintendent—or any of his men?"

Bristow took one or two puffs at his pipe.

"You mustn't ask me to condone murder, Charlie," he said, gravely, "but I certainly should not tell them unless I thought justice demanded it. Even then, I should ask *you* to tell them. My experience is that it isn't always wise to keep the police in ignorance. They are the last people to wish to get any innocent person into trouble. You must remember that even your damned Superintendent is human."

"All right," answered Charlie. "I've simply *got* to tell someone I can trust, and I know you're a sensible chap. I can't tell any of my people, and I simply *won't* tell the police, if I can help it. That's really the reason why I ran off today. I was afraid Kinch or that detective-sergeant would start cross-questioning me and pump it out of me. And I wanted to be alone."

"Go on," said Bristow.

"Well, you see, it concerns someone—well, I may as well say it—that I'm a bit keen on. And that's the trouble."

Bristow nodded.

"Better begin at the beginning—when you went out last night to get your cigarettes," he said.

"Very well. You saw me go out with the Vicar and Hurst. The Vicar said good night immediately, and turned off to the left to go out through the back gate in the stable-yard. Hurst and I walked on together for thirty or forty yards, and then he went off to the right—down the carriage-drive. Before he said good night—oh, but that doesn't matter—"

"Everything matters," interrupted Bristow. "Give me the smallest details."

"Well, he tore off the moustache and small beard he was wearing, and put them in his pocket."

"Did he say anything?"

"Only that he'd been wanting to get rid of them all the evening— they were so frightfully hot and uncomfortable."

"Oh!" Bristow had taken out a notebook and was making pencilled jottings in it. "Was that all?"

"Yes. So he went off. I walked on to the tent. You remember there was a small table in the corner of it? I thought I'd left my silver box of cigarettes on it, but it wasn't there. It was rather dark inside, you know—not quite, for there was a little moonlight. It must have taken me several minutes to find the cigarettes, and I finally did so on the table in the ladies' dressing-room part of it. The girls must have collared them."

"Did you strike a match?"

"Not then. I was going to, but found I'd only one left—and I wanted a smoke. That's what kept me so long. I had to blunder about in the semi-darkness. When I did find the box I used up my one match—there and then—in lighting a cigarette.

"Well, I came out of the tent, but I wasn't in a hurry. I'd had a bit of a headache, and I was enjoying the fresh air. So I strolled about."

"Where? Towards the bridge?"

"No. In the other direction—towards the stable-yard. I noticed the double gates leading into the yard were open—the Vicar had gone that way, you know. Dad is a bit particular about having them kept shut at night, so I thought I'd close them—for want of anything better to do.

"I reached the gates—it must have been quite a little while after I had left the tent; I'd been strolling in a round-about way, you see. Anyhow, I'd about finished my cigarette, and I chucked the stump away. I happened to turn round just then. And the moon had half broken through the clouds, so that you could see things quite plainly. And I saw someone coming from the house and crossing the lawn. I want you to understand that, at that moment, I was just inside the stable-yard, and saw this over the wall. The wall's about five feet high. So that all that was visible of me was my head."

"Did you see who it was?"

"Not for a moment or two. Then I did. The moonlight brightened still more. Roger, it was—Sonia Fullinger!"

"*Sonia!*"

Charlie nodded.

"Oh, yes—I wasn't mistaken. I wish I had been. It was Sonia right enough, still wearing that Edward the Sixth's dress—cap and all. Why, I could even see the gold lace on her little cape shining in the moonlight—you remember it? She'd got something in her hand—but I couldn't see what it was. I was some little distance away, you know."

"What did you do?"

"Well, of course I was a bit dithered. Anyone would have been, seeing a girl coming out of the house in the dead of night. Then the idea took hold of me that perhaps she was walking in her sleep. I think that must have kept me from calling out. Doesn't do suddenly to alarm a sleep-walker, you know. Anyhow, I *didn't* shout, and I was just coming out of the stable-yard to make for her, when she stopped, and waved a handkerchief."

"Waved a handkerchief!"

"Well, at all events it was something white. You couldn't mistake it."

"And then?"

"Things got still queerer. Some fellow came along—he must have been waiting by the bridge, for he came up the drive and across the lawn. Pretty fast, too."

Captain Bristow whistled.

"By George!" he said. "What did you do?"

"I was a damned fool, Roger. I did nothing. Only kept behind the wall and acted the spy. I was in a blinking rage—that was what was the matter with me. Sonia and I were pals, you see—and—and—I was going to ask her to be something more than a pal to me, and here she was, meeting some damn fellow at half-past one in the morning—meeting him by appointment, too. Can't you understand what I felt? I was just mad with jealousy, I suppose. Something more than jealousy, too. Pretty thick to see the girl you love go out to meet a man in the middle of the night when she's staying in your own house. I was sort of choking—and it wasn't all jealousy, Roger. It was something a bit stronger than that."

"Poor old Charlie!" murmured Bristow, sympathetically. "Tell me. What happened, next?"

"They went into the tent together—that's what happened. And that's all I saw. I'd had enough of it, old man. I thought, anyhow, she shouldn't see me sleuthing her—and I didn't want to sleuth her, either. I slipped along behind those shrubs on the left of the house, got on the terrace, and made for the front door. Then I let myself in, as quietly as possible. I noticed the light in the hall was out. I suppose she put it out when she came downstairs—thought someone had left it on by mistake. And, of course, I didn't lock the front door—I couldn't lock her out, could I? Now you know why I didn't go to bed. When you knocked on my door, I thought it was someone come to tell me Sonia was missing, or something of that kind, and I didn't want anyone to think that *I* knew anything about it. I told you, too, that I ran up to London to get away from the police—but it wasn't only that. I didn't want to see Sonia again, and I knew she would be going home today, so I made a bolt of it early to keep out of her way."

"I'm sorry, old man."

"Pretty rotten, isn't it?"

Bristow nodded.

"It is."

"And there's something more, Roger. Something I never thought of till Anstice dropped a remark on the terrace just now. Something that fits in with the rest of the wretched affair. That's Leonard Curtis, the damned young swine. You heard Anstice say that he was with us on that picnic last summer—and Sonia, too. And that they climbed those ruins? That wasn't all. They went off together, for a couple of hours or so. I was beastly jealous at the time. I'd had a bit of a tiff with Sonia in the morning—and that didn't make me feel better. You can see it now, can't you? They've been palling up together—and *that's* why he came here last night. I wouldn't even mind that so much—but that ass of a woman's damned pearls—and poor Hurst. What are we to do, Roger?"

Bristow blew a cloud of smoke, shook his head, and said, slowly: "Wait a bit, my boy. It doesn't fit in so closely as you say. How about the *two* men who went off in the car? Besides, I've other notions about young Curtis. And *they* don't fit in. No—I'm not going to tell you what they are. Pure conjecture at present. But look here, Charlie. The whole thing looks pretty black, I know. But do you remember what we were talking about last night with the Vicar and that poor devil, Hurst—the perfect criminal and the infallible detective? Well, you've also got to test your *clues* and find if *they* are perfect or infallible. I want to ask you a plain question. I know Sonia Fullinger a bit, and you know her pretty well. Granting that she was out there last night, do you believe that she connived, first at robbery, and then at murder?"

"I'm damned if I want to believe it."

"Of course you don't."

"But the worst of it is——"

"Oh, yes, I know. But it's fatal to jump to conclusions without all the evidence. I haven't thought it over yet, of course, but, on the spur of the moment I could give you an explanation that almost exonerates Sonia—though not quite."

Charlie looked at him in amazement.

"I'm not saying there is anything in it," went on Bristow. "I'm only giving you an instance to show we must be certain of our facts. Well, it's this. Mrs. Cresswell is a pretty rash bridge-player, isn't she? And likes high points. And she let out at luncheon yesterday that she dabbles on the Stock Exchange and hopes her husband doesn't know. Women who do these things often get into a nasty fix and want a good round sum to get out of it. And that sometimes means having to sell their jewelry. But Mrs. Cresswell daren't sell that necklace in the ordinary way. Even if she kept the transaction dark for a time, her husband would be sure, sooner or later, to find out they were missing, and you can see she's a bit afraid of him. So she plans a fake robbery. She is really selling the pearls, but she wants to make it appear they have been stolen. She takes Sonia into her confidence—they are pretty intimate, you know,—and they come down here together. It's a splendid opportunity—flaunting the pearls about in public, and, all the time, arranging for some agent to run down and receive them under cover.

"Sonia takes him out the pearls and goes back to the house. After all, it isn't exactly a *crime*. Mrs. Cresswell is selling what belongs to her. But something goes wrong. Hurst appears on the scene. Why, or how, we can't tell yet, but, for all we know, *he* may have been a genuine crook and have had his own plans with regard to that necklace. He gets knocked on the head—anyway. And they try to take him off the scene in the car, probably to get him out of the way for the time being. They would. Remember, he wasn't dead when they started with him. In the morning Mrs. Cresswell raises the hullabaloo, and plays the part of injured innocence—another little bit of acting. *Voilà tout!*"

"Gad!" exclaimed the younger man. "I shouldn't wonder if you've hit it, Roger. Why not follow it up, and—"

"There you go!" broke in the other, with a laugh. "One plausible theory, and centering everything on it. No, my boy, that's not the way to investigate. Have your theories, if you like, but put your facts first, otherwise your theories are pretty well bound to distort those facts. I only wanted to show you how easy it is, in a case of this kind, to jump to conclusions—just as you were so ready to link up Sonia with young Curtis. If you'd studied some of the facts, you might not have done that. But—to come back to the said facts, and to leave theories alone for a while. Things look ugly, I admit. You saw Sonia come out of the house, carrying something in her hand—presumably the jewel-case,—and meet some man who went with her into the tent. You've confided this to me—as a friend. Very well. I'll do my best to investigate it—as a friend—if you want me to."

"It's frightfully decent of you, Roger."

"Only,"—and he held up a warning hand—"you must be prepared to submit to any consequences—and they may be precious nasty."

"Yes—I see. I think I'd rather do that than have all this uncertainty."

"And there's another thing. You've got to give evidence tomorrow at the inquest. What are you going to tell the Coroner, Charlie?"

"Oh, Lord! yes. I know. That's been bothering me, too. What the deuce am I to do if the Coroner asks me leading questions?"

"You must answer them, my friend,—I'm afraid. But let me think for a minute."

He smoked silently, his brows knit. Charlie Lynwood watched him anxiously.

"Now, look here, Charlie," he said, presently. "Withholding evidence is a very serious matter. But I'm willing to take the risk."

"*You?*"

"Yes, I. I've got some sort of a reputation, I suppose, and if it comes to a push, I can tell the Coroner that you were acting on my advice. It's frequently done by the police when they confer with the Coroner beforehand. They often want certain evidence kept back till a later stage in the enquiry. It's quite certain that the proceedings tomorrow will only be formal—enough to justify an adjournment and to make out the Order for Burial. The *real* reason for the adjournment is to give the police time to make further enquiries, and they won't want much evidence just yet. They don't know enough. Why, they don't even know who Hurst was. I'll tell you what to do."

"What?"

"The Coroner will probably ask you to make a statement. Just say that, after parting from Hurst, you found your cigarettes and went back to the house. That's quite true. You might also volunteer the information that you saw no one in the tent. That's true, too. If he presses you with questions—why—you must answer him. But I don't think he will."

"Why?"

Bristow laughed.

"Because I fancy the police have an eye on you, my boy. And if they have, they'll want to watch you a bit and catch you tripping. *I* should, if I were Kinch. I shouldn't let on that I suspected you in any way, and I should explain matters first to the Coroner. I may be wrong, of course, but if Kinch is as wily as I imagine he is, that's what he'll do. Yes!"

James came in with whisky, tumblers and a siphon—followed by Harry Lynwood and Mr. Cresswell. Bristow glanced at Charlie warningly. The men helped themselves to drinks; pipes and cigars were lighted; and the conversation became general. Bristow was the first to say good night. But, when he reached his room, he made no attempt to undress. For over an hour he sat in an arm-chair, notebook in hand. And, from time to time, he made entries. At length he yawned.

"Can't see a way out, I admit," he said to himself; "but I have found a few tacks to go upon—anyway."

And then he went to bed.

8

Captain Bristow finished his breakfast early the next morning, and made his way to the Vicarage. He found the Vicar in a state of excitement.

"I've heard from Leonard—my nephew!" he said.

"Oh, *have* you? That's interesting. And what does he say?"

"Not very much. Certainly not enough to relieve my anxiety. Only a line on a postcard: here it is."

There was no address on the postcard. It read:

> "Sorry about your car, but I had to take her. Hope you got her all right. Will write soon. In great haste.
>
> Yrs,
>
> LEONARD."

Bristow turned the card over. The postmark was a London one: "S.W. 1." district. He smiled.

"Not over-communicative, is he, Vicar?"

The Vicar shook his head.

"He never is—on paper. He dislikes letter-writing exceedingly. What do you think of it, Bristow?"

Again Bristow smiled.

"I shouldn't worry too much, Vicar. Really, I shouldn't. But you must show this to the police, you know."

The Vicar sighed.

"I suppose I must." He took two or three notes out of his pocket-case. "Well, here you are, Bristow. Give this man Cyster what you think is fair. It's extremely kind of you to take the trouble to see him."

"Not at all. I'll be off, I think, now."

"Very well. We'll go to the garage."

Before he started the car Bristow looked at the dial of the speedometer.

"Had you set it?" he asked the Vicar, "Before your nephew collared the car, I mean?"

"No, I hadn't . . . let's see. . . . Oh, there ought to be plenty of petrol in her—I filled her up the day before yesterday." He looked at the petrol-gauge. "Oh, yes. Just over three-and-a-half gallons."

"How much does she hold?"

"Five gallons."

"And you say you filled her two days ago.—Used her since?"

"No."

"How many miles does she do to the gallon?"

"Not so much as she used to. I get about thirty-two out of her—I had to fit a bigger jet this summer."

Bristow made a rapid calculation. He was just about to start the car, when a voice exclaimed:

"Good morning, gentlemen."

They turned. Detective-Sergeant Mentmore was standing at the entrance of the garage, in plain clothes.

"I called at your house, sir," he said to the Vicar, "and they told me you were here. Are you taking your car out?"

"No. But Captain Bristow is. You've no objection, I suppose?"

"Not in the least, sir." He glanced quickly at Bristow. "But I'm glad I happened to come along first. Just a question. Did you set the speedometer before—"

Bristow laughed.

"It's all right, sergeant," he said. "I was after that, too. Curiosity, you know. The speedometer was not set, but the Vicar has been telling me he filled the petrol-tank the day before yesterday. She's used nearly one-and-a-half gallons, and she does thirty-two to the gallon. That's roughly speaking, a little under forty-eight miles. I've been looking at Yew Tree Bottom on the map. It's a matter of twenty-miles—forty there and back," he went on, dryly. "Got it now, sergeant?"

The sergeant had taken out his notebook, and was jotting the figures down.

"That's quite all right, Captain Bristow," he said, also dryly. "A useful bit of information. What do you deduce from it, sir?"

Bristow smiled affably.

"Probably the same as you," he retorted, "though there is more

than one way of looking at it. Possibly—later on—we may compare
notes. You don't want anything else—with the car, now?"

"You're not going far, sir? You'll be back for the inquest—at
eleven-thirty?"

"I'll be there. Meanwhile the Vicar has something rather interesting
to show you, Sergeant."

Bristow ran the car out and was soon speeding along the high-road.
It did not take him long to arrive at the village where Cyster resided,
and to find his cottage. The poacher was at home. At first he eyed the
Captain with some uneasiness, for Cyster lived, more or less, in an
atmosphere of suspicion. But Bristow quickly disarmed him. He
explained that he was a friend of the Vicar of Frimley, and had come
over to thank him for finding the car.

"Ah," said Cyster, suspicion giving way to greed. "I'd been hoping
the parson wouldn't forget me. I'm only a poor man, sir, and——"

"Quite so. Poor and deserving, I suppose. 'Honest' is also a quality
sometimes attached to poverty—not necessarily in *your* case, my
friend."

"I don't know what you means, sir," growled Cyster. "I works
hard for my living——"

"Yes, I know. Interesting work, too, I understand. But about what
you were saying. The Vicar is extremely obliged to you for finding his
car, and he wishes to show it. That is why I've run over."

And he produced the one-pound notes.

"I'm sure I'm very much obliged to him——"

"Oh, wait a bit, my man. I haven't given them to you yet. You see,
the Vicar has got his car back—but there are those tools and things,
and——"

"Tools, sir? I don't know nothin' about that."

"Yes, a hammer and——"

"I never see no hammer, sir."

"Wasn't it with the other tools?"

"No, sir."

"Oh—so you *did* have a look in the box?"

"I—well, sir,——"

"All right, Cyster. We won't argue. You give me the hammer and
the screwdrivers and the other things—*all* of 'em, mind,—and there's
three pounds for you. If not—well, you won't get 'em."

"But I never took——"

Bristow saw the furtive look in the man's eyes.

"That's enough," he said. "Take it or leave it. If you prefer to leave it, why, I shall advise the Vicar to put the police on the trail of those tools—and you won't get a halfpenny. You know you wouldn't be able to sell them for three quid. Better give 'em up—and then the matter is at an end."

Cyster eyed the notes and thought rapidly. Was it worth while?

"Supposin' I did find some tools—and took care of 'em, like," he growled, "likely as not if I was to give 'em to yer you'd tell the police all the same."

"You can take my word I won't, my friend. Hand them over—and the three pounds are yours. And a fourth, too, very likely."

Cyster looked at him suspiciously.

"You ain't a bloody policeman yourself, eh? One of those detective blokes?"

"I'm not. Now, get me those tools—sharp!"

Cyster rose from his seat. The stairs opened on to the room. He began mounting them. In the bedroom he opened a drawer and took out the hammer and the screwdriver.

"*Everything*, mind!"

He wheeled round. Bristow stood at the door.

"Blimey, guv'nor! You give me a turn."

"There were two sparking-plugs."

"All right, guv'nor—here they are."

Bristow risked it. He had been working up to the chance of there being something more.

"*And*—come—*you* know!"

"There ain't nothin' more—only this here handkerchief."

"*Sure?*"

"I'll take my oath on it, sir."

Bristow took the tools, and the handkerchief, and put them in his pockets without examining them.

"Here's the three pounds, then. And I'll give you another if you'll come with me in the car and show me just where you found her."

"I'll do that, guv'nor—willingly."

Before they got into the Morris, Bristow said:

"Now, show me exactly where that handkerchief was."

The man did so. Bristow made no comment. He ran the car to Yew Tree Bottom, and Cyster pointed out the spot where he had found her. Bristow asked him a string of questions, particularly about there having been the tracks of only one person.

"That's right enough, guv'nor. Here's where he came along—there's some o' his traces still, but the bobbies has been tramplin' the place down since. Here's where he come out o' the wood."

Bristow took a glance over the broad expanse of downland.

"And you say he was making in the direction of—what's the name of the place?"

"Linderton, sir. But, Lord bless 'ee! he might ha' been makin' for *anywhere*, once he got athert they downs."

Bristow had unfolded a map, and was studying it carefully. Presently he said:

"Look here, Cyster, I expect you know a few dodges about getting out of people's way when they're after you, eh?"

The man grinned.

"Well, now. Suppose you'd done something worse than poaching—this is murder, you know—and you wanted to save your skin. What would you have done if you had been the fellow who got out of the car here?"

Cyster thought for a few moments.

"Well, sir," he said, "I reckon *I* could hide myself for a month round about here wi'out bein' found. But I see what you mean, guv'nor. The only thing would ha' been to get right away. Where d'ye think this bloke wanted to get to?"

"Well, say London."

"Then I wouldn't ha' made for Linderton. 'Tis on the end of a single line o' railway and you have to change at Chiltonbury to get to London. Too much chance o' bein' spotted. I'd ha' kept along the downs, yonder," and he stretched out his hand, "and made westward, till I struck the main London road from the north. There's lorries comin' along that road to London all night, and I'd ha' got a lift on one of 'em. That's what I'd ha' done, sir."

Bristow nodded thoughtfully.

"I believe you're right," he said. "And now I'll run you home and get back to Frimley."

It was not till after he had dropped Cyster at his cottage that Captain Bristow took the handkerchief out of his pocket and examined it, stopping for a minute to do so. He whistled softly to himself. In the corner of the handkerchief, in marking-ink, was the name: "S. FULLINGER."

By the time Bristow reached Frimley, preparations were afoot for the inquest. At first this was to have been held in the hall of the Manor, but afterwards it was decided to make use of the Village Hall, which stood near to The Gables, the home of the murdered man. It was as well that this had been done, for the building was packed.

Curiosity in the neighbourhood was rife, and the number of reporters alone, London and local, formed quite a fair-sized group. Major Bainbridge was there with Superintendent Kinch and Detective-Sergeant Mentmore.

The modern Coroner's jury consists of not less than seven and not more than eleven jurors, the number being at the discretion of the Coroner. In this instance Mr. Lancefield, the Coroner, a shrewd, middle-aged lawyer of Chiltonbury, had summoned the maximum number and the eleven jurymen took the oath and elected their foreman. The modern jury also differs from the old one in that its members are not necessarily called upon to view the body of the deceased. The Coroner, who had previously done this, opened the proceedings briefly.

"You are met together," he told the jury, "to enquire into the circumstances of the death of Jasper Hurst, a tenant of Sir Harry Lynwood, occupying the house in Frimley known as The Gables. Unfortunately, at the present moment, very scant information concerning the identity of the deceased is obtainable. Partly for this reason, and partly for others—equally important—the proceedings this morning will be of the nature of a preliminary enquiry, and I must warn you that you must be prepared for an adjournment. I also wish to warn you of something else. You are on oath to find out the cause of death strictly in accordance with the evidence which will be given here, and on no other basis; and as that evidence may lead to serious charges against some person or persons, you must use every effort to keep your minds unbiased with regard to any gossip or theories which may be flying about. For this reason it is my duty to charge you not to discuss the case with anyone except yourselves during the interval which must necessarily elapse before we meet again. I hope you realise the importance of this?"

He paused. There was a murmur of assent among the jury.

"Very well, then. The evidence I shall call this morning will be more or less of a formal character. The witnesses will please understand that they will probably be wanted again at a later stage of the enquiry."

Bristow glanced at Charlie Lynwood, who met his gaze with a look of understanding. The first witness called was Sir Harry. After giving his name and address, the Coroner asked him:

"Jasper Hurst was a tenant of yours, Sir Harry?"

"He was."

"For how long?"

"Just over two months."

"You did not know him before he became your tenant?"

"I did not."

"You were satisfied, though, that he was a desirable tenant—I mean, financially?"

"Quite."

"Will you tell us why?"

"Certainly."

He explained how he had let the house through agents, that Hurst had given his Bankers as a reference, and that the reply from the Bank had been quite satisfactory.

"Thank you. Now, Sir Harry, you would describe Hurst—well, as a gentleman?"

"Yes."

"One, for example, you could ask to your house?"

"That is so."

"And you asked him, at the conclusion of the pageant which took place in your grounds the day before last, to come in to dinner with you?"

"I did."

"He had no idea beforehand that you were going to ask him?"

"None. It was at the very last moment."

"I see. Was there anything strange or suspicious with regard to him, while he was in your house?"

"Nothing."

"What time did he leave?"

"That I cannot say. I went up to bed, leaving him with some of the others in the smoking-room."

A juror began to interpose here. The Coroner interrupted him.

"We shall hear, presently, the time Hurst left the Manor," he said. "Thank you, Sir Harry. That will do, I think. James Barnes!"

Barnes, butler and chauffeur at The Gables, briefly stated what he knew of Hurst, which was very little. The Coroner asked him a few questions, and he stood down.

"Mr. Charles Lynwood!"

The young man seated himself in the witness-chair. Kinch looked up. He was seated, with the Chief Constable and the detective-sergeant, just on the right of the Coroner. The latter consulted his notes for a few moments.

"Suppose you tell us, Mr. Lynwood, to begin with, just what happened the other night when, as I understand, you left the house with Hurst. I will ask you any questions as you go on."

Bristow recognised the method. Sometimes, when a witness is asked to tell his own story, he makes slips which are useful in cross-examination afterwards. Charlie's story, however, was plain and straightforward. He told of the three men and himself in the smoking-room, of the Vicar and Hurst getting up to go, of how he had left his cigarettes in the marquee and went out to get them, of the Vicar saying good night, and of Hurst starting off down the drive. Then the Coroner began:

"Was Hurst out of sight when you went into the marquee?"

"Yes,—to me he was. When I got to the marquee I could no longer see down the drive."

"But he might not have kept walking on?"

"That is true. But I couldn't see."

"Well, you went into the tent. Did you find your cigarettes?"

"Not at once. Someone had moved them."

"And you looked for them?"

"Yes."

"That would take a little time?"

"It did."

Again the Coroner looked at his notes.

"There were three compartments in the tent?"

"There were."

"Did you go into each of them?"

"I did."

"Oh! Did you see anyone in the tent—in either compartment, Mr. Lynwood?"

"Certainly not."

At that moment Kinch leaned over and whispered to the Coroner. The latter nodded, and turned to Charlie again.

"I want to put this to you," he said. "Do you think it would have been possible, while you were in one of the inner compartments of the tent, for Hurst to have come back, enter the tent—thinking you were no longer there—and to have hidden himself in the other compartment?"

Charlie thought.

"Yes," he said, slowly, "I suppose it might have been. But, if he did, I didn't see him in the tent—nor anyone else."

"Very well. Go on, please."

"After I had found the cigarettes I came back into the house and went to my room. I was in bed when Captain Bristow came, later on, to tell me what had happened."

The Coroner looked at his notes again, and then, for a moment at the Superintendent. The latter shook his head—almost imperceptibly.

"Very well, Mr. Lynwood; that will do. I shall probably want you again—subsequently," he added, as the young man got up from the witness-chair.

The next witness was the Vicar. The Coroner only kept him a couple of minutes, simply getting him to corroborate the fact of the three men leaving the house together. The Vicar, who had expected more than this, hesitated.

"There was the question of my car—" he began.

"I know," broke in the Coroner. "At another stage of the enquiry, Mr. Ashley-Smith. I won't trouble you any further now."

One could distinguish a little thrill of excitement when Captain Bristow stepped forward, took the oath, and sat down in the witness-chair. Everyone knew, of course, that he had been the first to make the gruesome discovery, even before Hurst had breathed his last. Major Bainbridge looked at him with special interest. He knew the Captain's reputation. Kinch, too, watched his face. Mentmore had just a glimmer of scepticism in his eye. The astute detective-sergeant had, perhaps, more than an open mind about Bristow. He was by no means satisfied.

Bristow gave his evidence clearly, with no attempt at embellishment. He stated that, as he went up to bed, it was exactly half-past one—the clock struck the half-hour as he passed it. The Coroner asked him few questions till he had finished, and then began:

"Mr. Charles Lynwood did not leave the smoking-room when you were all there?"

"No."

He was quick to recognise the point of this question. So far, no mention of Mrs. Cresswell's pearls had been made in the enquiry. He saw, however, that the question meant the possibility of Charlie having gone into her room to get them. And added:

"He was with us all the time—I mean from the time we went in to dinner till he left the house with the Vicar and Mr. Hurst."

A flicker of a smile passed over the face of the Superintendent. He, too, knew the meaning of that question. In fact, he had suggested it beforehand to the Coroner.

"I see. And Hurst was still alive when you discovered him in the sedan-chair?"

"Yes."

"I am informed that he said something. What was it, Captain Bristow?"

"He was very incoherent and could only whisper. I caught two words—that was all. They sounded like 'the line.' "

"Have you any idea what he meant?"

"None whatever."

"About these two men, who were carrying the chair. Could you distinguish anything?"

"Nothing. I never got near enough, and it was only partially moonlight. The only thing about them I could make out was that one was taller than the other."

"You came closer to them, though, when they reached the car—and got in."

"Yes. But then I could only see the backs of their heads, till one of them, not the driver, turned round as I flashed my torch on the number-plate. I would not swear it, but I fancy he was clean-shaven. I was concentrating on the number-plate, you see."

"Yes. Well, we won't go into the matter of the car this morning— except—they drove straight away, I suppose?"

"Yes—but they stopped for a few seconds—I could hear. I suppose it was—to—open the gate leading from the drive—to the road— outside."

Bristow had become slow in his speech. A sudden thought had struck him—a point he had not thought of before. *Why* was the gate shut? Surely they would have left it open when they brought the car in—ready to get away quickly. Kinch, who was watching him narrowly, made a note in his book. Which ran:

"The gate—from drive to highway—was it open or shut?"

"Now, Captain Bristow"—the Coroner's clear, incisive voice brought him away from his thoughts—"tell us what you did next, please."

"As soon as I had satisfied myself that Hurst was dead, and that I could do no more, I ran back to the house and roused, first Sir Harry, and then Mr. Charles Lynwood."

"They were both in bed?"

"Yes."

"Asleep?"

"Sir Harry was. I'm not sure about Mr. Charles Lynwood."

"And then?"

"I telephoned for the police. Sir Harry and Mr. Harry Lynwood, whom he had called, came down—and Mr. Charles Lynwood. Mr. Harry went to fetch Dr. Forbes, and the constable who is stationed here."

The Coroner glanced at his notes, and at his watch, which was lying on the table.

"Thank you, Captain Bristow," he said. "I think that is all—at present. And now," he went on, speaking to the jury, "I propose only to call medical evidence, and then we will settle a date for adjournment. The police do not wish to say anything at this juncture—and I am in agreement with them. Will you take the oath, please, Dr. Forbes."

Dr. Forbes was brief, cautious, and professional. He stated that he had examined Hurst merely with a view to ascertaining whether life was extinct or not. It was extinct. Had only been extinct for a very short time. Yes, there was a contused wound on the left temple. Enough to cause death? He was not prepared to say. That matter was in other hands.

Dr. Burton, the police surgeon, was called next. He stated that he had made a cursory examination of the body when he had first been called to the scene of the tragedy, and corroborated the other medical man with regard to the wound on the temple, which had evidently been caused by some hard object.

"Did you arrive at any conclusion, then?" asked the Coroner.

"I did not."

"But you carried out a post-mortem on the body afterwards?"

"I did."

"Will you kindly tell the jury the result of your examination?"

"I found that deceased had been suffering from *arterio sclerosis* probably for some little time before he met with his death."

"Would you mind explaining what that means?"

"Yes. It means that the arteries supplying the wall of the heart—er—that is the muscle of the heart—were diseased. They were not working properly," he added, for the benefit of the jury.

"And the cause of death?"

"Cerebral hemorrhage, caused by arterial failure."

"But the blow on the forehead?" ejaculated the foreman of the jury. "Didn't that kill him?"

"As a secondary cause, yes. But the direct cause was what I have stated—arterial failure."

"I suppose, Dr. Burton," said the Coroner, who was quick to observe that one or two of the jury looked a little puzzled, "that the blow in question was not sufficient, in itself, to cause the death of an ordinary healthy man?"

"It *might* have done so," replied the police surgeon, with the caution of a professional, "but I should say that, with a person in normal health, that was not likely."

"It aggravated the disease from which the deceased was suffering?"

"Just so. It acted in the nature of a shock on the diseased arteries, accelerating the condition which caused death."

"Thank you, Dr. Burton. There is nothing more you wish to say?"

The doctor had some professional pride—the sort that asks for recognition.

"Except that I may mention that my diagnosis is confirmed by the report of a specialist, whom the deceased consulted some weeks ago. Superintendent Kinch will confirm this."

"That is quite right," said Kinch. "We can produce the physician in question if it is necessary," he went on, addressing the Coroner.

"Oh, I don't think we need do that. I imagine the jury are quite satisfied with Dr. Burton's evidence."

There was a murmur of assent. Dr. Burton looked pleased, and bowed.

"That is all the evidence for this morning," said the Coroner. "I will make out an Order for Burial, and then we can fix a date to resume the enquiry.—Yes?"

He had just begun to fill in the form when there was a slight confusion at the back of the hall, by the door, which was guarded by a constable. A man had come in, a tall, well-dressed man of about sixty, with iron-grey moustache and short, pointed beard. He was saying something to the policeman in a low tone of voice, and ended by pencilling something on a visiting-card and handing it to him. The constable pushed his way through the densely-crowded hall to the table at which the Coroner was sitting, and passed the card over. The Coroner looked at it, ejaculated "Oh!" and handed it to Kinch. That astute official's eyebrows lifted appreciatively.

The Coroner raised his voice, speaking to the man at the back of the room.

"Will you come here, please, sir?"

Jury, reporters and spectators stared at the stranger as he slowly made his way to the Coroner. Was a sensation about to be sprung on the Court?

The stranger came up beside the Coroner and conferred with him for two or three minutes in a low tone of voice. Then the Coroner turned to the jury.

"I must keep you a short time longer," he said. "This gentleman,"—indicating the stranger,—"is of opinion that the deceased is a relative of his. I have asked him to accompany Superintendent Kinch to The Gables, in order that he may view the body. We will await his return, please."

The stranger left the hall with Kinch, and the Coroner went on filling in the "Order for Burial." Then he leaned back in his chair, waiting. A buzz of conversation began to arise in the crowded court.

Presently the stranger came back. Superintendent Kinch conferred for a moment or two in whispers with the Coroner. Then the oath was administered.

He glanced at the visiting-card again, and then began:

"Your name is Stephen Westerham?" he queried.

The witness bowed.

"Your address, please?"

"The Red House, Tewkesbury."

"Your occupation?"

"I am a barrister, but I have not practised for some years, now."

"Thank you, Mr. Westerham. You have just seen the body on which this inquest is being held?"

"I have."

"Did you recognise the deceased?"

"I did."

"Will you tell us, please, what you know about him—concerning his identity?"

"He is Jasper Hurst. My half-brother."

"You are certain of this?"

"Absolutely."

A flutter of excitement went round the court. Reporters were scribbling hard. One of them was making a rapid pen-and-ink sketch of Stephen Westerham.

"We are grateful to you for telling us this, Mr. Westerham," went on the Coroner. "Up to the present moment, no information concerning your half-brother has been available. You will understand that, in the nature of this inquiry, the police will wish to consult with you before I can ask you to give any evidence at length?"

The witness bowed.

"Meanwhile, there are a few more questions I wish to put to you now. Will you tell us when you first heard of your half-brother's death?"

"Certainly. Only this morning, Mr. Coroner, I read the account of what had happened in Frimley in my morning paper, at breakfast. Jasper's—my half-brother's portrait was in the paper. Naturally I wished to place myself at your disposal without delay. The paper stated that the inquest was being held here this morning, and I lost no time. I motored straight here in my car."

"We are greatly obliged to you. You knew the deceased was living at Frimley?"

"Certainly."

"When did you see him last?"

"Monday in last week. I was spending the week-end in London, and he ran up and lunched with me at my club."

"Are there any other relatives?"

"Not in England. I have a married sister living in Canada. And there are cousins—but all of them are abroad."

"So you are the legal representative?"

"I am. And one of his executors. The other executor is his bank. I believe his will is deposited there."

"Thank you very much, Mr. Westerham. Your arrival here has simplified certain matters exceedingly. I will not go into any further details now, but, before I close the Court, I am sure the jury will join with me in an expression of sympathy for your bereavement—and the very sudden and tragic circumstances under which it has taken place."

The jury whispered together—the foreman got up, and said to Mr. Westerham, who bowed his acknowledgments:

"We are all very sorry for you, sir. And we hope the result of our being here may help to throw a light on what has happened."

The Coroner rose.

"The enquiry is adjourned," he said, "until this day week. We will meet here, at the same time—half-past eleven."

A little group remained in the hall after the rest had left. Sir Harry, who was always hospitable, went up to Mr. Westerham.

"I must introduce myself," he said. "I am your unfortunate brother's landlord. It was at my place, you know, that the affair happened. What are your plans?"

"Well," said the other, "I shall stay here for a few days, at my brother's house, I suppose. I packed a suitcase before I started. Of course there will be the funeral to see to—and other things."

"Let me offer you some luncheon now, at all events."

"It's very kind of you."

"Not at all. Major, won't you lunch with us, too?"

The Chief Constable accepted. Kinch came up, and spoke to Mr. Westerham.

"There's a lot I want to ask you, sir."

"You shall see Mr. Westerham after luncheon, Superintendent," said the Baronet. "Come to my house at half-past two—the library is at your disposal."

Sir Harry and his party started to walk to the Manor. Charles Lynwood dropped behind, with Bristow.

"You were right about my evidence, Roger," he said.

"Yes. I thought the Coroner wouldn't press you this morning."

"Have you done anything?" went on the young man. "Found out anything that will buck me up a bit?"

"I'm not going to tell you anything yet, Charlie. I'm still extremely puzzled. But I haven't been idle."

When they reached the Manor Mr. and Mrs. Cresswell, who were still there, were sitting on the terrace.

She began at once:

"Oh, Sir Harry,—what is the result of the inquest?—Did they discover who murdered Mr. Hurst?"

"I'm afraid they didn't get as far as that, Mrs. Cresswell. They are going to meet again—next week."

"What did they say about my necklace? Have they found out anything about it?"

Sir Harry shook his head.

"I don't know what the police have done," he replied, "but the matter of your necklace didn't come before the enquiry this morning."

"Oh, dear!" sighed Mrs. Cresswell. "I do hope they will trace it?"

"You have only yourself to blame if they don't, my dear," put in her husband, sardonically. Bristow, who was watching him, thought he detected a slight twitching of the man's lips.

In the hall they waited a few minutes till Hudson announced that luncheon was ready. Major Bainbridge lounged up to Bristow.

"Queer case," he said, laconically.

"Very."

"I suppose you are interested?"

"Extremely."

The Major nodded, a confidential, understanding little nod.

"I thought you would be," he said. "I know something of your reputation, Captain Bristow. You're really more of a policeman than I am," and he laughed. "I know my limitations, and I keep in the official background in a case like this. But my Superintendent is a capable fellow—and a sensible one," he added, slowly. "He's never above welcoming help—from anyone who can give it to him. Ah! Luncheon is ready."

Bristow smiled as he went into the dining-room. He understood perfectly well that the Chief Constable had thrown out an invitation.

9

Superintendent Kinch raised no objection as to the presence of others when he came, after luncheon, to interrogate Westerham. There was no reason why he should. Sir Harry, Captain Bristow, the Chief Constable, Westerham and Kinch went into the library.

"Now, sir," said Kinch to Westerham, "we want to know all you can tell us about your unfortunate brother. It often happens that the history of a person helps us considerably in tracing a crime. Sometimes it is impossible to find a motive until we know all about the persons concerned."

"I am as anxious as you are, Superintendent," replied Westerham, "that justice shall be done. I will place all I know of my half-brother at your disposal, and I hope it will assist you."

Kinch nodded. Westerham went on:

"Jasper was considerably younger than I. My mother, who was left a widow when I was a boy, married again, and Jasper was the only child of this second marriage. As a matter of fact, although he was my half-brother, I have really seen very little of him in the course of my life. When I left Oxford he was a small boy at school. Then my mother died. By my father's will I was left fairly well off, and preferred—well—to be independent. I mean," he added, "that I no longer made my home with my stepfather."

"But you kept in touch with your half-brother?" asked Kinch.

"Oh, yes. I saw him occasionally. We were always very good friends. We have met several times lately. He wanted my advice."

"What was your brother by profession?" asked Kinch.

Westerham smiled.

"He retired about six months ago. As to his profession,—well, have

111

you ever heard of Dewsbury & Hemmingford, Superintendent?"
Kinch looked up from his notebook with interest.

"Why, yes, I have," he replied. "I don't know that I ever came
across them—but we know of them, of course. Dewsbury &
Hemmingford, Private Enquiry Agents. Do you mean them?"
Westerham nodded.

"Yes," he said. "I thought you would know of them."

"I've heard of them," said Captain Bristow. "Didn't they recover
the Ashworth jewels—after the police had given up the case?" he
added, dryly, with a glance at the Superintendent.

"Ah!" put in the Chief Constable. "I remember. But it wasn't *my*
men who failed, you know. Another county, Captain Bristow—
another county."

"It was a smart job, I admit," said Kinch. "And this firm, sir?" he
went on, to Westerham.

"Well," said the latter, "my brother Jasper was Hemmingford,
Superintendent. He took that name for professional purposes when he
went into partnership with Dewsbury. He really began life as an
architect, but he always had a *penchant* for detective work. As a
matter of face, he solved one or two rather delicate problems as an
amateur while he was in business as an architect. That's how he met
Dewsbury, and it led to his giving up his business and going into
partnership with him. Dewsbury died about a year ago. He was a
bachelor, with no near relatives, and he left his share in the agency to
Jasper. But Jasper's health was failing. An opportunity arose of selling
the agency, and he took it. He had means enough to retire upon.
That's why he came here."

"A detective, eh?" said Sir Harry, who had been intensely interested
in Westerham's recital.

"In a way, he was," replied Westerham, "but the cases he handled
were often delicate matters which do not come into the category of
police work. The firm, I believe, had a good reputation."

"Excellent," said Bristow. "I was never actually in touch with
them. But I know they were sometimes consulted by the powers that
be."

"This is very interesting, Mr. Westerham," said the Superintendent. "It may even help us to throw some light upon what has
occurred here. I suppose, now,"—he was thinking rapidly—"that
Mr. Hurst made enemies in the course of his work?"

"It is possible," replied Westerham, "but he never mentioned any
to me. Indeed, he never spoke of the details of his work—or of persons

connected with it."

"Yes—I see," said Kinch. "Now, can you tell me anything about his private life which might be useful?"

"Not very much. Except that he has not had a happy life for the last few years. I suppose I shall be breaking no confidence in telling you?"

"I think you can rely upon our discretion, Mr. Westerham," said Sir Harry, "but if you prefer to entrust your confidences to the representatives of the police only, Captain Bristow and I will——"

"No, no," broke in Westerham. "That is not necessary. I would really like you to know. Well, then, about four years ago poor Jasper did a very foolish thing. He became infatuated with a woman considerably younger than himself—and married her. I only knew of this afterwards. As I said, we seldom met. He seems, from what he told me some months ago, to have met this woman when he was spending a short holiday at Annecy, in Haute Savoie. Anyhow, he married her within a few weeks. I believe things were fairly right for a couple of years—and then he made a very painful discovery. He told me that, in the course of some investigations he was carrying out—a robbery, I think,—that, almost by accident, he found that his wife, before he married her, had been mixed up with a gang of thieves—in fact, that she was an adventuress. But this was not all. He began to suspect that she was still associated with crooks. The irony of it all was pretty terrible, for Jasper was a man of great integrity. Well, he charged her with it. He was still fond of her, and told her this discovery should make no difference, if she would promise, once for all, to break from her old associates. For a time she appeared to have done so. Then, to make a long story short, the climax came. She left him—ran off with a man who was a thorough bad lot—Jasper never told me who he was, but he knew about him. Then she wrote to him and asked him to divorce her, so that she could marry this other man. He came to consult me about it."

"What did you advise?" asked Kinch.

"Naturally, that he should divorce her and get rid of her altogether. But he wouldn't. He was still infatuated with her, so much so that he seemed to have the notion that as long as she was his wife she might come back to him in a state of penitence—and he would forgive her. My poor brother was a strangely chivalrous man where women were concerned. In spite of my advice, he actually wrote and told her this. And, so far as I know, he never heard of her since. But it helped to break him. And he told me that the chief reason why he gave up his work was not really that of failing health, but the fear that haunted him that in the course of some criminal investigation he might find himself on the track of his own wife. It was a tragedy."

"Poor chap!" exclaimed Sir Harry. "I'm sorry for him."

"You will understand," went on Westerham, "that I have no wish to make all this public. My evidence at the adjourned inquest——"

"That ought to be all right, sir," broke in Kinch, glancing at the Chief Constable, who nodded in acquiescence. "I don't think there will be any need to enter into Mr. Hurst's private life at the inquest, though, if all this has any bearing on the crime, it will have to come out. I'm greatly obliged for your information. It throws a new light on matters."

"May we ask how?" said Sir Harry.

Kinch thought for a moment or two, and then said:

"I don't see any reason why I should not tell you. In fact, it's obvious. Well, I mean that from what Mr. Westerham has told us of his brother's character, it does not seem probable that he was after those pearls."

"Good heavens!" exclaimed Westerham. "You never suspected *that*, I hope?"

"Well, I don't know, sir," replied Kinch, consulting his notebook. "There were certain points to be considered. Your brother was hanging about in the corridor upstairs, close to Mrs. Cresswell's bedroom, for some little time before he came down to dinner the night before last. And, at dinner, he questioned Miss Fullinger—who was to have driven Mrs. Cresswell back to London yesterday—about the necklace. He asked if Mrs. Cresswell would be taking it with her in the car. There were other things," he added, looking again at his notebook, "but I prefer not to mention them now—except that what you have told me about Mr. Hurst having been a private detective throws a light upon them. Thank you very much, Mr. Westerham. I think that's all, for the present."

Westerham then took himself off to The Gables, saying that he should be making arrangements for the funeral and should be staying in Frimley until the adjourned inquest, at all events. The Chief Constable ran Kinch back to Chiltonbury in his car, and went with the Superintendent into the latter's private office.

"Now, Kinch," he said, "tell me what you think of the case—as far as you've gone into it. It's pretty complicated—and it's deeply interesting."

"It is that," replied Kinch, "but I fancy what we've just heard this afternoon about Hurst explains some of the points in it."

"I'd like to hear."

"Well, sir, we've got to remember that Hurst was connected with this firm—Dewsbury & Hemmingford. He *was* Hemmingford. I daresay you know the kind of work Dewsbury & Hemmingford undertook?"

"I've heard something about them—yes."

"They were a high-class firm of private enquiry agents. People in a good position consulted them on delicate matters which are either outside our province, or because they didn't want to call in the police. Cases of evidence for divorce, blackmail, missing valuables—*you* know, sir. And Hurst must have had a pretty deep knowledge of the private affairs of lots of people—society folks, and so on. Some of it, you may be sure, *criminal* knowledge. It's *our* business, of course, to bring every criminal case we know of before the law. But Hurst's profession was different. In many instances he would be employed in keeping matters private—not letting them get into a court of justice. You can't blame him. We are the servants of the public. *He* was employed in a purely private capacity. I've no doubt he could have told us of people whom we should never have suspected of being criminals—crimes which never saw the light of day. There are any amount of them about."

Major Bainbridge nodded.

"I follow you," he said.

"Well, now, sir, Hurst retires. He is living a quiet life in a small village. He has given up his work, but he's still got his knowledge. He is asked to take part in this pageant. I've ascertained that there were a number of rehearsals—when of course, costumes were not worn and they didn't make up their faces. But none of the members of Sir Harry's house-party were present at these rehearsals. They all came down the day before and took part in one *dress* rehearsal. I've ascertained, further, that Hurst, like many of the others, dressed and made himself up at home—before he came to the Manor grounds. And his make-up would disguise him—he wore a moustache and beard. And he was called *Hurst*—not Hemmingford."

"Ah!—I see what you mean, Kinch," said the Chief Constable. "You mean that anyone who had known him as Hemmingford, the private detective, would not have recognised him as Hurst, a Puritan of the sixteenth century?"

"Exactly, sir. None of the house-party would have done so, either at the rehearsal or at the actual pageant. Now, of that house-party, we can eliminate all except Mrs. Cresswell and Miss Fullinger. Of those two, he had Miss Fullinger's address written in his notebook. *Why?* It's been puzzling me all the time, sir, till our interview with Mr. Westerham just now. Hurst, you may depend upon it, knew something about the girl Fullinger—at least, it's a fair inference that he did. Possibly something not exactly to her credit."

"Oh, but—" Major Bainbridge began. And then stopped short.

"Wait a bit, sir. It's only an inference, I admit. But it fits in. At the pageant he notices two things. First, this Fullinger girl. Secondly, the foolish way in which Mrs. Cresswell was asking for trouble by flaunting those pearls about. For all we know, that necklace may have been familiar to him. I had a chat about it with Mr. Cresswell, and he told me that, once or twice, he had employed a private detective to keep watch when his wife had worn the thing in public. And I shall ask him if he ever went to Dewsbury & Hemmingford for a man. Well, Hurst's interest is aroused. He accepts Sir Harry's invitation to dinner. When he goes upstairs to wash, he reconnoitres that corridor. He's on the look-out for something. He sits next to Miss Fullinger at dinner and asks leading questions about that necklace. And he takes care not to remove his moustache and beard till he gets outside the house. He didn't want to be recognised by someone inside the house."

"You think he suspected theft—and that he wanted to frustrate it?"

Kinch shook his head.

"That I can't say, sir. I only go so far as to suggest that his interest was aroused."

"But how does this bear on what happened after he left the house—the murder, and so on?"

"Possibly we shall never know that—even if we find the culprit, sir. But, following out this theory: Hurst leaves the house, probably with nothing more in his mind than that certain circumstances were peculiar, perhaps that Mrs. Cresswell was in danger of being robbed. And then, accidentally, he runs into the thief. If young Curtis, and whoever was with him, had that car waiting round the bend of the drive, Hurst would stumble upon it just after he had crossed the bridge. And then we don't know exactly what *did* happen, though it's plausible to suppose that he didn't interfere *then*. Probably hid and watched. He got that blow from the knuckle-duster inside the tent. At least, it seems so. Captain Bristow saw the sedan-chair carried out of the tent—and Hurst was in it. And they got the pearls right enough. The empty case in Yew Tree Bottom proves *that!*"

The Chief Constable nodded his head, thoughtfully.

"Yes," he said, slowly. "There's a lot in what you say. If I might offer a suggestion, though, Kinch, the jigsaw puzzle doesn't all fit in. What do you make of that wrecked car at Drifford? Do you think it has any bearing on the case?"

"Well, sir," replied Kinch, "from one point of view it looks like it. We have to remember that there are *two* men to be accounted for who were not members of the house-party—the two whom Captain Bristow saw carrying the sedan-chair and then making off in the car. One of them was the Vicar's nephew—young Curtis. He took the car out of his uncle's garage."

Major Bainbridge frowned a little.

"Go on," he said. "Who was the other, then?"

"We know, pretty well, that whoever was driving the wrecked car came on to Chiltonbury by train. The finding of the number-plates on the line proves that. And there's another thing. Sergeant Mentmore discovered this morning—the amount of petrol consumed proves this—that the Vicar's car ran more than the twenty miles to Yew Tree Bottom that night—eight or nine miles more, sir."

"Well?"

"If it were driven from Frimley to Chiltonbury and back *first,* that would just account for those eight miles. Suppose young Curtis drove in here and fetched the other man out?"

The Chief Constable frowned again.

"Plausible. But there are difficulties. How could young Curtis *know* that the other fellow had broken down?"

"It must have been arranged that the other man should only run as far as Chiltonbury in his car, sir,—and Curtis was to pick him up there."

Major Bainbridge shook his head.

"I don't like it, Kinch. That's a fact. The difficulty to my mind is that this nephew of the Vicar's was far too open and above-board in what we *know* he did—his calling at the Vicarage and waiting there for his uncle. But go on. Follow out this theory a little further. Suppose it *did* happen as you put it. What then? The two men make off in the car with the jewels. Whoever they were—whether Curtis was one of them or not—they separated. Only *one* man ran the car into Yew Tree Bottom, according to that poaching fellow. He took the pearls, of course. Pocketed them, I suppose, and left the case behind. But how about the other man? Where did he leave the car?"

Kinch laughed.

"I think I've found that out, sir—at the inquest, this morning."

"How?"

"I ought to have thought of it before. It was when Captain Bristow was giving his evidence. He told me, previously, what he told the Coroner—that the car stopped for a moment or two, apparently at the gate leading from the drive to the main road. And I noticed that he hesitated, as if a sudden thought had struck him. It struck me, too. Was it likely that, when they drove the car in from the road they would have left the gate shut? And, if it was open, why did they stop? After the inquest—before I came to the Manor to interview Mr. Westerham—I made enquiries. As luck would have it, I came across a man who had been out late and was returning by the main road a little before midnight. And he was ready to swear that the gate was open. He noticed it as he passed. That's why the car stopped, sir,—to put down one of the two, *there!*"

"Oho!" exclaimed the Chief Constable. "You think that, do you? What have you done about it? It's important, if it's true. It means that this fellow, whoever he was, may be still in the neighbourhood—unless he walked into Chiltonbury and got off by train."

"Couldn't have done it—the last train, up or down, had left long before. Oh, I've taken measures, sir. Mentmore is on the job, making enquiries to find if any man was seen in the neighbourhood."

"I see. No news of young Curtis—the Vicar's nephew,—I suppose?"

"No, sir. Stevens is on that job—in London. The Metropolitan Police are helping him—enquiries at night-clubs, and so on. We ought to get on his track."

The Chief Constable got up.

"I must be off," he said. "I'll drop in tomorrow morning." He hesitated. "May I offer you a suggestion, Kinch?"

Kinch knew the phrase, and that there was generally something in it when Major Bainbridge made use of it.

"Certainly, sir. I'll be glad to have it."

"I always think it's worth while trying to pick a fellow's brains if his brains are in good order, you know."

"Certainly."

"I imagine Captain Bristow's brains come under that category. I don't want to interfere, Kinch, but it might be useful to try to find out what he thinks of things."

"I rather agree with you, sir. But he's a bit of an oyster, isn't he?"

Major Bainbridge laughed.

"Part of our business to open oysters—diplomatically," he said. "I don't suggest that you should hunt in couples, but I do fancy he's sniffed a little of the scent—maybe a whiff or two that you haven't nosed yourself, and if you—"

"Excuse me, sir."

The telephone-bell had rung. Kinch took up the receiver.

"Hullo . . . yes . . . yes. Superintendent Kinch of Frattenbury . . . that's right. . . . Yes . . . Oh . . . Splendid . . . good business . . . Yes, by all means, bring him along. . . . No, you can't help that, of course. . . . Yes—merely detention at present. . . . Right! . . . I see . . . Yes. My man, Stevens, is in London . . . I'll try to get through to him presently and tell him to meet you—what time? . . . Yes . . . Eight-thirty-three at Charing Cross. And if he's not there, you'll come straight on here yourself? Right. Thank you very much!"

He replaced the receiver and turned to his superior officer triumphantly.

"That's the best bit of news we've had today, sir. Trunk call from Dover. They've got him right enough."

"Who?"

"Young Curtis, sir. The Vicar's nephew. Making off by the Boulogne boat."

"Good!"

"They're bringing him up to London by the next train—arrives at Charing Cross at eight-thirty-three. He'll be here tonight, sir. I think the train gets in about half-past ten." He looked at his watch. "I ought to get on to Stevens—he was to ring up about six. I want him to meet Curtis at Charing Cross and bring him down. *Now* we ought to get a bit ahead, sir," and he rubbed his hands briskly.

"I shall be anxious to hear what Curtis has to say."

"Ah! I wonder! I suppose I ought to let his uncle know—poor old chap! I'll get through to Frimley presently."

The Chief Constable still lingered.

"You won't charge him?"

"Not yet, I think, sir, . . . only, that scarf of his, you know. *In the tent* it was. I should be justified."

"I know," replied Major Bainbridge, thoughtfully. "I'd forgotten that scarf, for the moment."

"I hadn't," replied Kinch, grimly. "And whatever yarn he spins, it will take him all his time to explain *that!*"

10

Captain Bristow had found a secluded spot in the grounds of Frimley Manor, a small summer-house, and there he sat, by himself, working out in his mind the problem he had set himself to try to solve. The Chief Constable was right when he hinted to Kinch that Bristow had ideas with regard to the double crime which might be worth ascertaining. He had. But he was by no means sure of the veracity of most of them, and it was doubtful whether, in the present state of his mind, he would have been willing to open out had Kinch endeavoured to pump him just then.

When in the Secret Service he had always been adverse to taking any action until he had satisfied himself as to the stability of the grounds for doing so, and, until he had reached his conclusion, was, as Kinch had remarked, as secretive as the proverbial oyster. He was blessed with a singularly clear and logical brain, a brain that took in not only the facts of any cases he had investigated, but the psychology of any persons who were concerned in it. And he had always been more wont to devote himself to severe and thoughtful analysis, than to spend all his time on the actual spade-work of an investigation.

Once he had told a friend, when speaking of his methods, that there were two ways of solving a jigsaw puzzle.

"The first," he had said, "is to work on the shapes of the pieces, fitting them together irrespective of the picture. The other is to get hold of a bit of the picture to begin with, and build the thing up from colour and design rather than from shapes. Personally, I prefer the latter, because, in a way, the thing shapes itself. Besides, it's more true to type. In a crime you rarely have all the pieces to begin with, but you generally have enough to start a picture."

The particular bit of the picture that was engaging his mind centred around Sonia Fullinger. He had said nothing to Charlie about the discovery of Sonia's handkerchief in the Vicar's car; he did not want to upset the young man. For the finding of the handkerchief corroborated what Charlie had seen. There could be little doubt that Sonia was mixed up in things pretty deeply.

And yet, to use the simile of the jigsaw puzzle, though the pieces in this particular part of it seemed to fit, the "colour scheme" was not exactly harmonious. Somehow or other, knowing the girl fairly well, as he did, he could not associate her with barefaced robbery and participation in a murder—it seemed so preposterous. On the other hand, however, it was evident that the greater crime was unpremeditated, and rested, so it appeared to Bristow, on chance all along. For it was only by chance that Hurst had been invited to dinner that night—only by chance that he left the house at that late hour. Yet, even to connect Sonia with a robbery seemed preposterous. Unless— and it entered his mind more than once—his own suggestion to Charlie was true, that Sonia was really helping Mrs. Cresswell to dispose of those pearls under the semblance of a robbery.

The two pieces of evidence against her, too, seemed so damning. Charlie was certain that he saw her come out of the house that night, and then there was her handkerchief—found in the Vicar's car.

Then, in the conflict in his mind between psychology and facts, he allowed, for the sake of argument, psychology to predominate, and looked at the problem from the point of view that Sonia was innocent. That would, of course, entail another explanation of the facts—for they *had* to be explained. Sonia, though innocent, meeting a man by that tent at half-past one in the morning, and Sonia's handkerchief being found in the Vicar's car. *What* could be the explanation? He took out a notebook, wrote in it a list of all the persons in the house that night, and studied it carefully.

An interruption came, however. Footsteps sounded on the gravel path. Anstice Lynwood was coming slowly along it. He got up and went to meet her.

"Hullo, Roger," she said, glancing at the notebook he was still holding. "I hope I didn't disturb you. You look as if you were composing poetry with that notebook—and your rather solemn expression."

"Never wrote verse in my life, Anstice," he replied with a laugh, "but I *was* trying to compose something, all the same."

"What? Is it allowed to ask?"

"Of course. I was trying to figure out the problem of this tragedy."

"Ah! I'm not surprised at that, Roger. Are you trying to emulate—or to rival—the good Superintendent Kinch?—For I rather like him."

"Not exactly. But I'm naturally interested, you know. To a certain extent it's in my line."

"I felt sure you were, Roger. I couldn't help noticing how you've been watching the police enquiries. Are you going to help them?"

"They haven't asked me. No, I'm puzzling over a few ideas of my own. And I want you to tell me something."

"*I* don't know anything about it, I'm afraid."

"I know. But, look here, Anstice. You're a bit observant; you made a list of the hired costumes and properties for this Superintendent fellow. Did he do anything about it?"

"*He* didn't, but his sergeant,—Mentmore is his name, I think—examined the lot, in the tent, after I'd sorted them. He did that yesterday morning—when you went into Chiltonbury with the Superintendent."

"Oh—did he? Were you there, Anstice?"

"No, but he saw me afterwards. He wanted to know something."

"What?"

"He asked me whether there were any other costumes—belonging to us or the house-party. I showed him mine, and daddy's and the rest—Paul Singleton's and Frank Underwood's, you know. They were in the house. Then he asked where Sonia's was. I told him she'd hired it herself and taken it back with her."

"Oh! Did he want to know where she'd hired it?"

"Yes. Rather funny of him, I thought."

"Did you tell him?"

"Yes. She got it from Sparkson's, you know."

"I see."

They were strolling slowly along a garden path. For a minute or two he was silent. Then he said:

"I'm going to ask you rather a curious question, Anstice. And please don't think that I am suspecting anyone. Can you tell me whether either of the maids here went into Sonia Fullinger's room, to call her, on the morning after the pageant?"

Anstice looked surprised.

"Why, no, I don't suppose either of them did. It would be her own maid,—yes, of course it was. I remember now. She was coming out of Sonia's room when I went in."

Roger Bristow stopped short, and turned towards her.

"Oh, but that's capital," he said. "You can tell me just what I wanted to know. *You* went into her room, did you?"

"Yes. You see, I was up early. I meant to have had a canter. And I just went in to wish her good morning."

"Excellent. Was she awake?"

"Certainly. She was sitting up in bed and drinking her early cup of tea. I suppose her maid had brought it up."

"And did she say anything about what had happened in the night— or did you?"

"Neither of us knew about it then. I didn't hear of it till I came downstairs, so of course we never spoke of it."

"And she was quite normal—not flurried, or anything like that?"

"Why, of course she wasn't, Roger. Whatever are you driving at?"

He ignored the question.

"Now, can you remember," he went on, "whether that Edward the Sixth's costume she had been wearing the day before was lying about the room? Did you see it, I mean?"

"Yes, I did—part of it, anyhow."

"Oh, *damn!*" he exclaimed.

"What's the matter?"

"You've done me! Never mind. Go on, please, Anstice. You say you saw *part* of the costume?"

"Yes, but I expect it was all there. Her box was at the foot of the bed and was open. The costume lay on the top of the things, folded up. So of course I only saw the bit of it that was visible."

"Oh, it was all there, right enough. Yes, I see. I've got to think things out again. They don't fit, somehow. Frightfully decent of you to tell me all this, Anstice."

"Why do you want to know, Roger? Is—is there anything wrong about Sonia?—no, I don't mean that, of course—but do you think that detective-man had something in his mind—when he asked me about her costume?"

Again he stopped—and looked at her gravely.

"I do think so," he said, "and I'm going to take you into my confidence, because I think, perhaps, you can help me later on—when I've thought things over a bit. I may?"

"You can trust me, Roger," replied the girl.

"I know. You mustn't ask me how I know, but I've found out"— he was alluding to the handkerchief, and not to Charlie's story—"that Sonia Fullinger is in great danger."

"Roger! She *couldn't*—"

"I don't say she *did*," he interrupted. "You mustn't drop a hint of this to anyone—least of all to Charlie."

"Charlie! Poor boy—yes, I see. Of course I won't."

"Well, if the police knew as much as I do, they'd have no choice. They would be bound to arrest her, or at any rate to detain her or keep her under strict observation. I should myself, if I were a policeman. As it is, I suppose I'm not justified in keeping what I know from them, but I'm taking the risk."

"But this is simply terrible, Roger!"

"Don't worry. I'm going to do my best to put things right—if they can be put right. But the point is that it seems to me the police have their suspicions. What you've told me about Mentmore being after that Edward the Sixth costume has made me think a bit. And this Superintendent fellow is a might cute chap. Well—I'm going to run up to London tomorrow and see Sonia Fullinger."

"To warn her?"

"Not exactly. I want to ask her one or two questions. And then I may ask your help. I don't want anyone here to imagine I am making enquiries."

"Of course I'll do anything I can to help Sonia—but what can I do?"

"We'll see. It won't be anything very difficult. Keep this to yourself, please, Anstice. I must go and use the telephone now. By the way, when are the Cresswells leaving?"

"Tomorrow. But Mrs. Cresswell will have to come down again next week—they've told her she will be wanted at the adjourned inquest."

"Ah! I thought she would."

They were nearing the house now. Out of the front door came Detective-Sergeant Mentmore.

"Ah," said Bristow, "I'll have a word or two with this fellow."

Anstice went into the house, and Bristow stopped Mentmore.

"Still on the job, sergeant?"

Mentmore looked at him a trifle suspiciously. He still had not fathomed this ex-Secret Service man.

"By the way," went on Bristow, pleasantly, "we both got a notion over the amount of petrol used in the Vicar's Morris, this morning, didn't we? You wanted to know what I thought about it. Well, I'll tell you. The distance over and above the run to Yew Tree Bottom would have been—well—to Chiltonbury and back, eh?"

Mentmore was cautious.

"A very good guess, sir," he replied.

"I expect that applies to both of us, sergeant, eh?"

"Very likely, sir."

Bristow laughed.

"And you infer from this that young Curtis drove her into Chiltonbury and brought the other blackguard out, eh?"

Mentmore was nonplussed. That *was* his inference, of course, but he hesitated to admit it. He meant to be cautious with Bristow.

"It might have happened," he admitted.

Again Bristow laughed.

"Oh, well," he said, "let's suppose it did. Now, may I ask you a question, sergeant?"

"I don't promise to answer it, sir."

"Quite so. But I'll ask it, all the same. Only one man drove that car into Yew Tree Bottom. Which do you think it was—the Vicar's nephew or the other fellow?"

"I don't mind telling you that I'm hanged if I know what to think about that, sir."

"Oh, well, I wouldn't mind betting a fiver that it wasn't young Curtis. And I'll go on to say that the key to the puzzle lies in the personality of the other fellow. May I give you a hint, sergeant?"

"I'm always grateful for information, sir."

"Well, where did this fellow make for after he abandoned the car? Isn't it just possible that instead of making for a railway he may have cut over the downs to the main London road and got a lift on a lorry or something?"

In reply, Detective-Sergeant Mentmore laughed.

"We're not all fools, sir," he said. "Give us credit for a little sense. It's a big job, but we're trying to make a list of vehicles running along that road from three o'clock the other morning onwards. Don't suppose we shall get 'em all, but a couple of dozen drivers have been interviewed already."

"Good business!" said Bristow. "I beg your pardon for mentioning it, sergeant."

"That's all right, sir," replied Mentmore, relaxing a little. "It was smart of you to think of it, if I may say so."

Bristow wished him good day and passed on. In a few minutes he was in the hall of Frimley Manor, making a trunk call on the telephone.

"Hullo— Are you Sparkson's?"

"Yes. What is it?"

"Captain Bristow speaking. I want a word with Mr. Sparkson, if he's in."

"Hold on, sir, please."

In a few moments Sparkson himself spoke.

"Oh—Captain Bristow? Yes, sir. What can I do for you?"

"You supplied me with costumes for the pageant here—I'm speaking from Frimley Manor—near Chiltonbury."

"Yes, sir. That's right."

"I believe some of the actors hired their own costumes from you, Sparkson?"

"Yes, I think they did."

"There was a Miss Fullinger—she had a male Tudor dress—she played King Edward the Sixth."

There was a slight pause. Then Mr. Sparkson said:

"Oh! . . . Yes."

"Has she sent it back?"

Another slight pause . . . then the answer:

"It came in this morning."

"Well, I wish you'd reserve it for me, Sparkson. I may be wanting it. I shall be in London tomorrow, and I'll call."

"I'm not sure, sir, . . . whether I can let you have it. I'll see."

"It isn't hired, is it?"

"N-no. Not exactly."

Bristow smiled. He guessed pretty shrewdly what was in Sparkson's mind. Kinch *was* after that costume, then.

"Oh, all right," he said. "I'll call tomorrow, anyhow."

"I've another Tudor dress—same size—" began Sparkson, but Bristow interrupted him.

"Never mind now—see you tomorrow. Good-bye."

"Now," said Bristow, to himself, "who is going to be the first to see that costume? Kinch's man or I? It doesn't much matter, though. I don't suppose Kinch is after what's in *my* mind. I wonder what he *is* after!"

It was after dinner that night that the Vicar called. He asked Sir Harry if he might speak to him privately. He also asked if Captain Bristow might be present. The three men went into the library.

"I've come to tell you something," said the Vicar, when they were alone. "I've had a message from Superintendent Kinch. My nephew has been found."

"Oh!" exclaimed Sir Harry. "Where?"

The Vicar shook his head, sadly.

"From what Kinch tells me I don't like it at all," he replied. "He was on his way to the Continent—just about to embark on the afternoon boat from Folkestone to Boulogne."

"Ah," remarked Bristow. "Of course they'd be looking out for him at all the ports. That's a foregone conclusion. I suppose Kinch told you he'd be brought to Chiltonbury?"

"Yes. He expects him here late tonight, by the train arriving at ten-forty."

"Have they arrested him?" asked Sir Harry.

"Kinch didn't use that word. He said they were bound to detain him."

"That means," explained Bristow, "that they have made no formal charge against him as yet. They'll question him, of course. And you mustn't be surprised if they arrest him. It all depends upon whether he can give an account of himself and prove an alibi, if he was not here at the time poor Hurst was done in. Of course you'll be allowed to see him, Vicar."

"Yes. Kinch told me that. I've come round to ask your advice. Do you think I ought to go to Chiltonbury tonight and see him?"

Mr. Ashley-Smith turned instinctively to Captain Bristow as he asked the question.

"I should wait till tomorrow. He won't be here till late tonight, and Kinch will want to put him through a catechism. Better see him after that has happened."

"I suppose you wouldn't go in with me, Bristow? It would be kind of you."

"I'll do that with pleasure—providing you don't mind going in early—directly after breakfast. I want to catch the ten-twenty to London."

"Very well," said the Vicar. "I'll run you in. I'll call for you here at nine o'clock. It is exceedingly good of you."

"Not at all," replied Bristow, with a smile. "I'm very curious to see your nephew and to hear what he has to say for himself. I've been formulating my own ideas about him, and I want to see if I'm anyway right."

"Looks rather nasty, though," said Sir Harry, "trying to get away by the Channel boat, eh?"

"Not necessarily," said Bristow. "Hundreds of people cross the Channel every day without anything against them. Anyhow, Vicar," he went on to Mr. Ashley-Smith, "I shouldn't worry too much. Wait and hear what sort of an explanation he has to give."

"Well, there's one thing about Leonard," said the Vicar, getting up to go. "He's given me a deal of trouble, but I've never known him tell a lie."

"Look here," said Sir Harry, "why not telephone to the police-station now to tell them you'll be there early tomorrow?"

"Thanks very much. I will."

Kinch replied.

"Very well, sir," he said; "that will suit quite nicely. I'd like to be here when you come—and I have to catch the ten-twenty train. I'll expect you a little after nine."

"I'm bringing Captain Bristow with me," went on the Vicar.

There was a little chuckle in reply, and then Kinch said:

"I thought probably you would. Good night, sir.—I'm very sorry to cause you all this trouble, but I've got my duty to do."

The Vicar replaced the receiver and turned to Bristow.

"That's settled," he said. "An early interview suits Superintendent Kinch. *He* wants to catch the ten-twenty train, it appears."

Bristow smiled.

"Oh, he does, does he? We may be bound for the same destination."

"Why, of course you will be," said Sir Harry. "The ten-twenty's an express—to London. Doesn't stop anywhere."

Captain Bristow lingered in the smoking-room with Charles Lynwood that night after the others had retired. He did not tell Charlie of his discovery about Sonia Fullinger's handkerchief, but he questioned the young man minutely about his seeing Sonia outside the Manor House on the night of the tragedy. He seemed particularly anxious to know if she was wearing the cap belonging to the Tudor costume, as well as the rest of it. Charlie said she was. He begged Bristow to tell him whether he had found out anything that would help. But all that Bristow would say was:

"I haven't made much progress, Charlie, but I've got an idea. Mind you, it's a *very* hazy one—and may come to nothing. It's far-fetched— but there's a chance in a thousand that it may help, and I'm going to see if the chance exists. It's something that happened years ago in an investigation with which I was concerned—a bit of detective work which a colleague of mine carried through, so it's not original. I chanced to remember it, and I'm going to put it to the test. Apart from that, I'm more than ever puzzled concerning what you've told me about Sonia."

Someone else was sitting up late that night, to wit, Major

Bainbridge, the Chief Constable. His wife had gone to bed, leaving him poring over a particularly stiff crossword puzzle. He was fond of crosswords, and hated being baulked by them. With the help of a big dictionary he had just solved the last two clues, and gave a sigh of satisfaction as he pencilled in the words, leaned back in his chair, and re-lighted his pipe.

Then he opened a drawer of the knee-hole table at which he was seated, and produced a notebook. Had Kinch, or any other subordinate officer of the County police, seen that notebook, they would probably have been a little surprised. In his dealings with them the Major was always so diffident, so self-effacing in the matter of investigation of criminal or other cases. He so often said he was not a "policeman," and that it was their work to probe the mysteries of their craft.

And yet, in that fat, carefully-written notebook, were records of a hundred and one cases; and Kinch and others, had they read them, might have found the bases of some of those "suggestions" which the Chief Constable sometimes threw out so unobtrusively, "suggestions" which, somehow or other, were generally worth following out.

Certainly Kinch would have been surprised had he seen what was freshly written under the heading of "Frimley Manor—Murder and Robbery." There was the case meticulously tabulated in every detail that had come under his notice from the Superintendent's notes or his own observation.

Every person who had been connected with the drama was tabulated, with remarks against each, many of them having only a brief word or two, such as "Knows nothing," "Stupid ass," "Nonentity," and so forth.

Against Bristow was written:

"Fellow who solved the Roumanian Treaty theft. Also the disappearance of Paul Koravitch. Very clever. Evidently is working quietly and has theories. Ought to be taken into confidence at the right moment. Have suggested this to Kinch."

Charles Lynwood did not come out of it quite satisfactorily.

"Believe he is sweet on Sonia Fullinger. Remember noticing when dining at Frimley Manor last Christmas, when both of them were staying there. He doesn't seem comfortable about something. Would shield the Fullinger girl if he suspected anything about her.

"Sonia Fullinger. Kinch has got his knife into her. Suspicious. Not much to go upon yet. Possible developments."

Mrs. Cresswell would not have cared to have seen the note against her name.

"Silly female. Serve her damn well right."

Major Bainbridge proceeded to add to his notes a précis of the Inquest that morning. Also the account which Westerham had given of Hurst. He read them over. Then wrote:

"Suggestion. Try to find Hurst's wife. She might be induced to throw some light on matters."

He was about to close the book and go to bed, when, glancing at it once more, he took up his fountain-pen again and made a further note:

"Hurst's last words—'the line.' What did they mean? A point which seems to have been overlooked by all of us, so far. Worth considering, though."

He leaned back in his chair: his glance fell on the nine bulky volumes of the "Century Dictionary," in their own little book-case. He was constantly using the Dictionary in solving those abstruse crosswords which were his hobby. He picked out one of the volumes, opened it, and turned to the word "Line." There were six long columns devoted to this little word, containing every possible meaning and combination. "A cord—a rope—a lot or portion—a limit—a short letter—a row—a service . . . a line of shipping—a railroad—a telegraph-wire. Line of direction—line of health—line of life. . . . To draw the line—to drop a line." All kinds of phrases in which the word "line" occurred, with its various meanings.

There was nothing to help him. Then he tried "Lime. . . ." The sound of an "m" might easily have been mistaken for that of an "n" in that faint whisper made by a dying man. "Lime-burner—Lime-flower—Lime-hound—Lime-juice—Lime-kiln—*Lime-tree!*" Ah! Here was a possible clue to its meaning. There were plenty of trees about that marquee. He would find out if one of them was a lime. Even then it was all very vague.

But it was as good, if not better than a crossword puzzle.

"I'll get to the bottom of it *somehow,*" he said, half-aloud. Then he put the volume of the dictionary back in the book-case, and took himself off to bed.

11

Superintendent Kinch received Mr. Ashley-Smith and Captain Bristow in his office the following morning.

"You'll find your nephew in my house, sir," he said to the Vicar. "I'll take you to him at once, but I'd like a word with you afterwards. I've made him as comfortable as I could," he added.

"You haven't arrested him?" asked Bristow.

"I have not, Captain Bristow,—so far; though I think I should be justified in doing so."

"Hasn't he given an explanation?"

"Oh, yes,—he's got a story. Told me it last night. Of course, if it's true . . ." and he shrugged his shoulders.

"Don't you believe him, then?" asked the Vicar.

Kinch laughed.

"We have to be skeptical, Mr. Ashley-Smith, in our profession. Still—I admit there *is* something in his favour." He turned to Captain Bristow, and went on, dryly:

"I believe you were making enquiries at the railway-station here the other morning about the signalling of the train, Captain Bristow?"

"Ah," replied Bristow, "you found that out, did you? Well, had it anything to do with Curtis' story?"

"You go with the Vicar and hear what he's got to say, sir. Anyhow, I can compliment you on a shrewd guess as to possibilities. Come along, gentlemen, please."

He led the way from his office into the part of the building which was his private residence. In a small room, overlooking a courtyard, sat a young man, reading a newspaper and smoking a cigarette; a young man with fair, curly hair, fresh complexion and blue eyes, who

131

sprang up from his seat as they entered.

"Hullo, uncle! I say, this is frightfully decent of you to come and see me after all the bother I seem to have caused you; especially as the Superintendent here thinks I've done a man in."

"Now, now, Mr. Curtis," said Kinch, "I never said that, you know."

"You never *said* it, but you implied it. He put me through the third degree last night, uncle. And I'm expecting him any moment now—after he's got all he can out of me—to arrest me and warn me that anything I say may be taken down and used in evidence—that's the right formula, isn't it, Superintendent?"

At last his uncle got a word in.

"I'm very sorry to see you here, Leonard. I hope with all my heart that——"

"Not guilty, uncle! Not guilty! The foreman of the jury added that he wished to say that his colleagues were of opinion, however, that the prisoner was a bally fool—so the learned judge discharged him with a caution."

Kinch shook his head.

"I hope you may be able to prove that, Mr. Curtis, but I warn you that you are in a very serious position—and now," he added, "I'll leave you for a little while."

"He's really quite a decent chap," said the imperturbable young man, when Kinch had gone out of the room. "Gave me a stunning breakfast. I'm frightfully sorry about it all, uncle, but, honestly, I haven't done anything really wrong."

"I'm glad to hear you say that, Leonard. And now, let me introduce you to Captain Bristow. He is staying at Frimley Manor, and I think I may say you can rely upon him to help you."

"Oh, I say," said Curtis, shaking hands with Bristow, "I've just been reading about you. You're the chap that discovered the thing, aren't you? And saw me driving my uncle's car down the drive?"

"I never said so," replied Bristow, smiling in spite of himself.

"No, but it *did* look like it, didn't it? *I* should have thought it was me—excuse bad grammar—if I'd seen it. You know, uncle," he went on, "until a fellow in plain clothes gave me a start by clapping his hand on my shoulder at Folkestone yesterday afternoon, I'd never even heard of this affair at Frimley Manor."

"But—surely you saw it in the papers?" asked Bristow.

Curtis shook his head.

"Never read 'em," he replied, "except the sporting page. And for the last three or four days I haven't even bothered about that. Till the Superintendent brought me in all these papers with my breakfast I'd never read a word about the case. I say, though, I *have* been and gone and done it! No wonder they were after me!"

"Now, Leonard, I want you to tell me all about it," said the Vicar. "I've been terribly worried—more than I can say. I want your explanation first, and then we'll see what is best to be done. And I know Captain Bristow will advise us."

"Very well, then, uncle," replied the young man. "I'll tell you the whole thing from the beginning. I know," he went on, with a more serious tone in his voice, "that I'm in a nasty hole—and that it's my own fault I'm there. So I'll be glad of any help to get out of it. Let's see: I'll begin at the beginning."

"Go on," said his uncle.

"Well, you know last time I was down with you, you gave me a hectic discourse on my degenerate life, and ended up by saying you'd have nothing more to do with me till I turned over the proverbial new leaf and qualified for sainthood."

"You deserved all I said, Leonard."

"I agree—entirely. Frightfully bad hat and all that sort of thing, wasn't I? Stern uncle—ungrateful nephew. Quite all right. But, you know, that lurid lecture of yours touched me on the raw, somehow. And I went away with the heroic determination to turn over that new leaf. Worst of it was, the leaf itself wasn't so easy to find—you can't get 'em at Woolworth's for six-pence—and it was a long time before one put in its appearance. When it did, I began the turning process."

"You aren't very explicit, Leonard."

"Well, it was like this. I met a johnny connected with the wine trade—a sort of sleeping partner in a vineyard near Bordeaux. He lives at Exeter, but has an office in London—imports wine, you know. His brother-in-law, the actual partner, is a Frenchman—at Bordeaux—and he wrote and asked for an English clerk to go over to the business there—one who could speak and write French fluently. And that's one of my few accomplishments. The end of it was that Hazell—that's the Exeter johnny—offered me the post, but I was to go in a deuce of a hurry—yesterday, in fact. It meant a frightful rush, getting a passport, and so on, and I had to run down to Exeter the day before I left to get final instructions.

"Well, the day all this caboodle happened at Frimley I suddenly made up my mind I'd run down and see you—repentant prodigal and all that sort of thing. And I won't deny I was going to touch you for a tenner—I was desperately hard up. I acted on the impulse of the moment, took the next train to Chiltonbury, and walked out to your Vicarage. That rummy old housekeeper of yours—Mrs. Ayres—told me you were playing the giddy goat up at the Manor."

"Oh, come," broke in the Vicar, "she hardly put it like that!"

"Well, she said you were acting in a pageant, but that she expected you home to dinner. It wasn't much use trying to see you while you were—er—"

"Playing the giddy goat?" suggested Bristow.

"Exactly! So I thought I'd wait. Mrs. Ayres got me some dinner. She said she was sure you'd be in soon, and as I never knew you as a dissipated night-bird, I went on waiting—even after Mrs. Ayres and the maid went to bed, about ten. Then I began to be a bit anxious— you see, I had to get back to London that night because of starting off to Exeter early the next morning. And the last train left Chiltonbury at eleven-twenty-three. It got towards that time—I still hung on. I thought if you *did* come back, you'd run me into the station."

"Oh!" exclaimed the Vicar. "You did, did you?"

"Well, it's always up to a parson to act the Good Samaritan. Then—I'd had a busy day—I suppose I must have dropped off to sleep for a few minutes—in that comfortable arm-chair of yours. I woke with a start and looked at the clock on the mantelpiece. And I saw I could only catch that train by the skin of my teeth."

"Rather a mixed metaphor," remarked the Vicar.

"Isn't it? But it explains. I couldn't rouse Mrs. Ayres to give her a message—not decent. There was not time to write one. I made a rush for your garage and got your old 'bus out."

"Would you mind telling me what you meant to do with her?" asked the Vicar, dryly.

"Oh, that was all right. I thought I should have time, before catching the train, to run her into the yard of the King's Arms, ask them to garage her for the night and either drive her out to you in the morning or send for you to come in for her. But there wasn't time. As I ran over the railway bridge I saw I should have to drive like the devil."

Bristow interrupted.

"You mean you saw the train was signalled?"

"You've hit it, sir. There's a signal-post just by the bridge, and the green light was showing for the up-train. I ran her through Chiltonbury to the station at about forty—not so bad for your old 'bus, uncle. And the train had come into the station as I pulled up outside. There wasn't any time to see anyone. I just left her standing there, dashed on to the platform, and caught the train while she was moving off."

"And what did you suppose was going to happen to my car, I should like to know?" asked his uncle.

The young man lighted a fresh cigarette, shrugged his shoulders, and replied:

"What do you suppose? I knew no one was likely to steal a dilapidated five-year-old Morris. And it was a perfectly fine night. I thought, of course, that someone would find it standing there—the police, very likely,—and, of course, they'd soon discover, by her number, whose she was. It didn't seem to me there was anything to bother about. I say, though," he went on, turning to Captain Bristow, "it seems someone *did* run off with her, though?"

"Just what I suspected all along," replied Bristow, "and that's the trouble, my young friend!"

"But you believe me?" asked Curtis.

"Yes, I do. You see, putting two and two together—especially what your uncle here told me about the sort of chap you are—I'd formed the conclusion that something of the kind had happened."

"You've told all this to the Superintendent, I suppose?" asked the Vicar.

"Rather. But he's skeptical. Besides—there's another thing. That scarf of mine."

"Oh," said Bristow, "Kinch has tackled you about that scarf, has he? What did he say?"

"Told me it was found in a tent at the Manor, and asked me if I could account for it."

"And you said?"

"I couldn't. I missed it after I'd got into the train. I remember taking it with my overcoat from the hall in the Vicarage, but I didn't put it on. Whether I dropped it in the garage in my hurry or left it in the car, I don't know."

"No doubt about that," said Bristow. "You left it in the car, of course."

"But," exclaimed the Vicar, "surely you can prove all this, Leonard? And that ought to convince the Superintendent."

"Unfortunately I can't," replied his nephew.

"Better finish your story," said Bristow. "What happened later?"

"As soon as I reached London I took a 'bus along the Harrow Road. A pal of mine had lent me a tiny flat for a week—while he was away. There was absolutely no one else in the place when I got there;

otherwise, of course, I could prove an alibi."

"Oh, but there are other ways of doing that," said Bristow. "Naturally an alibi next morning wouldn't do, but wasn't there anyone you spoke to—in the train, for instance?"

"There was. A testy old fool, who lectured me when I scrambled into the compartment. Unfortunately, I told him to go to blazes, so he's not likely to be much help."

Bristow laughed.

"On the contrary," he said, "he'd remember you all the more. We've got to get hold of him, somehow, if we can. Have you told Kinch about him?"

"Oh, yes,—of course I have. But he didn't seem to take much notice. Look here, sir,—what do you think is going to happen? I ought to be on my way to Bordeaux, you know. I don't want to lose that job. How long are they likely to keep me here?"

"That I can't tell you," replied Bristow. "The Superintendent can only *detain* you for a limited time, and even if he lets you go, it's pretty certain he'll want you for the adjourned inquest—and that he'll keep you under observation meanwhile. But he may go further than that— he may charge you formally, and then it's a question of a magistrate's court, at least. You'll admit you've been foolish?"

"I know I have. But—suppose I'm arrested?"

"We must do our best, Leonard," said his uncle. "You may be sure I'll do all I can. Do you think," he went on, speaking to Bristow, "that I'd better consult a lawyer?"

"I shouldn't do that yet, Vicar. Wait and see what happens. There'll be time enough to call in legal aid when Kinch charges him—if he does. But, somehow, I don't think the Superintendent is quite so sure of things as he was, and you must remember that the police are not stupid—they never want to bring a charge unless they think they can prove it. Kinch may not have said as much to you," he went on, to the young man, "but I shall be very much surprised if he hasn't already taken steps to see if there is any truth in what you have told him. And I shall ask him presently."

"It's frightfully good of you to help me, sir; isn't it, uncle?"

"More than you know, Leonard. Captain Bristow is accustomed to probing criminal cases. I may tell you he made a reputation—when he was in the Secret Service."

Bristow laughed.

"Oh, well," he said, "this particular case interests me—more so than ever now, because one bit of my theory has proved correct—Yes?"

"Sorry, gentlemen," said Kinch, who had come into the room, "but I shall have to ask you to leave now. I shall see you this evening, Mr. Curtis," he added, to the young man. "I'm afraid you must remain here, but I've given orders to make you comfortable. Would you like some books to read?"

"Yes," said Curtis. "I'd like a good detective story—about some poor devil who gets arrested for what he hasn't done by a Superintendent who repents his folly in sackcloth and ashes later on, when Captain Sherlock Holmes Bristow solves the crime."

Kinch laughed.

"I wouldn't mind a bit if he did," he replied. "All right. You shall have something to read."

"The Chief Constable is in my office," he went on, to the Vicar, as they left the room. "He'd like to have a word with you, sir."

Major Bainbridge greeted them.

"I'm very sorry for your trouble, Vicar,—about your nephew."

"Kinch has told you—" began the Vicar.

"Yes, yes. I've just read the young man's statement. I'm not going to comment on it just now, but you may be sure, if there's anything in it, we shall do our best. But I just want to ask you something, Vicar. You know the grounds of Frimley Manor pretty well, don't you?"

"I ought to, Major. I've been Vicar of Frimley for over fifteen years."

"I know. Well, can you tell me—Has Sir Harry got any lime-trees—near where that marquee stood?"

Captain Bristow looked at the Chief Constable curiously. It sounded such a strange question.

"Yes—I can tell you that," replied the Vicar. "There isn't a single lime-tree in the grounds of Frimley Manor."

"Oh!" ejaculated Major Bainbridge. "You're quite sure?"

"Absolutely."

"You'll excuse, me, sir," broke in Kinch, speaking to his Chief, "but I have a train to catch."

"I know, Kinch. See you later. Don't go yet, Vicar,—or you, Captain Bristow."

"Ah—but I have a train to catch, too," said Bristow. He turned to Kinch, who was in plain clothes. "We might travel together, Superintendent, if you're going to London?"

"Good," muttered the Chief Constable, beneath his breath.

"I suppose you *are* going to London?" said Bristow to the Superintendent as the two went out to the street.

"Well, yes. As a matter of fact, I am. Glad of your company, sir," he added, with a swift glance at his companion.

Bristow talked about ordinary topics on their way to the station. At the booking-office he asked for two first-class return tickets.

"All right," he exclaimed, as the other expostulated, "we are more likely to be alone if we go first—and there are one or two things I want to ask you."

As soon as the train moved off, Bristow began:

"I haven't said much to you about this Frimley case, Super-intendent," he said, "and I don't want to interfere with you in any way—I know you're doing smart work. Also, I'm not trying to get anything out of you, but I just wanted to say a word about this young Curtis."

"Right, sir," replied the Superintendent. "I suppose he told you his story?"

"Yes. What do you think of it?"

Kinch smiled.

"In a serious case like this we have to be cautious, Captain Bristow. And I like to have things verified before I express an opinion. What do *you* think of it, sir?"

"Well, to begin with, I think every effort should be made, from pure justice, to try to get corroboration—if it's possible. That old gentleman in the train, for instance,——"

Kinch interrupted with a laugh.

"Give me a little credit, sir," he said. "I'm doing my best. The evening papers will have a note of that—asking for the old gentleman in question. Reporters are a bit useful sometimes. The ticket-collector on duty at Chiltonbury that night will be seen presently, and asked if anyone rushed by him to catch the train as it moved off. The guard of the train will be questioned. I've already 'phoned the divisional superintendent of the district in which that flat off the Harrow Road is situated, and asked him to enquire if anyone saw Mr. Curtis enter it late that night. And we're in communication with this fellow at Exeter, who—so Curtis says—was sending him to Bordeaux. I tell you, sir, I don't want to charge a man with participation in a serious crime unless I honestly have good reason to believe he is implicated. *You* know that."

"Bravo!" exclaimed Bristow. "You're thorough!"

Kinch smiled with pleasure at the well-deserved compliment.

"Now, perhaps, you'll tell me what *you* think, Captain Bristow?"

"I will. I believe young Curtis' story in every detail, because it is the only one which fits in with the facts of the case. I daresay if I could read your mind I should see that you've a pretty strong leaning to that opinion yourself. Look at what took place. Curtis comes down to Frimley Vicarage in an unpremeditated way——"

"We don't know that, sir."

"Not absolutely. But he evidently wanted to see his uncle."

"He might not. He might have known beforehand that the Vicar would be at the pageant."

"Granted. But he didn't know the Vicar would be staying so late at the Manor, did he?"

"No—I suppose not."

"Very well. Then imagine that his uncle had returned while he was there—wouldn't that have put the lid on any nefarious plan?"

"Not necessarily. He could have left the Vicarage in time—to keep an appointment."

"With whom?"

"The other man—whoever he was."

"But this other man was wrecked in the car, on his way down to Chiltonbury. And Curtis couldn't have known *that*."

"Yes—but the arrangement might have been for Curtis to meet him with a car, at Chiltonbury—and drive him out."

"But, in that case, with the Vicar at home, he'd hardly have taken his uncle's car from the garage."

"Um—perhaps not."

"I tell you, Superintendent, that, from the first, I never suspected young Curtis of complicity. I asked myself the simple question, *Why* did he want the car, and *what time* did he take her out of the garage? There were several answers to that question, I admit, but the most obvious one was that he wanted to catch the last train from Chiltonbury to London. It was the only answer to the fitting-in of the times. Now then?"

Kinch looked at Bristow, a twinkle in his eye.

"I thought that was your theory, Captain Bristow."

"Why? I never said anything."

"No, but you made enquiries about that train—and when she was signalled."

Bristow laughed.

"One to you," he said.

"And I *may* say, sir," Kinch went on slowly, "that it is one of the theories I formed myself. I express no further opinion at the moment. But go on, Captain Bristow. Put this young man on one side, then. Is it too much to ask you what you think really took place?"

"No. Especially as, up to a point, I believe we shall be in agreement. Don't tell me anything you had rather not——"

"You may be sure I shan't do that, sir," broke in Kinch, dryly.

"Quite so. But—as far as you choose—let's see where we are in agreement. In the first place, then, you probably admit that this was a premeditated crime?"

"The robbery of the necklace was—most decidedly. The murder, though,——"

"Exactly. I quite agree. Well, then, you'll probably go on to admit there was someone on the spot beforehand who was in collusion?"

"Don't you think so?" asked Kinch, cautiously.

"Certainly I do."

"And I believe," went on Bristow, with a twinkle in his eye, "that you have a theory as to who that person was."

"I may have," retorted Kinch.

"Well, we'll agree to leave that alone."

"Ah—but, excuse me, sir,—have *you* got a theory?"

"I may have." Bristow answered him in his own phrase, and laughed.

"So we agree again, then, sir."

"Not necessarily. But to go on. Then there was the actual person who was to come and take the jewels away. He starts in a car bearing a false registration-mark. On the way down it is wrecked. He has just time to take the last train from Drifford on to Chiltonbury, having first removed the registration-plates, which he throws out of the window. An artful fellow, this, Superintendent. And a dangerous one. He is prepared for all emergencies, and seems to have carried a very useful little weapon—that knuckle-duster. A professional, this chap,—don't you think so?"

Kinch nodded.

"Go on," he said.

"Well, he has to get out to Frimley Manor by a certain hour—that was arranged with that person whom neither of us will mention. He would probably have done so if he had sprinted on foot, and possibly meant to do this. It would be dangerous to hire a car at Chiltonbury that time of night. But, on coming out into the yard outside the station, he sees the Vicar's Morris standing there, unattended. He looks about. The few passengers off the train disappear. So he gets into that car and runs out to Frimley, entering the Manor grounds from the main road—through the gateway. The gate, by the way, was open."

"How do you know that, sir?"

"By the same means *you* know it, Superintendent. I made enquiries."

Kinch slapped his knee. "By George, you're a deep one, sir! Well, what then?"

"He runs the car part of the way along the drive, gets out, and leaves her there, having reversed her first. Now, what exactly took place after that is not so easy to surmise. But I can't help thinking that, in some way or other, Jasper Hurst had had his suspicions aroused. What do you think?"

"Well, there's no harm telling you. I *know* he had!"

"Ah! I thought so. Recognised someone—at the pageant, eh?"

Kinch nodded.

"And, being disguised by a false beard and moustache, was not recognised himself?"

"Ah—well," remarked the Superintendent, "quite possible. But now that we know who he was, it is also possible that the person he recognised never even knew him. He was in our profession, so to speak. A private inquiry agent knows many individuals with something shady about them, without it being necessary that they even know him by sight."

"Somehow I thought you'd have that sort of theory," said Bristow.

"Why?"

"Oh—I may be wrong. But to return to our reconstruction. Let us suppose that Hurst, on his way down the drive, sees this other fellow, without being seen by him, shadows him, and, finally, when Mrs. Cresswell's pearls are brought out to him, suddenly attacks, with the hope of rescuing them—with the fatal result we know. He wasn't dead, and they never meant to kill him. But he knew too much, and they daren't leave him there to recover his senses and split on them. The sedan-chair was the easiest way to carry him to the car. At that stage it was kidnapping, not murder. Don't you agree?"

Kinch nodded.

"Yes," he said, slowly, "I think there's a lot in what you say, sir. Only you've made one mistake all along."

"What's that?"

"You kept on talking about *one* man who came down in the car. But there were two of 'em, Captain Bristow."

Bristow put on an air of puzzled innocence.

"Were there?" he asked.

"Well, you said two men—to begin with."

"When?"

"Why, when you telephoned that night—and when I came out to the scene of the crime—and in your evidence at the inquest. You said you distinctly saw *two* persons getting away in the car."

"Oh, yes. So I did."

"Well, *didn't* you, sir?"

"Yes."

"Well, then,——"

"Look here, Superintendent," said Bristow, "what I said was perfectly correct. But I fancy the solution to the riddle lies in the fact that the gate leading into the high-road was open. Think it over—I'm not going to say anything more about it now. Anyhow, only *one* man ran the car into Yew Tree Bottom—and got away from there with the pearls—leaving the empty case behind. And that's the beggar you want."

"I wish to the Lord I could get him, sir. I believe, however, I've heard of him since."

"How?"

"My sergeant—Mentmore—came in to report this morning. He's a good man, that. Last evening he got hold of the driver of a lorry—from Birmingham to Oxford, on the night of the murder, or, rather, in the early morning. He says he gave a man a lift from Dinworth to London—or, rather, as far as Ealing, where he got off. And Dinworth is only three miles, across the downs, from Yew Tree Bottom."

"Could he describe the man?"

"No, worse luck. There was no room by the driver's seat, and the fellow scrambled up behind. The only thing he noticed about him was that he spoke with a peculiar accent. Might have been a foreigner, he says. He had his hat drawn over his face, and the lorry-driver didn't get a good look at him."

"Interesting. Done anything about it?"

Kinch shrugged his shoulders, but made no reply. The train was running through tunnels and nearing the terminus. Kinch looked at his notebook for a minute or two, replaced it, and said:

"Well, I've enjoyed the run, sir. As a matter of fact, I knew of your reputation, and I wondered, more than once, what your ideas about things were. Once or twice I was on the point of asking you. There's nothing else you'd like to tell me, I suppose?"

In reply Bristow said:

"Has Mr. Cresswell offered a reward for those pearls?"

"Mr. Cresswell? No, sir. Not that I know of. . . . Well, I'll be wishing you good morning, sir . . ." for the train was drawing up at the platform.

"Oh," said Bristow nonchalantly, "is it worth while to engage two taxis when one will do? Won't you share mine?"

"It's very kind of you, Captain Bristow, but—er—I won't bother you to go out of your way."

"I shan't be going out of my way," retorted Bristow, with a laugh. "At least, I don't suppose so. I expect we're both bound for the same destination, aren't we?"

"Where's that, sir?"

"Oh—Sparkson's."

"Well, I'm damned!" ejaculated Superintendent Kinch.

12

Superintendent Kinch suffered himself to be led by Captain Bristow to a waiting taxi, and got in with him. Bristow gave the destination to the driver, and they moved off. Then Kinch began:

"Look here, sir," he said, "I don't mind accepting your offer of a lift, but I do want to know how we stand."

"Fire away, Superintendent," replied Bristow. "You're quite justified in asking. We're on the same quest, so to speak, only whereas it is your chief desire to secure the guilty, I'm only acting in a purely private capacity out of consideration to the innocent. My primary desire is to exonerate my personal friends."

"Well, then, how do you know I am going to Sparkson's, Captain Bristow?"

Bristow laughed.

"That's very simple. I happened to be on the same track, and your traces turned up. You see, I class you as a smart man, Superintendent, and I know you don't do things without a very good motive. Your sergeant, Mentmore, examined those costumes in the tent pretty closely—as well as those in the house. It was evident to me that you were after *something* in connection with one of the costumes, though I give you my word I haven't guessed what it is. But it wasn't *there*—at Frimley Manor. Then Mentmore asked where Miss Fullinger had hired her Edward the Sixth's dress. That was significant, wasn't it? Now *I* had a reason for wanting to see that particular costume—"

"Why?" snapped Kinch.

"I'll leave you to guess for the present—no, it isn't my intention to withhold information, but I'm acting on a surmise I want to put to the test—though it may very likely come to nothing. Well, I 'phoned through to Sparkson, asking him to reserve that Tudor costume for me—first finding out from him that it had been returned—I pretended I wanted to hire it. His answer was evasive, but, anyhow, Sparkson wasn't going to let me have that costume just yet. The inference was obvious. He had been already asked to keep it back pending a visit from you or Mentmore. Am I right?"

Kinch nodded.

"My congratulations," he replied. "A very pretty little bit of work. And I may tell you, Captain Bristow, that I intend to handle that costume before anyone else gets a chance of doing so."

"Of course you do. I haven't come up with any idea of interfering with you or frustrating you. I'll stay outside in the taxi while you go in to Sparkson's and make your examination, if you like. I only want to see the thing after you've done with it."

Kinch looked at him, shrewdly, for a moment.

"I don't know that there's any need for that, sir," he replied. "I wish, though, that I knew exactly how far I can go with you. You'll excuse my saying so, but, although you declare you're not withholding information, it looks very much like it, and I can't be a respecter of persons—even with *you*, Captain Bristow. It's up to me to tell you that it is your duty, if you know anything bearing on the case, to tell me. And if you refuse—well, you wouldn't come very well out of a cross-examination in court. Excuse my saying this."

"You are quite justified in doing so. And I give you my word, Kinch, that directly my surmises turn into facts—or, rather, that I get very fair proof that they are correct,—I'll tell you all, gladly. As it is, if you find anything in connection with that costume which confirms any suspicions you may have in your mind, I'm prepared to give you a bit of information which may still further confirm them. Only—I was going to say I'd make a condition in telling you, but of course I can't do that—I shall ask you to take my advice, though. May I ask you a question?"

"I don't promise to answer."

"I know. But I'll ask it. Have you got anyone up here shadowing Miss Fullinger?"

"Oh!" said Kinch. "We're much of a mind, it seems. Well, I shan't tell you that, sir."

"I think you have told me, all the same," replied Bristow, dryly. "Well, here we are. Shall I stay outside till you've finished?"

"No, sir," answered Kinch, with the air of a man who has made up his mind. "You seem to know so much already that I'll ask you to come with me."

"That's very good of you."

Kinch asked to see Mr. Sparkson himself, and, when that individual came, presented his official card. Sparkson looked at Captain Bristow, with whom he had frequently done business, with a puzzled air.

"Of course I couldn't tell you—" he began.

"That's all right," said Bristow. "I quite understand."

"Now," went on Sparkson, turning to Kinch, "you've come about that Edward the Sixth's costume you 'phoned to me to keep back, I suppose? I hope there's nothing wrong?"

"Nothing for you to worry about, Mr. Sparkson," the Superintendent assured him. "I want to have a look at it, that's all. Have you unpacked it since Miss Fullinger returned it?"

"No. Directly it came in, I put it, just as I received it, under lock and key."

"Good. Now this gentleman and I would like to be alone, if we may?"

"Certainly. You shall go into one of our private dressing-rooms . . . This way, please . . . I'll fetch the parcel for you."

He showed them into a small room, went out, and returned, presently, carrying a brown-paper parcel.

"As I told you," he remarked, placing it on the table, "it has not been opened since I received it. I presume it is complete."

"Wait a moment," said Kinch, as Sparkson was about to leave the room. "I should like to know if it is complete. I'll open it, and you can check the contents, if you will."

"Yes," said Sparkson, as Kinch opened the parcel and drew forth the pieces of the costume, one by one. "A pair of tights—the breeches—doublet—cape—cap—and a pair of shoes. All are there. I don't know if it's worth while mentioning it, but this is a made-up costume—I mean, the cape and doublet and tights are part of the original one—the breeches and cap are new."

Bristow turned to him.

"Do you mean this is the first time the breeches and cap have been hired?"

"That is so," replied Sparkson. "The old ones were torn and shabby, and I had them replaced. Well, I'll leave you now."

"Doesn't much matter whether they are old or new," said Kinch, when he had gone, proceeding to look them over.

"There I differ with you, Superintendent," replied Bristow, dryly.

Kinch glanced at his companion. The latter had sat himself in a chair and was lighting a cigarette.

"Why?"

Bristow laughed.

"Oh—it helps me to establish my theory—if there's anything in it: that's all."

"I don't understand," began Kinch, and then suddenly stopped. "Ah!" he exclaimed. He was examining the cape now.

"Found anything?" asked Bristow.

"I have," said Kinch, cheerfully. "What I rather expected to find, too."

Bristow asked no further questions, but went on smoking quietly. Presently there was another exclamation of triumph on the part of the Superintendent. He was holding the breeches now.

"Ah!" he remarked again. "They generally bungle somewhere or other. And this is a bad bungle. What a fool!"

"I doubt it," said Bristow, almost beneath his breath; but the Superintendent heard him.

"Look here, sir," he said, "there's no reason why I shouldn't take you into my confidence now. I've got quite sufficient evidence to go ahead with, and there's no reason for concealment as far as you are concerned."

Bristow inhaled and blew out a cloud of smoke.

"Enough evidence—against Miss Fullinger, I suppose?" he said, very quietly.

"That's it, Captain Bristow. Now, tell me—wasn't it Miss Fullinger you had in your mind all the time?"

"More or less," admitted Bristow. "What made you suspect her, though?"

Kinch smiled.

"We have a formula, you know, sir,—'from information received'—that's as far as I'll go now with reference to others. But I want to show you something," and he held out his hand. "You see this bit of gold lace, eh? Well, I found it lying on the floor, by the door, inside Mrs. Cresswell's room, the morning after the robbery."

"By Jove!" exclaimed Bristow.

"I very soon satisfied myself that Mrs. Cresswell had no costume with gold lace on it—nor had the others, or, if they had, none of it was torn off. That's why I wanted to have a look at these clothes. You can see for yourself, sir," and he took up the little cape, "there's where it was torn off—look, it fits exactly," and he laid the little bit of lace on the cape.

"Yes," admitted Bristow, examining it carefully. "There isn't much doubt about that."

"Is there? But that's not all. I've just found this in the pocket of the breeches."

And he held out a small key.

"Well?" asked Bristow.

"It's the lost key of Mrs. Cresswell's suit-case—the duplicate. Here's the other. I kept it, and had one made for Mrs. Cresswell to use meanwhile."

"I say," exclaimed Bristow, "you're pretty thorough, Kinch! Yes— I see—there's no doubt about that, either—they're a pair right enough. What are you going to do about it?"

"What do you think, sir? Miss Fullinger will have to give me an explanation about all this—and, if she can't—well!" and he shrugged his shoulders.

"I see," answered Bristow, gravely. "And now I'm going to give you that bit of information I promised you. You will add it to this evidence, I expect."

He took, out of his pocket, an envelope, opened it, and produced a small white handkerchief, which he handed to Kinch.

"Read the name in the corner," he said.

"S. Fullinger," read Kinch. "Where did you find this, sir?"

"I didn't find it. Your sergeant, Mentmore, made one little slip— quite excusable. Apparently he forgot to ask that poacher fellow, Cyster, if he had found anything in the Vicar's car."

"Oh, no, he didn't, Captain Bristow. Cyster stuck to it that he had found nothing."

"Ah, well, I had other means to prevail upon Cyster to tell the truth. He'd pocketed some of the Vicar's tools—*and* this hand-kerchief."

"You mean he found it in the car?"

"That's so."

"Good Lord! That rather clinches things!"

Bristow was in the act of lighting a fresh cigarette. He looked up, a humorous little twinkle at the corners of his mouth.

"Only you must remember," he said, "*I* didn't see Miss Fullinger in the car that night."

"But it's her handkerchief?"

"I think so. And I fancy I can tell you a little more about it, something I found out from Sir Harry. Miss Fullinger had lost her handkerchief while she was acting in the pageant, and sent her maid to the house to get a clean one. The maid brought it out just after the pageant was over. Sir Harry, who was talking to poor Hurst at the time, saw her give it to Miss Fullinger."

"Well," said Kinch, "the main thing is it's Miss Fullinger's handkerchief. When and where she first put it in her pocket doesn't matter."

"Now, do you know," replied Bristow, "it might matter considerably—to my mind."

"Can't see it, sir. The point is it was found in the car, you say?"

"Yes. But another point is, how did it get there? And, again—it may have been the handkerchief she lost earlier in the evening, eh?"

The Superintendent brought his open hand down on the table with a smack.

"It seems to me, Captain Bristow," he said, "that you are trying to confuse the issue."

"Not at all," answered Bristow, "I've given you the handkerchief for what it's worth, but I want you to see it's only presumptive evidence against Miss Fullinger, not conclusive. I know perfectly well you are building up a strong case against her, and I agree with you that you are justified. But I do suggest that you keep all the facts in your mind, Superintendent."

"Well, I'm trying to, sir, am I not?"

He spoke a little testily.

"Not quite. You might bear in mind what I told you about Sir Harry seeing a handkerchief given to Miss Fullinger, while he was talking with Jasper Hurst—and that the gate from the drive to the main road was open that night. I'm not going to explain further at the moment because, as I told you, I'm only surmising. And now, if you've quite finished with those togs, it's my turn."

"Here you are, then, Captain Bristow—take a look at 'em, by all means. And I'll stay and watch you, if you don't mind—you've roused my curiosity. Afterwards," he went on, grimly, "I'm going to pay a call on Miss Fullinger. Now, sir,—which will you have first?—the breeches?"

"Thanks," replied Bristow, "but I only want to see the cap."

"The *cap?*"

"That's all."

"And what do you expect to find there, sir?"

"I'm not sure. Ah, pretty little head-dress, isn't it? And Sparkson tells us it's quite new. That may be fortunate. Have a cigarette, Kinch, while I take a squint."

Kinch, laughing, accepted the proffered cigarette, lighted it, and sat watching Bristow. The latter, cap in hand, went to the window and produced from his pocket a magnifying-glass.

"Sherlock Holmes!" ejaculated the Superintendent.

"Quite—Dr. Watson," replied Bristow, dryly.

He peered into the interior of the cap, examining it minutely with his glass. Kinch smoked placidly, the smile still on his face. Bristow, without a word, went on with his examination, standing, almost motionless, at the window. Presently he came back to the table, and laid the cap down on it.

"Finished?" asked the Superintendent, quizzically.

"I think so—for the present."

His face was inscrutable. If he had discovered anything, he made no sign.

"Well?" asked Kinch, "and what of it?"

"I suppose you won't be wanting to take this away?" said Bristow, in reply, pointing at the cap.

"No," replied Kinch, "but I shall want this cape, though."

"All right, then. Shall I ask Sparkson to come in? Then we can get a move on."

"But aren't you going to——"

He broke off. Bristow had opened the door and gone out. Kinch took the cap off the table, looked at it carefully, and shook his head.

"Now, what the dickens did he mean?" he said to himself. Then Bristow returned with Sparkson. The latter addressed the Superintendent.

"Well," he said, "have you found what you wanted?"

"I have, Mr. Sparkson. I shall have to take away this cape with me—I'll give you a receipt for it, if you want one. And it may very likely happen that you may be wanted to give evidence later on."

"Evidence?" exclaimed Sparkson. "What on earth could I give evidence about?"

"Only to prove that Miss Fullinger hired these clothes—and returned them," replied Kinch, wrapping up the cape as he spoke."

"And I want the cap, Sparkson," said Bristow, "just for a few days. Get me a cardboard box to put it in, will you, please?"

Outside, the taxi was still waiting. Kinch hesitated.

"This is your taxi, Captain Bristow," he said. "I'm much obliged to you for the lift. And now, I suppose, I'd better get one for myself."

"I suppose you are going to see Miss Fullinger, aren't you?"

"I am that, sir."

"Well, that's the chief reason why I've come up today, though I wanted to have a look at that costume before I called on her." He glanced at his watch. "Now, look here, Superintendent,—I didn't mean to have put all my cards on the table this morning, but now we've begun to understand each other, I think I'd better. I suggest you come with me to my club and have luncheon with me before you pay your call on Miss Fullinger. An hour won't make much difference—if she's being kept under observation. And I don't think you'll regret it."

Kinch hesitated, and then said:

"Very well, Captain Bristow. I'll accept your invitation. But I can't see anything you've got to tell me can make any difference to my performing rather an unpleasant job afterwards. The evidence stares one in the face, and, unless Miss Fullinger can give an explanation, well—I've no option in the matter."

"At present you haven't, I know. But I'd like to put a suggestion before you—when we've lunched."

It was after luncheon that Bristow took Kinch to a quiet corner of the smoking-room of his club, and began:

"Suppose," he said, "you were able to produce a witness who saw Sonia Fullinger meet a man outside Frimley Manor that night, after Mr. Charles Lynwood went out to get his cigarettes, what would you say?"

"Why—obviously—that she must have been mixed up in things. Only one more proof of what seems to me now to be a certainty."

"Yes. Well, it isn't a certainty to me, Superintendent. I don't believe for a moment that Sonia Fullinger had anything to do with either the robbery or the murder. She was probably fast asleep all the time—like most of the others."

"There I think you make a mistake, sir. I have good reason for believing that, though she went to her room early, she didn't undress. She was still wearing that Edward the Sixth's costume after eleven o'clock—I have that from the last person who saw her that night."

"May I ask who that was?"

"Her maid."

"I see. That looks very queer, certainly. Now, apart from this—and the bit of gold lace, the key and the handkerchief—have you any other evidence against her?"

"Yes, I have. Something that put me on the track to begin with. There is a notebook belonging to Mr. Hurst—Mentmore found it at The Gables. It's an address-book. Well, Miss Fullinger's address was written in it. How do you explain that, Captain Bristow, if there was no collusion?"

"Collusion between Hurst and Miss Fullinger?"

"Yes."

"But you don't suspect Hurst of conspiring—"

"No, but what did I tell you coming up in the train this morning, sir? I said I *knew* Hurst had had his suspicions aroused. Why should he have written down that address otherwise? He had his eye on Miss Fullinger—knew something about her to begin with—and then, when he saw her at the pageant . . . well, there you are!"

"Now, this is most interesting," said Bristow. "I'm very glad you told me about it. Well, listen to my side of the case. I admit all the evidence—the address in Hurst's notebook—the torn bit of lace—the key—and the handkerchief. *I* found out the handkerchief, remember. That—and something else—pointed to Sonia Fullinger. And yet I *couldn't*, somehow, associate the girl with such a crime. You see, I've known her for years."

Kinch grinned.

"I never let sentiment interfere with facts, sir," he said.

"Quite so. But sentiment sometimes helps one to establish facts, or put a new construction upon them. I thought things over, and, after a bit, it seemed to me that there was just one person, quite easy to overlook, but to whom the facts—so far as I knew them—could apply."

"Who was that?"

"I'll tell you a story before I answer that question. In the time of the Great War, a colleague of mine, in the Secret Service, was spy-hunting—at one of our naval bases. There was a young military officer, invalided home from the front, who was performing light duty in the town, and was strongly suspected of treachery. He was quartered on a family where there was a son who was a civilian—medically rejected from service. The reason why the young officer was suspected was because he had been seen pottering about in places and among people which rather pointed to the seeking for information. But my colleague wasn't satisfied. He had an idea at the back of his mind that someone was impersonating that young officer, and he put his idea to the test. He was right. The civilian was the spy—half-German, it turned out—and he'd been wearing the officer's spare uniform."

"What was the test?" asked Kinch.

"Same as I used this morning—that's where I got the notion from. Here's that Tudor cap"—he unpacked it. "Now, look at the inside of it through this magnifying-glass. . . . See anything?"

Kinch looked carefully.

"Bear in mind that Sparkson said it was a new cap," went on Bristow. . . . "Well?"

"I can't see anything—except a few hairs," replied Kinch.

"What colour? . . . Here, take 'em to the window—there's more light there. Now?"

"Looks like three or four dark ones—and a couple of fair ones."

"And Miss Fullinger's hair—dark or fair?"

"By George!" exclaimed the Superintendent. "I see what you mean, sir. Hers is dark hair, of course. You think someone else——?"

"Wore the costume? Exactly. Now then—who was the fair-haired individual who had easy access to that costume when Miss Fullinger took it off that night?"

"Ah! Her maid! She's got fair hair."

"Quite so."

"But . . ." began Kinch.

"Stop a moment. Let me work it out. The first thing is—suppose my theory is correct,—why did the maid want to wear the costume? The answer to that lies in the story I've just told you . . . in case she was *seen* she would be mistaken for Sonia Fullinger. Follow it out. Some time previously—probably while the pageant was on—she goes into Mrs. Cresswell's room and gets that duplicate key. Later on, when she takes the handkerchief out to her mistress, Hurst was there, and recognised her—that would account for *her* address—not necessarily Miss Fullinger's—being down in his notebook. He knew of this woman and had made a record of her whereabouts. Well, when she went up to her mistress' room that night, she took away the costume—possibly saying she was going to pack it——"

"But she told me Miss Fullinger hadn't undressed."

"Ah—but never mind what she told you. She'd *want* you to think that, wouldn't she? Anyhow, let's go on. She rigs herself up in those togs—enters Mrs. Cresswell's room and gets the jewels—puts the key back in her pocket—and slips out of doors to meet her confederate. Now, here is where *I* went wrong to begin with—and you've gone wrong since in hunting for *two* men. There were not two men, Kinch, depend upon it. I naturally *thought* I saw two, but suppose one of them was this woman—dressed as a man, eh? I was never near enough to distinguish what their clothes were like in detail, you know."

"But if that's right, Captain Bristow, then this woman—Bates is her name—must have driven off in the car when you chased them?"

"Well, doesn't that fit in? It was while I was giving evidence at the inquest that the significance of the gate leading from the drive to the main road being open or shut suddenly struck me."

"Ah—I saw something was in your mind," exclaimed Kinch, "by

the way you hesitated all at once. And I made a note then and there to enquire about that gate—though I couldn't quite see how it bore on the case."

"But it does, doesn't it? I distinctly heard the car stop when it must have been close to the gate, and then go on again. If the gate had been closed, why, they stopped to open it. But it *wasn't* closed. Then why did they stop? Don't you think it was to let down one of the two people in her? Again, it all fits in with that handkerchief. Miss Fullinger probably left it in the costume, and Bates may have used it while in the car, and muddled matters in putting it back."

"Then," said Kinch, "you infer that Bates—if it was she—got out of the car by that gate—and then?"

"Made her way back to the house. I can't be certain of details—but there was plenty of opportunity for her to slip in afterwards. The front door was undone for some considerable time. Well, what do you think of it all?"

"I think more than ever," said the Superintendent, "that the sooner I see Miss Fullinger the better. Your theory is a very clever one, sir, and I'm not denying that it may be true. But you've got to remember that every blessed thing you've just told me fits Miss Fullinger equally well."

"Except those two yellow hairs," said Bristow, dryly.

"I grant you that," replied Kinch. "But it takes a bit of risk to put two hairs in one scale and a pile of evidence in the other, doesn't it?"

"Come, come, Superintendent," said Bristow, with a laugh, "you're too old a hand at the game to be only ready to judge of evidence by the bulk of it. And, anyhow, you've got to account for those two hairs as well as the rest. They're a part of the jigsaw puzzle, and you can't complete the puzzle without them."

Kinch looked at the other for a few moments. Then he said:

"I'm not convinced. But I'll try to put your theory to the test. Look here, sir,—will you come with me now to see Miss Fullinger? Only, if you do, I must ask you to let me do the questioning."

"Of course. You're in charge of the case, not I. I'll be only too glad to go with you."

"Right, sir!" And he got up. "Then the sooner we start, the better."

13

"Wisteria," the residence of the Fullingers, was a large house, standing back from the quiet road—one of those many quite secluded by-streets in St. John's Wood—with a garden in front and a curved carriage-drive leading to the entrance. It was Captain Bristow who enquired of the butler whether Miss Fullinger was at home, Kinch considering it preferable that the servants should remain ignorant of the fact that a police visit was being paid.

They were both shown into a drawing-room and, in a minute or two, Sonia came in, with her mother, a pleasant-looking, middle-aged lady, who greeted Captain Bristow as a frequent visitor to the house—as, indeed, he was.

"But I thought you were still at Frimley—" she began, but stopped. Sonia had recognised the Superintendent. Captain Bristow explained.

"So I am," he said, "but I've come up today with Superintendent Kinch—you've met him, Sonia, you know."

"Oh, I know," said the girl, bowing stiffly to Kinch. "Mother—this is the policeman who put me through the third degree—isn't that what you call it?"

"I hope I was not so bad as that," said Kinch.

"And may I ask—?" began Mrs. Fullinger, turning to Bristow for an explanation.

"It's all right, Mrs. Fullinger," said Bristow. "Some more facts have come to light, and the Superintendent wants to ask Sonia some further questions."

"But I told you all I knew—which was very little," exclaimed Sonia.

"Ah," replied Kinch, "I know. Still, you may be able to throw a little more light on matters."

"I think you will, too, Sonia," said Bristow, cheerfully. "Now, Superintendent, go ahead. I'll not interrupt you."

Kinch, who had been undoing the parcel, produced the velvet cape.

"Is this part of the costume you were wearing at the pageant, Miss Fullinger?"

"Looks like it," she replied. "What of it?"

"You will observe that a small piece of gold lace is missing from the edge. Here is the bit. I found it inside Mrs. Cresswell's room the morning after the robbery. Can you explain how it got there?"

"Explain? I'm sure I don't know."

"Did you go into her room while you were wearing the cape?"

"I may have done so. But what of it, if I did?"

Kinch did not reply to this question. He produced the key.

"This," he said, "is the key of Mrs. Cresswell's dressing-case, in which she placed the necklace; missing off her bunch. I found it this morning."

"That's interesting. Where?"

"In the pocket of the breeches belonging to the costume you were wearing that night," he replied, slowly, looking straight at her. For the first time a serious expression stole over her face.

"But," she said, "how on earth did it get there?"

"Ah! Can you explain that, Miss Fullinger?"

"I? Of course not."

"But," interjected her mother, "do you mean to suggest——"

"One moment, please." He took the handkerchief out of his pocket. "Is this yours?" he asked the girl.

She looked at it.

"Certainly it is."

"This handkerchief was found in the car which was driven off after Mr. Hurst was killed—the one Captain Bristow saw. Can you explain *that*, Miss Fullinger?"

She shook her head.

"I don't understand it in the least."

"Why," broke in her mother, "you were in bed when all this happened, weren't you, Sonia?"

"Of course I was."

"Oh!" said Kinch. "You didn't go outside the house that night— about half-past one? You needn't answer, you know, if you prefer not to."

"*Go outside the house?* Certainly not. . . . You . . you . . . don't mean you think *I* had anything to do with it?—No, mother—let him go on. But this is all nonsense!"

"Very well," said Kinch, referring to his notebook. "You don't seem able to give me an explanation about this key and the handkerchief. I'll go a little further, then. I suggest that you were acquainted with Mr. Hurst, in some way, before this affair happened. Is that so?"

"You suggested that before," replied Sonia, "and I told you then that I knew nothing whatever about him. What makes you ask?"

"Because the name and address of this house were found written in a notebook belonging to him—after the letter 'F.' You will admit that I have a reason for asking."

"This is preposterous," said Mrs. Fullinger. "None of us in this house knew him. I know my husband didn't."

"Is there anything more?" asked Sonia.

"Yes. I want to ask you about your movements after you went to your room that night at Frimley Manor. Mrs. Cresswell stated that she knocked at your door and that you didn't answer——"

"If she did, I was asleep. I told you so."

"I suggest you were not asleep—not even in bed. That you were sitting in your room, still wearing your Edward the Sixth costume, and that you did not undress until much later. What have you to say to that?"

Sonia, indignant, turned on him.

"That it's a lie!" she exclaimed. "If you want to know, I'll tell you just what happened. I was in bed by eleven o'clock that night, just after my maid left the room.—I heard the clock on the stairs strike the hour—and that was the last thing I remember till I awoke in the morning. As for that costume, not only was I not wearing it, but it wasn't even in the room."

Bristow leaned forward. At last Sonia had touched on a point that had puzzled him. For Anstice Lynwood had told him that costume *was* in Sonia's room when she had gone in early the next morning. Kinch looked up from his notebook. He, too, recognised the importance of this statement.

"Where was it, then?" he asked, sharply.

"My maid had taken it away to fold ready for packing. She brought it back the next morning, when she called me."

"Ah!" muttered Bristow, beneath his breath. "Now I understand!"

"Wait a bit," said Kinch, slowly. "Miss Fullinger, tell me, please. When your maid went to your room that night, were you in bed?"

"No. I was smoking a cigarette. I undressed while she was with me. I *can't* understand why you are asking me all this."

"I've been trying to keep quiet," broke in Mrs. Fullinger. "But now

I must insist upon your telling me—who gave you this information about my daughter? I mean, *someone* must have been talking about her to you. Who was it?''

Kinch hesitated. He was just going over to Bristow's views. He did not reply at once to Mrs. Fullinger, but studied the note he had taken when questioning Sonia's maid. And then it occurred to him that Bates, with her doll-like innocence of expression, had made her statement in such a way that two constructions could be placed on it: the first—that which had been in his mind all the time—that Sonia had *remained* dressed after Bates had left her for the night; the second, Sonia's own explanation. They both fitted. A lie suggested by a half-truth is generally the most dangerous kind of lie.

He turned to Mrs. Fullinger.

"Who told me?" he said. "Well, apart from the bit of lace, the key and the handkerchief, I had some information from Miss Fullinger's maid." He turned again to Sonia. "Your maid told me," he went on, "that when she went into your room that night you were wearing that costume and smoking a cigarette."

"Quite right. I've just told you that. And then?"

"She led me to believe that you were still dressed—in that costume—when she left you for the night."

"Well, I wasn't. I couldn't have been. She took the costume out of the room when she left."

Bristow nodded at Kinch suggestively.

"Right, sir," said the Superintendent; "it looks now as if it's one up to you. Now—before I go any further—a word or two about that maid of yours, Miss Fullinger."

"But, surely,——"

"Oh, yes," interrupted Kinch, "I'm beginning to think so. When I came up to London this morning, I don't mind telling you that I had a notion I should have to ask *you* to come back with me."

"Oh!" exclaimed her mother.

"The Superintendent was justified," said Bristow. "Knowing what he did up to a point, he was bound to be suspicious about Sonia."

"Thank you, sir," said Kinch. "But now," he went on to Sonia, "I'm prepared to accept your explanation."

"But I *haven't* explained anything," said Sonia, a little puzzled. "I still haven't the slightest idea about that key—or the handkerchief."

"Ah—I almost forgot that. Did you leave the handkerchief in one of the pockets of your costume—when you took it off?"

Sonia thought for a moment.

"I believe I must have done so; anyhow, I don't remember taking it out. But do you really think that Bates——"

"Bates? Yes." He referred to his notes. "I see she came to you on Lady Challington's recommendation. Did you see her ladyship—or have any correspondence with her?"

"No," replied Mrs. Fullinger; "neither. Lady Challington was abroad. Bates brought her testimonial with her when she applied for the post, and we engaged her, to a great extent, on the strength of it."

"Ah! Now tell me, Mrs. Fullinger . . . she took the place of another maid here?"

"Yes."

"And did that maid leave rather suddenly?"

Bristow nodded, approvingly.

"Yes—she did. She even forfeited a month's wages."

"Let me have her name and address, please."

Mrs. Fullinger gave it to him, and he wrote it down.

"And now," he said, closing his notebook with a snap, "I'll see this woman—Bates; if you don't mind."

Mrs. Fullinger got up.

"You're only just in time," she said.

"Why, madam?"

He wheeled round sharply, as she spoke.

"Because she is leaving us this afternoon."

"Oh! Wait a minute, please, madam. This is important. When did she give notice?"

"She didn't," said Sonia. "A telegram came for her today, saying her mother was desperately ill and was undergoing a serious operation—so of course we have to let her go."

"Did she say where she was going?"

"Horsham, wasn't it, mother? Yes—of course. I helped her look up a train in Bradshaw—leaving Victoria at 4:05. And Perkins—our butler—rang up a garage and ordered a taxi to be here at a quarter past three—and it's past three now."

"I'll go and fetch her at once, then," said Mrs. Fullinger, making for the door.

Kinch sprang up.

"Not on any account, please, madam," he said.

"But—!" began Bristow, and suddenly stopped.

"Now, madam," went on Kinch, "will you please do exactly what I tell you? It's most important. Go to her now—you can make an excuse to say good-bye to her—don't arouse her suspicions, whatever you do——"

"Oh," broke in Sonia, "mayn't *I* go? I'd love to help, if she's really the scoundrel you think she is."

"Either of you, then," replied Kinch. "What I want is that she shouldn't catch sight of me when I leave this house. She probably knows by this time that Captain Bristow is here, and it's lucky my name wasn't mentioned when we came in. Just keep her engaged for a couple of minutes while we step out. You'll like to come with me, Captain Bristow?"

"I would—immensely."

"Be quite natural with her, Miss Fullinger," was the Superintendent's last injunction as the girl left the room. "Now, sir—Good afternoon, madam—and many thanks. We'll let ourselves out, please."

In two or three minutes Captain Bristow and the Superintendent were getting into their waiting taxi and driving off.

"Stop!" said Kinch to the driver, when they were halfway along the quiet street. On the pavement a man was lounging, a nondescript-looking fellow, smoking a pipe. Kinch opened the door.

"Hop in, Morgan," he said. "This job's up. But there's another one coming, unless I'm mistaken. Ah—look there, sir," he said to Bristow, as he glanced back, "there's the taxi just gone into the gate to fetch Bates."

Bristow laughed.

"I like your smartness, Kinch," he said. "For just a moment I was fogged, but, of course, I saw immediately afterwards what your game was. Give her a bit of rope before you arrest her. Same as in the war we sometimes caught the big boss in the spy business by letting one of the little ones make the scent."

"That's right, sir," replied Kinch, grimly. Then he gave the driver directions.

"Draw up to the kerb there—on the left-hand side of the road, with your front wheels turned out ready to swing round. Watch for that taxi coming away from the house we've just left. If it comes along here, get a move on, let it pass you, and then follow it. If it goes in the other direction, swing round and do the same—yes—you can see my card if you want to—it's a police job. Now, sir," he turned to Bristow, "she mustn't catch a glimpse of us, or the game will be up. Lean well back, and bend your head down—we must trust to the driver."

In a few minutes the other taxi appeared again in the street, turned in their direction, and passed them, their driver throwing in his clutch and following.

The chase led up the Finchley Road, past Lord's Cricket Ground into Upper Baker Street. The driver followed at a distance of some twenty yards. At the junction of Baker Street with the Marylebone Road the traffic was held up for a couple of minutes by the police on point duty. Kinch said to Morgan:

"Look here, Captain Bristow and I must remain in the background. She mustn't see us. Now, do you think she knows you, Morgan?"

"I've been mighty careful, sir. Of course I wasn't keeping an eye on her—but I don't think she's noticed me. I've only seen her once."

"Very well. I shall probably depend on you. Miss Fullinger has told us she said she was going to Horsham, but that remains to be seen. Anyhow, wherever she goes, you've got to keep in touch with her. You shall have help as soon as I can manage it—ah—*that's* not the way to Victoria!"

For the traffic in front, released, was moving forward. But the taxi they were following, instead of crossing into Lower Baker Street, swung round to the left into the Marylebone Road. They followed.

Past Madame Tussaud's—the top of Tottenham Court Road—straight on—past the entrance to Euston station—past St. Pancras, and then into the entrance of that very squat-looking station, King's Cross. Kinch had the speaking-tube in his hand.

"Stop!" he commanded the driver. "Don't go inside—draw up by the kerb, here. Off you go, Morgan—quick, man. If there's time, run back and report—if not, 'phone or wire destination to Scotland Yard—we'll go there and pick it up."

Morgan nodded, and was off. They waited. In a few minutes he was back.

"Just time," he said. "She's booked to Letcham—so have I. Train starts in five minutes."

"Right!" ejaculated Kinch. "Get on with it. I'll 'phone Letcham."

He waited for a few minutes, and then went into the station. On his return, he said to Bristow:

"I got onto the Inspector at Letcham; man I know, too. He'll have the train met, so Bates—or whatever her real name may be—will be kept in sight. Something ought to come of it. What do you think, sir?"

"I agree with you," replied Bristow. "The only question, to my mind, is whether it wouldn't be better for us to follow on to Letcham."

"Morgan is a smart man, sir,—and so is the Inspector there. I don't think there is any fear of her giving them the slip."

"I'm not doubting them, Kinch, for a moment. It's my curiosity that's at work. I confess I'm interested in the lady's movements—and where they may lead."

Kinch thought for a moment. Then he said:

"I'll tell you what, Captain Bristow. There's no reason why you shouldn't take the next train to Letcham. After all, it's due to you that we've got a line on Bates. I'll write you an introduction to the inspector, and you can give him full particulars. Only . . . well, I can trust you not to barge in and spoil the game, can't I, sir?"

Bristow laughed.

"I see what you mean," he said. "Of course, if she caught sight of me, there, it would rouse her suspicions. I'll be careful. But what are you going to do?"

"Oh, I shall drop in for a few minutes at Scotland Yard. It's just as well to let them know there what is happening—especially as the Metropolitan area has come into the case. Then I want to get back to Chiltonbury."—He laughed. "I expect young Curtis won't be sorry to see me."

"Ah," replied Bristow, dryly, "I don't suppose you'll want to keep him any longer. Well—give me that note, Kinch, and I'll see about the next train."

Kinch tore a leaf from his pocket-book, scribbled the introduction, and handed it to Bristow, who, at once, made for the station.

"Scotland Yard," said Kinch to his chauffeur, and the taxi started off. When he arrived at his destination the Superintendent asked if Chief Inspector Hadley was in, and, if so, could he see him.

The Chief Inspector was in, and was willing to see Kinch. He rose from the table at which he was sitting as Kinch came into his room, a thin, delicate-looking man, with refined features, hair worn rather long, and soft, silky moustache. He looked far more like an artist than the astute criminologist. He welcomed Kinch, whom he knew, with a smile.

"Ah," he said, "quite a pretty little drama you've been having out Chiltonbury way, I understand, Kinch! I was wondering only this morning whether we might be invited to take part in it."

"I don't think you will, Hadley," replied Kinch, grinning. "I fancy we're on the scent—and may, with luck, be in at the death."

"I congratulate you," answered Hadley. "Queer business, isn't it?—carrying off that poor chap Hurst in a sedan-chair."

"Did you know him?"

Hadley lighted a cigarette, and leaned back in his chair.

"Oh, yes,—slightly. Ran across him once or twice. Clever fellow.

Ought to have been here, really. And you think you know who did him in, eh?"

"No, I don't—yet. But I hope to get him—through a woman."

"Ah! I've always taken the line of concentrating on a woman if there's one in a case we're investigating. May I ask who she is?"

"There, again,—I don't know—yet. It's what I've called about. Shall I tell you what's happened, so far?"

"I'd like to hear."

Kinch told him. Hadley smiled once or twice during the recital, and, when it was finished, remarked:

"Captain Bristow, eh? Quite a good man, that. Lucky for you he happened to be on the spot, old man."

"I admit it."

"And now—what do you want of me? I take it you haven't simply blown in for a friendly chat?"

"No, I haven't. I want to have a look at your collection of portraits."

"Ah! To see if this woman, Bates, is among them?"

"Exactly."

Hadley took up the telephone-receiver and gave an order. In a few minutes a clerk brought in a couple of bulky volumes.

"You see," said Kinch, "it's perfectly obvious now why Hurst jotted down the Fullingers' address in his notebook. He knew this woman was there. And he spotted her at the pageant and she roused his suspicions. Now let's have a look."

He searched through the array of photographs and reproductions. And finally shook his head.

"No," he said; "I can't find her here."

"Very likely," replied Hadley. "Hurst, I know, had a line on some folks who are not in our records. Well," he went on, as Kinch got up to go, "I wish you luck—if there's anything I can do, let me know."

Kinch went out to his waiting taxi and caught the next train back to Chiltonbury. When he arrived he found that, during his absence, information had come in with regard to young Curtis. The ticket-collector on duty at Chiltonbury station on the night in question remembered a young man dashing past him and only just catching the train; the guard had seen him getting into the compartment; a wire had come from Exeter confirming his statement about going to Bordeaux. Finally, after Kinch had arrived, an elderly gentleman, a well-known resident of Chiltonbury, called at the police-station and asked to see the Superintendent.

"Good evening," said Kinch. "What can I do for you, Mr. Hemmingway?"

"Well," said Hemmingway, "I read the evening paper on my way down from town, and the question seems to be what can I do for you, Mr. Kinch? You are advertising for an elderly gentleman who travelled up to London by the last train on Monday, and who saw a young fool scramble into his carriage at the risk of committing suicide. So I thought I'd better call in."

"Oh," said Kinch "it was you, was it, Mr. Hemmingway? All right. You're sure it was Monday night—and the last train?"

"Perfectly. My niece met with an accident that night in London, and I was telephoned for late. That's why I happened to be going up. As a matter of fact, I've been staying in town till she was out of danger, and have only just returned."

'I'm glad to see you. I won't keep you five minutes. I only want to see if you can identify the young man who got into your carriage that night."

"Oh, is that all? Yes, I think I can do that."

"Just wait a few moments—and I'll have him paraded. Excuse me," and he left the room. After a short interval he came back, and led Mr. Hemmingway to a corridor in which half-a-dozen men were standing side by side, Leonard Curtis among them. Mr. Hemmingway went straight up to him.

"This is he," he said to the Superintendent. "I'm not likely to have forgotten—I don't often, at my age, experience being told to go to blazes. Ah—I see you remember, young man?"

"I'm sorry, sir," said Curtis; "though, in a way, it seems to have helped matters—it made you remember me, anyway."

"H'm!" Hemmingway turned to Kinch. "Cheeky still, I see. May I ask what he'd done, Mr. Kinch?" he went on, as the Superintendent led him away. "I suppose he was escaping from justice?"

Kinch laughed.

"I'm able to say now, sir—after you have identified him—that he's done nothing. You've proved his alibi, and, in a few minutes, I shall set him at liberty and send him out to his uncle, the Vicar of Frimley. I know he was cheeky"—Kinch laughed—"but you've helped to clear him from a worse charge than that."

"What is it?"

"Murder," replied Kinch, dryly.

"God bless my soul! I'm very glad—very glad. You may tell him I forgive his impudence. Good night!"

14

Captain Bristow, as soon as he reached Letcham, made for the police-station and presented Kinch's scribbled introduction to the Inspector. The latter, a rather stout, good-natured-looking individual, but with a certain penetration in the glance of his brown eyes, which betokened another side of his character, said:

"I'm pleased to see you, Captain Bristow. Any friend of Kinch would be welcome, for I worked with him in past years—you especially, sir, for I happen to have heard of your reputation. Before we go any further—where are you staying here?"

"I really don't know," laughed Bristow. "I came here on the spur of the moment, and may have to ask your sponsorship for an hotel—being luggageless."

"I'll do better than that, if you'll allow me, sir. I've got a spare room in my house, and shall be only too pleased to put you up, and," he added, with a laugh, "I think you'll be able to get into a spare suit of my pyjamas."

"That's very kind of you, Inspector, and I accept, gratefully, if I have to stay the night. It is pure curiosity which has brought me here. I'd like to be present if there's an interesting *dénouement*. Otherwise, please remember I'm only an outsider so far as this case is concerned."

"Oh—I don't know so much about that! Kinch put me wise to a certain extent when he 'phoned. Now, sir! You'd like to know what's happened since then?"

"I should, very much."

"Well, one of my men and I met that train—a couple of hours ago. And I very soon spotted the quarry when she got off."

"This woman Bates? The dickens you did! Did you know her, then?"

165

"Not by that name, Captain Bristow. And not much about her by any other name. But we do happen to have a little information. You see, she's been living here for a short time—she and her husband. Name of Charlier, partly French, so I imagine. About two months ago, they moved into a small house here—Weston View is the name of it. Charlier seems, from what I've had time to make out, to have been going up to town most days. Of course we've scores of men living here who are 'something in the City.' Quiet, respectable folks, no children, and a charwoman going in for the day. Mrs. Charlier, though, has, apparently, been away from home for a month or more."

"Ah!"

The Inspector smiled.

"Fits in, eh? Well, Charlier stayed on—by himself. At least, that seems to have been so, but you'll understand, of course, that, having no line upon them, they haven't been under observation in any way—only I like to know something about residents here. There are queer fish in this garden city of ours at times. Since I met that train and spotted the woman I've had a few enquiries made, and a preliminary report has come in. Charlier, as I say, has been living there alone during his wife's absence, but, three or four times, he's been visited by a woman. He was away from home Monday and Tuesday nights last—yes—I see the significance of that—he came back on Wednesday, bringing this woman with him. I can't be sure, but possibly she stayed there.

"Well, to make a long story short, when Mrs. Charlier arrived this afternoon she made straight for the house, and let herself in with a key. Kinch's man, Morgan, and one of my men here followed, of course. They've got the place under observation. It's an easy house to watch; stands by itself, and has a few trees about the garden. Also, there's a telephone-booth at the end of the road, and that's handy. My man has 'phoned me from it already. He says Mrs. Charlier is alone—the charwoman had left before she came. And that's as far as we've got, sir."

"What do you propose to do?"

"Well, we've got to be careful. From what Kinch said, he'd enough information to justify an arrest. Isn't that so?"

"Oh, quite. But you don't want——"

"Of course not," broke in the other. "Not just yet. And, so far, you've got nothing against the man, have you?"

"Didn't even know who he was."

"Exactly. Besides, there's another thing. That pearl necklace. I take it Kinch would like to get hold of that, if it's possible. Anyhow, I've made up my mind, as a precautionary measure, to have a search-warrant ready. I was just going round to a magistrate to get one when you came in. And I think I'll do so now, sir.—You let my missus get you a cup of tea, and I'll be back soon. Anyhow, we can't make any move till Charlier turns up. And his wife won't get away before then—you bet!"

"I'll be glad of the tea. May I use your telephone, Inspector?"

"Certainly."

Bristow got on to Frimley Manor. Anstice answered his call. He told her he should not be returning that night, and asked if Charles Lynwood was in. In another minute Charlie spoke.

"What's up, Roger?" he asked.

Bristow laughed.

"Too long a story to tell you, Charlie. Except one thing. I thought I'd like to put you out of your misery, old chap."

"What do you mean?"

"That you needn't worry any more about what you told me. It wasn't Sonia Fullinger you saw that night—outside the house."

"Good Lord! But—but—I *did* see her."

"No, you didn't. You can take that as a certainty, my boy!"

"Who was it, then?"

Bristow chuckled.

"Ask Sonia," he replied. "She knows. And I think it's due to her that you should explain why you ran away the day after the murder."

"You're not joking, Roger?"

"Never was more serious."

"By Jove!" A pause, and then:

"I'll get out the two-seater and run up and see her this evening."

"Good."

And he rang off, smiling to himself.

It was later on that evening that the telephone-bell rang. The Inspector took up the receiver and listened. Then he turned to Bristow, and said:

"That was from my man. He says Charlier has just returned and gone into the house. There was a woman with him. I think I'll go there at once."

"I'll come with you."

The Inspector hesitated.

"But—it won't do for you to be seen, sir. They——"

"I know. I'll keep in the background. I presume you'll go in—with your search-warrant?"

The other nodded.

"Very well," he said. "It's only a few minutes' walk."

Weston View was a picturesque villa situated in a quiet street of similar houses, mostly detached. It stood well back from the road in its own grounds. The next-door house was unoccupied.

Lounging about the road, at a little distance from the house, was a nondescript-looking man, smoking a pipe. The Inspector stopped to speak to him.

"It's all right, sir," he said. "The three of them are in the house. Morgan is in the next-door garden. There's a good view from there of one of the rooms, and plenty of cover. A low fence divides the two gardens."

"Right!" said the Inspector. "You join him, Simmonds. You can go with him, Captain Bristow, only please keep out of sight to begin with. Can you and Morgan," he went on to Simmonds, "manage to get over that fence into their garden without being seen?"

"Quite easy, sir,—at the further end."

"Very well. Do that—both of you. I'm going to have a look round first, and then I'll call—at the front door. Watch for me. As soon as I'm inside the house, you two are to see to it that none of them make a get-away by the back door or the windows. Got that?"

"Yes, sir."

"All right, then. Off you go."

Bristow followed Simmonds into the next-door garden. Morgan was crouching there behind a tree, peering through a knothole in the dividing fence. He looked round at their approach, and a look of surprise passed over his face as he saw Bristow.

"Is Superintendent Kinch here?" he asked, in a low voice.

Bristow shook his head.

"No," he said. "But I've come to have a look—as a spectator."

Morgan grinned.

"You'll get a fair view through that hole, sir. You can see right into the room where the three of them are. They seem to be rather excited."

Simmonds briefly repeated to Morgan the Inspector's orders, and the two men, crouching low so as not to be seen over the low fence, made their way to the bottom of the garden. Bristow watched them climb the fence. Then he put his eye to the knothole.

Morgan was right. He could see into the room opposite through a French window. It was, evidently, a dining-room. Seated, facing the window, on the further side of a table, he could make out a man, apparently young, and wearing a black moustache. On his left, also seated, was a young woman, in hat and coat, her elbows on the table, her chin in her hands, motionless, looking straight in front of her.

Looking at "Bates." And it was upon "Bates" that Bristow concentrated his gaze, after a brief glance at the other two. For the ex-lady's-maid appeared to be "holding the stage." She stood, on the other side of the table, her shingled golden hair rather dishevelled, excited, talking volubly. Bristow could even hear her raised voice, though he caught no words. Every now and then her arm shot out— towards the man—or the other woman—as if she were denouncing them. Every now and then she brought her hand down on the table, emphasising her remarks. Not for a moment was she still. Once or twice the man leaned forward and spoke. Each time he did so, "Bates" turned on him like a virago.

Bristow cautiously shifted his position, got behind the tree, stood up, and, keeping the tree between him and the window opposite, glanced over the fence. From where he stood he could just see the front gate. The Inspector, in uniform, was coming in through it. The psychological moment was arriving.

Stooping once more, Bristow put his eye to the knothole again. The man had risen from his chair, come round the table, and was standing by the window. He unhasped it, and threw it open. Then turned towards the interior. And Bristow heard him say:

"Look here, you little devil! I've had enough of it. You've bungled the whole thing, and I'm sick of you. The sooner you clear out the better I shall like it."

"Clear out!" Bates's voice rose into a shriek. "You thought *you* were going to clear out, with that strumpet of yours, before I found out anything, didn't you? That's why you told me to stay on where I was, eh? You wouldn't have cared a damn if the cops had traced me. But I guessed you were hiding something from me, and I came down here and found I was right. Oh, yes! I'll clear out! Only—before I go—"

She was standing at the back of the room now, and Bristow could not see her plainly. But he could make out that, suddenly, her arm went up—there was a flash of red fire—a report—and the man at the window spun round and pitched, head-long, onto the gravelled path outside. There followed a piercing scream, another stab of flame, and then Bristow vaulted over the fence just as the two policemen came tearing up the garden.

Bristow bounded across to the window, over the prostrate body of the man, into the room, which reeked with an acrid smell, through the door into the hall, and then—

"Bates" was in the hall, cramming her hat on. She opened the front door, and then started back, with a cry. The big Inspector stood in the doorway, blocking her path. She ran back—straight into Bristow's arms, and he seized hold of her wrists. She looked at him.

"*You!*" she shouted. "Damn you! I ought to have known—Ah!—"

She wrenched her hands free, struggled—bit—kicked. It was two or three minutes before the Inspector had the handcuffs on her and was holding her down on a chair in the hall. As he said afterwards, a really vicious woman gives more trouble than a prize-fighter.

Panting, half-sobbing, she turned to Bristow again.

"Tracked me down, have you?" she cried. "But I don't care if I swing for it. I mean for what I've just done now. I'd have given myself up rather than he should have got away with that minx. I hope I've killed them both. I—"

"Here!" said the Inspector. "Just keep quiet, will you?"

She looked up at him."

"I won't keep quiet—I—"

"It's for your good I'm telling you," he said, firmly. "You're under arrest for being concerned in the murder of Jasper Hurst and the robbery of Mrs. Cresswell's pearls," he went on, formally. "And I warn you that anything you say—"

She laughed hysterically.

"You won't stop me saying what I choose," she cried, "and it doesn't matter now what I say. Only—"

Impatiently the Inspector took her by the arm and led her back into the dining-room, Bristow following them. Lying in an arm-chair was the other woman, Simmonds bending over her. Outside the window Morgan was kneeling beside Charlier, who was stretched on the ground.

"Get a move on, quick," ordered the Inspector. "Is she dead, Simmonds?"

"No, sir. Not even hit, I fancy. Looks like a faint."

"Right. See if there's a telephone in the house—if not, use the one at the street corner. Call up Dr. Leslie and tell him to hurry. Then call the ambulance and a taxi. Mind this woman, will you, please, sir?"

Bristow came over to Bates and stood beside her. The Inspector went outside. Morgan looked up.

"I don't think he's dead, sir," he said. "The bullet seems to have struck him behind the ear—and glanced off."

"Humph! Can't tell till the doctor comes. We'll carry him indoors, though. Lucky that next-door house is vacant, or we'd have had half the street in by now. . . . Yes—lay him on the floor. Put that cushion under his head."

He slipped his hand under the man's waistcoat.

"You may be right," he said to Morgan. "I believe his heart's beating."

The Inspector turned to "Bates." She was sitting in a chair, silently looking on, pale of face and breathing heavily. But her rage seemed to have subsided.

"Now," said the Inspector to her, "I've got a taxi coming for you. Are you going to give me any more trouble, or will you go quietly if I send you to the police-station with one of my men here?"

She looked at him, half-defiantly.

"Oh, you needn't worry about me," she replied. "I've come to the end of things now and there's nothing more to be done. I wish I'd killed them both, though!" she added, her eyes blazing for a moment.

"I should have thought that being charged with one murder was enough," said the Inspector, dryly.

"There you are wrong," she retorted. "I never killed Jasper. And, what's more, you say I'm charged with being concerned in the robbery of that pearl necklace. Well," and she pointed with her manacled hands at the man who was stretched on the floor, "if there's any truth in *his* story, the necklace never left Frimley. But I want to make a statement: I want to tell you the whole. . . ."

"Look here," broke in the Inspector, sternly. "I've warned you once, for your own good, about saying anything. If you choose to do so, you must take the risk yourself. Only, I'm not going to hear you now. That sounds like the taxi—yes—Take her away, Simmonds,"— he stepped outside the French window and looked towards the gate— "ah, and here's the doctor, too."

The doctor, after a brief question or two, made very short work of his two patients. The woman, who was already recovering, he pronounced to be in no danger—merely suffering from the results of shock—and the Inspector made arrangements for having her taken to the police-station to be detained pending enquiries. A swift examination of Charlier, who was still bleeding from a wound behind the ear, confirmed Morgan's suspicions that the bullet had not penetrated his brain.

"Concussion," he said, "but I don't think he's in any danger. I'll just fix a bandage on his head, and then we'll have him taken to the hospital—you say you've 'phoned for the ambulance? Good. He ought to regain consciousness after a bit. May one ask what it's all about, Inspector?"

The Inspector laughed, shortly.

"I don't know, yet," he replied, "except that it's a case of attempted murder, to say nothing of an actual one. We've got to put the jigsaw together a bit before we can make a clear picture. What do you think, sir?" he added, turning to Bristow.

"I think," said Bristow, dryly, "that it won't be very long before that picture stands out, and that Bates—or Mrs. Charlier—or whatever her name is, will put the pieces together. Jealousy acts on a woman very much as, according to the old proverb, '*In vino veritas,*' alcohol acts on a man. And I fancy you'll find, in this case, that she'll tell the whole truth, whatever it costs her. She's out for revenge— especially as she failed to get it—with *that!*"

And he pointed to a small revolver which the Inspector had picked up from the floor, and which now lay on the table.

"And how about that search-warrant?" he went on.

"Ah!" said the Inspector, "as soon as we've got these people away, we'll have a look over the house. Though I don't expect to find those pearls here—after what she said."

Nor did he. Neither did he find anything incriminating. Finally he and Bristow went back to the police-station.

It was late that night, and the two men were smoking a pipe in the Inspector's sanctum. The latter had visited Charlier in the hospital. Charlier had, as the doctor foretold, recovered consciousness, but had refused to answer the few questions the Inspector had put to him. The latter left a policeman on duty by the patient's bed. He had also interviewed the woman whom Charlier had brought with him to Weston View, but she, too, had refused either to disclose her identity or to give any information, except that she protested against being detained and declared that there was no possible charge against her.

A knock came at the door, and, in answer to the Inspector's "Come in," a policeman entered.

"It's about this woman—Charlier, sir," he said. "She's asking if she can see you and Captain Bristow tonight."

"Oh! How is she now?"

"Perfectly calm, sir. She's eaten her supper. Mrs. Rose, who is seeing to her, says she is giving no trouble."

"Oh, very well. Shall we go and see her, Captain Bristow?"
Bristow nodded.

"It might be as well," he replied.

The policeman was right. "Bates" was sitting on her bed in the cell, all traces of rage and excitement departed. Still dressed in the plain black frock she had worn in Sonia Fullinger's service, she looked more like a demure lady's-maid than a potential murderess. Her fair hair was carefully brushed and she had powdered her face and touched up her lips.

She looked up as the door opened and the two men stood in the entrance of the cell.

"Thank you for coming," she said, in even tones. "No," she went on, as the Inspector was about to speak. "I know you have to caution me—and you've done so already. I'm perfectly aware of my position, and you are welcome to make any use you like of what I may say—though it won't be much now. I suppose," she went on, to Bristow, "I have to thank *you* for tracking me down?"

Bristow shrugged his shoulders.

"I am not a policeman," he said, "but I may have helped the police—yes."

"I thought so. Jules warned me to be on the look-out for you."

"Jules?"

"Jules Charlier. The man I shot this evening."

She made the statement coolly and evenly, as though the shooting of Jules Charlier was the most casual thing in the world.

"Your husband?" said the Inspector.

"No. Not my husband."

"But you were living with him here?"

"That may be. You have him under arrest?"

The Inspector hesitated.

"I have detained him," he replied.

"Ah! You want a definite charge, I suppose? I can give it to you, Inspector. Jules Charlier killed Jasper Hurst—I daresay you have guessed that already?" she asked Bristow.

The latter nodded.

"Do you wish to make a statement to that effect?" said the Inspector. "You are not obliged to do so, but——"

"Oh, yes, I'll make a statement—enough for you to charge him. I'm not going to spare him. But, what I want to know is this: Can I give evidence at the adjourned inquest?"

"You can if you wish to," replied the Inspector; "but it is my duty to warn you, for your own interests, that anything you say then——"

"Oh, yes, I know," she interrupted. "But I don't care what I say. I want to make sure that the truth is known. You give me pen and paper now, please, and I'll write out what you ought to know up to the present. And the rest I'll make plain at the inquest."

"You may not be wise," put in Bristow.

She laughed bitterly.

"I'm past the time when it's a question of wisdom or folly, Captain Bristow. I'm a woman who only wants—revenge!"

And her eyes flashed.

15

There was, if anything, more excitement about the adjourned sitting at the Coroner's Court than when it had first opened. The hall was crowded, and a buzz of anticipation sounded over the room as those present waited for the Coroner to come in. Sir Harry and his two sons were there, Charlie seated next to Sonia Fullinger. Mr. and Mrs. Cresswell were present, and so was the Chief Constable.

The Coroner came in, took his seat, and the roll of the eleven jurymen was called. The Coroner addressed them, gravely.

"Since the last time we met, gentlemen," he said, "certain extremely important events have arisen which will materially assist you in arriving at your verdict. I have no doubt that some of those events are known to you through the public press, but I want you to keep your minds clear of all that, so far as this enquiry is concerned. The functions of a Coroner and his Court have, recently, been severely criticised in certain instances, in some cases, perhaps, with a measure of justice, but I, for one, while strictly guarding the prerogatives of this court, should be sorry if, in any way, it merited similar criticisms. I wish you, therefore, to understand that your and my sole duty is to record the manner in which the deceased, Jasper Hurst, met with his death. I understand that the police have further objects in view, but those objects do not concern this court. The evidence that you are asked to hear, therefore, will be strictly confined to the purpose of this enquiry. Events which have transpired since you last met have affected the course of this enquiry, and it will be, I think, unnecessary to call certain witnesses I had in my mind.

"I should also like to add," he went on, consulting his notes, "that there is one witness whom I cannot compel to give evidence in this Court, but who, I am told, wishes to do so. In order that her evidence, when given, may be properly judged as to its worth and reliability, I shall call certain other witnesses first. Rose Ellington, please."

There came forward a young woman of about thirty years of age, plain of face, and quietly dressed. She took the oath.

"Your name?"

"Rose Ellington, sir."

"Your home?"

"My home is at Pinner, sir. But I am not living there. I am employed in the service of Mrs. Andrews, of Tudor House, Elm Avenue, Amersham."

"Quite so. As lady's-maid, I believe?"

"Yes, sir."

"Before then, however, you occupied the same position in Miss Fullinger's service?"

"Yes, sir,—I did."

"And left very suddenly."

The girl reddened.

"Yes, sir."

"Will you tell the jury why?"

"I had—an inducement to do so, sir."

"Ah! In what way?"

"An offer of money."

"Yes? How much?"

"Fifty pounds, sir."

"And who made you this offer?"

"I—I don't know, sir."

"You don't know? Well, tell us how it came about."

"It began with a letter—asking me to meet the writer—under the clock at Charing Cross station—and saying it meant something to my advantage. So I went. There was a woman——"

"You would know her again?"

"Yes, sir."

"Go on."

"She offered me fifty pounds if I would leave my place— somehow—I don't know how—she seemed to know I was badly in want of money. . . . I was in debt. . . . She gave me half the sum then and there, and I made an excuse to leave Miss Fullinger—and the other half came by post."

"That is all?"

"Yes, sir."

"Very well. Stand down, please. I shall want you again later on.

Miss Fullinger!"

Sonia came forward, smiling at something Charlie had whispered to her. All eyes were directed towards her, for a whisper had gone forth that she was closely connected with the case. She gave her name and address, and then the Coroner asked her:

"When you were staying at Frimley Manor for the pageant, you had your maid with you?"

"Yes."

"Her name?"

"She called herself Phyllis Aurelia Bates."

Some of those present exchanged significant glances, foreseeing a mystery.

"You engaged her when your late maid, Ellington, left your service?"

"I did."

"How?"

"She called, saying that a Registry Office had given her my name."

"Yes—and her testimonials?"

"She produced a written one from Lady Challington, with whom she had been—so the testimonial said—four years."

"And you engaged her on the strength of this?"

"Yes."

"Thank you. Now, Miss Fullinger, you were acting in the pageant. Tell us what costume you were wearing?"

The girl did so. The Coroner went on:

"When you retired for the night, you were still wearing this dress?"

"I was."

"When you had taken it off, did it remain in your room that night?"

"No. My maid took it away to fold ready for packing."

"What time was that?"

"Just after eleven."

"When did you see the costume again?"

"My maid brought it back in the morning, and packed it in my room."

"Thank you. That will do, Miss Fullinger. Mr. Charles Lynwood, please."

"I believe," went on the Coroner, dryly, when Charlie had taken his place, "that you have something to add to the evidence you have previously given. Will you tell the jury what that is?"

Slowly and deliberately Charlie unfolded the story he had told in the first instance to Captain Bristow. Quite an audible gasp of astonishment burst from the listeners as he calmly recounted how he had seen someone in that Edward the Sixth's costume emerge from the house and meet an unknown man at the entrance to the marquee.

"And you believed her to be Miss Fullinger?" asked the Coroner.

"Naturally," replied Charlie, with great coolness. There was another gasp of astonishment. Several of the jury turned and looked at Sonia. She was actually smiling. The Coroner leaned forward and said, a little severely:

"Why did you not tell us this last time, Mr. Lynwood?"

"You did not ask me," answered Charlie.

"I hardly think that was the reason," snapped the Coroner. "But I will say nothing about that, except that I am bound to observe that no excuse suffices for withholding evidence. However, we are glad, now, to have heard what you have told us. That will do, Mr. Lynwood."

Charlie, quite unabashed by this rebuke, resumed his seat next to Sonia. The Coroner looked at his notes for a few moments, and then called Superintendent Kinch.

"Just one question, Superintendent. Miss Fullinger has told us she engaged Bates, her maid, on the strength of a testimonial from Lady Challington. Have you anything to say on this matter?"

"I have, sir," replied Kinch, tersely. "I ascertained that Lady Challington is in India; I obtained her address and cabled to her for verification. This is her reply."

He produced a cablegram and read:

"Have no knowledge of Bates. Did not give testimonial."

"Thank you," said the Coroner. "That is all."

Again he consulted his notes. Then he leaned back in his chair and spoke to the jury, in his somewhat sententious manner:

"The evidence you have just heard," he said, "may perhaps appear irrelevant. But I assure you it is not. It has been given mainly for the purpose of preparing you for a witness I have already mentioned, and who, as I told you, cannot be compelled to give evidence, for the reason that she is under arrest on a serious charge connected with this case. I understand, however, that it is her wish to make a statement, and, that being so, I shall, of course, allow her to give evidence. I wish, before doing so, to point out to you that, in connection with the death of Jasper Hurst a robbery appears to have taken place. The investigation of that robbery, however, is not the business of this court. I mention this, in case any of you might feel disposed to put questions concerning the matter. Such questions I shall disallow.

Yes"—he nodded to Kinch—"you may bring her in."

Kinch stepped to a door at the back of the hall which opened into a dressing-room. All eyes were fixed on it. Jarvis, the local policeman, emerged, escorting a woman dressed in black, a fair-haired, pretty woman, whose complexion owed something to art as well as nature. But her prettiness was marred by the hard, steely look in her blue eyes, and the little downward curves at the corners of her tightly-compressed mouth.

The Chief Constable, who had watched her intently as she came forward, turned and whispered to Bristow:

"By gad, Bristow, I shouldn't like to be up against that woman! Devilish fierce, eh?"

"She is," retorted Bristow, "suffering from the worst passion a woman ever falls under—jealousy. She's a bad lot, anyhow, but—as you say—she's a regular devil now. She's tried murder, and failed. *Now* she means to invoke the hangman."

The Coroner spoke to her, gravely.

"I have to warn you," he said, "that you are not compelled to give evidence in this Court. If you determine to do so, you must take the risks. You had better consider carefully before the oath is administered."

"I have considered," she replied, in a firm, even voice. "I understand perfectly that I am here to speak of my own will and accord. And I wish to do so."

"Very well," and he nodded to the Clerk, who administered the oath.

"Your name?" he asked.

"Francia Hurst."

"We are inquiring into the cause of the death of Jasper Hurst. Are you related to him?"

"He was my husband."

"Ah-h!" A long-drawn sigh went forth from the spectators. She never moved, but stood there, her eyes fixed on the Coroner.

"You were not living with him?"

"Not for the last two years."

"And can you throw any light upon his death?"

"I can tell you everything," she replied, quietly. "The only question I wish to ask is, need I give my reasons for doing so?"

"Not if you don't want to," said the Coroner. "The facts will be sufficient. And I think I will ask you to tell us in your own way. I have already warned you, and I have no wish to make the position in which you have voluntarily placed yourself more difficult by pressing you with questions. Go on, please."

She paused, just for a moment, and then, from time to time glancing at a paper she held in her hand, in a low, but perfectly modulated voice, made her statement amid a strained and intense silence.

"I first met my late husband in Annecy—in France—and we were married a very short time afterwards. He made few enquiries about me, but knew that I was an orphan, born of English parents. But what he did not know was—well—my associates, and, as I had purposed to put them from me on my marriage, I told him nothing. Resolutions, however, are sometimes difficult to carry out, and—well—these associates of whom I have spoken—would not altogether allow me to put them out of my life."

"One moment," interrupted the Coroner. "Will you—er—tell us the nature of these associates?"

She regarded him steadily.

"They were crooks," she replied. "Some French and some English."

The Coroner nodded.

"Go on."

"Jasper Hurst's profession was that of a private enquiry agent. I did not know exactly what he was until some little time after our marriage. Then, from hints which he dropped, I got to know that he had discovered something about my past. But more followed. He began to suspect that I had not entirely dissociated myself from the past—which was true. And then—well, he spoke to me about it. He was, I suppose, justified in doing so, and I bear him no ill-will—but—it began an estrangement, which widened. I take the blame. Women dislike to be ordered to do things—and—well, I resented it. He didn't understand me. He forced me more and more to go back to my old companions—and—and . . ." she faltered a little now, "there was one of them who—before I married—had been more than a companion—and—well, I left my husband, and went to him. I asked my husband to divorce me. But he would not. I—I—think he must have cared for me still. And I *knew* he kept himself aware of my movements. I had proof of it."

She paused for a moment, and looked at the Coroner, as if, almost, she was asking him to help her along. But he remained silent. Then she went on:

"Jules Charlier—the man I have told you of—" A hard look came into her eyes as she spoke his name—"was a clever jewel thief, so clever that he had never been detected, though I knew that my husband suspected—what was the truth—that he took the Countess of Chelmsford's diamonds. My husband was engaged on the case. Well, to make a long story short, Jules Charlier knew about Mrs. Cresswell's pearl necklace—and he—*we*"—and she emphasised the word— "were determined to get it. Jules was clever, and he laid his plans carefully. We got to know about the pageant that was to be acted here. Mrs. Cresswell was foolish enough to talk to her friends about her part and how she was going to wear her pearls. And we also got to know that Miss Fullinger would be staying with her here. I bribed Miss Fullinger's maid to leave her at a moment's notice, and secured her place by a forged testimonial. Everything was arranged. Jules was to motor down from London the night after this pageant, and I was to get the necklace and take it out to him between half-past one and two. I very soon found out Mrs. Cresswell's habits—I had every oppor-tunity in the two or three days here before the pageant—and I knew she kept the necklace in a case in her dressing-case and her bunch of keys in her left-hand drawer. I also found she had duplicate keys to the dressing-case, and I took one of them off the ring.

"That night Miss Fullinger went to bed rather earlier than the others. She rang for me. I helped her to undress, as she was not feeling well. Among other things, she asked me to take the costume she had been wearing and fold it ready for packing. That gave me the idea. I went to my room and changed into the costume. It was partly a precaution, because, if I were seen, I should be mistaken for Miss Fullinger, and, in any case, a male costume was easier in which to move about quietly.

"It was something after one o'clock that I went into Mrs. Cresswell's room, unlocked her dressing-case, and took out the pearls. It was quite simple, and hardly took a minute. When I came out on the corridor I heard men's voices downstairs. I waited—listening. Then I heard them saying good night in the hall—and the front door shut— and someone came up the stairs. I slipped into the lavatory at the end of the corridor, and waited till all was quiet. Then I went downstairs. The hall light was still burning, and I imagined they had forgotten to turn it out, so I switched it off myself. Then I went out of the house."

"By the front door?" put in the Coroner.

"No. I was afraid of making a noise by unlocking it—and I did not know, then, that it was already unfastened. I went into the library and opened one of the French windows, at the side of the house."

Jarvis, who was listening, suddenly started. Something seemed to have occurred to him. The witness went on:

"I went out on the lawn. I suddenly remembered that I was to wave my handkerchief as a signal, but, in changing into the costume, I had forgotten to bring one. I felt in the pockets in case there was one there. There was. It was Miss Fullinger's, of course. So I waved it. Then I saw Jules coming from behind some trees—at least, I supposed it was Jules, though I couldn't see his face as he came up—he had a muffler round the lower part of it and his hat was pulled down over his eyes. But, when he spoke, I recognised his voice. He said, 'Have you got it?' and I replied, 'Yes.' Then he whispered, 'Come inside that tent—there's too much light here, and we might be seen from the house. I want a word with you.' I handed him the jewel-case, and we went inside the tent. Then he told me he had had a breakdown with the car, and had begun to fear he wouldn't get here in time. He said he had come on by train to Chiltonbury, where he had found a car outside the station, and had taken it. This, he said, had altered his plans, as he dare not drive back in it to London. I was to have met him the next evening at Letcham, where we had taken a house, but he told me to remain with Miss Fullinger till he let me know—I didn't understand then," she went on, bitterly, "but I did afterwards. As he talked he was holding the jewel-case in his hand. He took off the muffler. 'Found it in the car,' he said, 'but it's frightfully hot.' Just then he gave a start, dropped the scarf, and gripped my arm. I turned. Standing at the tent door was the black silhouette of a man. Before we had time to think he had bounded forward and seized the jewel-case. Then he made for the entrance of the tent, but Jules was too quick for him—he put out his leg and tripped him. He was up in a moment, but by this time Jules had his back to the opening, and I saw, as the moon shone in, something shining on his clenched hand. The other man had retreated to the back of the tent. Then, as far as I was concerned, it was all confusion. Jules went for him—he seemed to dodge him—then they met face to face—and the other struck out. But Jules is a clever boxer—I saw him parry the blow with one hand while the other shot forward—there was a crash—and the man fell to the ground.

" 'Oh!' I said. 'What has happened?'

" 'Keep quiet,' whispered Jules—flashing a small electric torch—'at any rate I've got the pearls'—and he picked up the case, which was lying on the ground, and put it in his pocket. Then he turned the light on the face of the man who lay there—and I saw. It was my husband."

There was a thrill of intense excitement in the Court. Perhaps, of all there, Francia Hurst was the most detached. She was telling her story in such a calm, lucid manner, as though she had not been one of the principal characters in its action. But there were those there, Captain Bristow among them, who realised that it was strong passion—the passion of jealousy and revenge—raging in her heart which really produced that calm demeanour.

She went on:

"He was dressed in a black velvet suit—and then I knew. I had seen him among the performers in the pageant, and had noticed something familiar. But he was wearing a beard then, and I suppose that is why I did not recognise him.

"I was terribly frightened. I had no quarrel with my husband: he had always treated me well . . . only . . . well, I suppose I never really loved him—and so I had left him. I thought he was dead. But Jules stooped down and laid his hand on his heart—and then—my husband moved slightly, and tried to speak. 'He brought it on himself,' said Jules. 'I had to knock him out—but now—we mustn't leave him here. If he comes to, he'll give the alarm.'

"Then he made up his mind. We did not know he was living in the village here. Nor did we think, then, that he was so seriously hurt. Jules' only thought was how to get him out of the way while he made his escape. Finally he said we must get him to the car—which Jules had left in the drive. Then Jules would drive the car away to some quiet spot he knew of, and leave him there. He said he was sure to be found . . . and . . . well, I was so frightened that I agreed to everything.

"The sedan-chair was my idea. I saw that, once we got him inside, we could carry him much more easily. So we lifted him in, seating him there. He tried to speak—even then. Then we started, carrying him off. We had reached the bridge when we heard something behind us—and we looked round and saw someone running from the house. Jules was always quick of action—and he didn't hesitate for an instant. 'Run for the car,' he whispered, and we set down the chair and took to our heels—just in time. I looked round as Jules started her, and saw our pursuer had almost overtaken us. I couldn't make out who he was, for he was flashing an electric torch.

"At the gate, Jules stopped the car for a moment, and told me to get back to the house as well as I could. I asked him to take me with him—but he wouldn't. I know *why* now!"

As she spoke, Bristow, who was watching her closely, saw, for a moment, a change spread over her set face. Her eyes flashed—and she caught her breath. Then she went on:

"He said it would allay suspicion if I returned, and give him a better chance to get away. But—but—*that* wasn't his reason."

The Coroner, at this point, interrupted her, saying, dryly:

"You remember you said your were only going to give us facts—not reasons, Mrs. Hurst?"

She turned on him. She was losing her self-possession a little now. "I shall tell my story how I choose!"

"By all means. I only reminded you."

Captain Bristow whispered to the Chief Constable:

"She'll break down before she's finished—getting to the end of her tether."

And the Chief Constable nodded in reply.

"I did get back to the house—after a time," she went on. "But I saw what was happening first—I was behind some trees. And I guessed— my husband was dead. I was afraid to move into the open till they had all gone—back to the house. Then I made my way round the grounds, and let myself in by the window—which was still unfastened."

At this point Jarvis turned to Detective-Sergeant Mentmore, who was standing beside him, and whispered:

"I *told* you I saw that French window flash in the moonlight!"

There was a pause. Francia Hurst put one hand to her throat, the other grasped the back of a chair—and Bristow noticed the chair began to shake slightly.

"Is that all?" asked the Coroner.

"No!" Her voice rang out, but sank as she went on. "It isn't all. My God, it isn't all! Jules Charlier killed my husband, but even then I would have stood by him. I *did!* You and your policemen"—she suddenly turned towards Kinch and pointed at him—"found nothing from *me,* did you? Oh, I knew how to put you off the scent! But—but—I waited. And Jules never wrote—or wired—as he said he would—and I went to him at last—I guessed where I should find him—and I *did.* And *you,*" she turned now to Captain Bristow, "know what happened then—and *why!* I'd—I'd only been a catspaw! But he didn't get the necklace—oh, I'm *glad* he didn't get it. The case was empty when Jules opened it—and he said that was all the more reason why he'd done with me—but—but—he killed my husband— and—he—threw me over . . . he——"

It was Kinch who caught her as she shrieked and sank to the ground, and Kinch and Jarvis who lifted her between them and carried her out of the hall. And, when order was restored, and the Superintendent had come back, the Coroner said:

"I propose to call no more witnesses. But before I ask the jury for their verdict, the police have a statement to make."

And Kinch said, briefly:

"In the ordinary course of events, sir, the man, Jules Charlier, would have been present at this enquiry—I mean, of course, in custody. But he is lying in hospital, suffering from an injury. He is, I may say, under arrest."

"Thank you," said the Coroner, and then proceeded, but not at any length, to charge the jury.

The verdict, after such evidence, was a foregone conclusion. The jury, however, before giving it, asked a question, by their foreman, of the Coroner. They were satisfied that Jules Charlier had caused the death of the deceased, they said, but as, apparently, he did not mean to kill him, would it be in order to leave out the expression "wilful murder" and simply state that Jasper Hurst died from heart-failure— they had remembered the medical evidence—brought on by a blow given by Jules Charlier?

"As you please," snapped the Coroner. And that was their verdict.

"All the same," said Kinch, to Mentmore, as they came out, "*our* charge will be murder, I think!"

The company of relatives and friends were gathered in the hall at Frimley Manor, waiting for the butler to announce luncheon. Mr. and Mrs. Cresswell, Sonia, Captain Bristow, the Vicar and Major Bainbridge were all there, with Sir Harry and his two sons and Anstice. The sedan-chair stood in the corner of the hall—in its usual place.

And the Chief Constable had detached himself from the others and was standing, his hands in his pockets, regarding that chair intently. Presently he glanced over his shoulders. They were all talking. Very quietly he opened the door of the chair and stooped over the interior. Then he shut the door again, a little smile on his face. Bristow came up to him at that moment.

"What's amusing you, Major?"

"Oh—just an inspiration. I say—Sir Harry!"

"Yes?"

There was a sudden silence—for the Chief Constable had raised his voice.

"I'm not *really* a policeman, or a sleuth, you know," he said, "but a suggestion came into my mind this morning. Something that wretched woman said at the inquest set me thinking. The question is, what became of those pearls, if Jules Charlier never had them?"

Mrs. Cresswell burst out:

"Oh, Major Bainbridge, if only you could find them!"

The Chief Constable smiled.

"What was it poor Hurst said to you—just before he died?" he asked Captain Bristow.

"Why, I never could make it out. What he seemed to say was, 'The line.' But I can't, for the life of me, imagine what he meant."

"Well, perhaps I can," replied the Chief Constable, with a smile. "I think he was telling you where to find that necklace. Suppose I try to prove that. Wasn't it Sherlock Holmes who said that when you've struck out all that's impossible, what remains must be true—or something to that effect? Well, figure it out. The pearls were in their case when you locked it up, weren't they, Mrs. Cresswell?"

"But, of course. I can swear to that."

"Very well. This woman we have been listening to took the case—with the necklace inside it—handed it to Jules Charlier— necklace still inside. Hurst took it from him—necklace still inside. Jules got it back—*but*—was the necklace still inside? When he opened the case afterwards, it wasn't there!"

"Where was it, then?" chorused the group.

"It could only have got out of the case when Hurst had it. You remember she told us he went to the back of the tent? His object, we all agree, I suppose, was to prevent his wife being implicated in the robbery. He discovered she was staying here, and that roused his suspicions. As he went down the drive he must have seen Jules Charlier, and that car. He had, you remember, discussed Mrs. Cresswell's necklace with Miss Fullinger while he was at dinner here. All his suspicions were confirmed, and he followed up Jules with the intention of getting back the necklace and restoring it. When he found himself in a tight corner in the tent, he slipped the pearls out of the case."

"But what did he do with them?" asked Sir Harry.

"The obvious thing. He put them in his pocket."

"But they weren't there!" chorused the group.

"Ah!" retorted the Chief Constable, "I never said he *kept* the necklace in his pocket. Remember, when they put him in the sedan-chair he was semi-conscious—so he was when you found him, Bristow."

"Ah!" exclaimed Bristow, "was it——"

The Chief Constable stopped him.

"He *told* you where it was," he said. "It was, really, quite simple, all the time—if we'd only thought to study that chair carefully, as I was doing just now. Look!"

He opened the door of the sedan-chair and pointed within. They all crowded round.

"Now, then," he went on, " 'the line'—Wasn't what he was trying to say 'the *lining*'?"

Inside, the old chair was lined with faded blue silk. And in one place, on the side of the chair, the lining was torn—there was quite a big hole.

Major Bainbridge plunged his hand into this hole and reached down, behind the lining, to the bottom of the chair. The next moment he drew out the pearl necklace.

"There!" he said. "My reputation is saved. Allow me, Mrs. Cresswell. I *am*, I suppose, a policeman in the official sense of the word, and it's always a pleasure to the police to be able to restore stolen property. Will you give me the reward of wearing it?"

And, with great courtesy, he undid the clasp—and then fastened the string of pearls round the neck of the delighted lady, while the audience clapped approval.

"Gad!" exclaimed Sir Harry. "You're too modest, Bainbridge. No policeman, eh? You're a super-sleuth! But, suppose the pearls *hadn't* been there? It was a bit of a risk, wasn't it?"

"Not at all," said the Chief Constable, with a smile. "You see, I have to confess that I satisfied myself that they were there before I produced them. I plead guilty if I was melodramatic."

"Luncheon is served, Sir Harry."

The butler, staid and impassive, had come into the hall. They trooped into the dining-room. Captain Bristow, who had been watching Mr. Cresswell, a little smile on his face, took him by the arm and managed to keep him back for a moment.

"Cresswell," he said, "are you going to let your wife wear those pearls at the next pageant?"

"Why not?" He looked at Bristow. "I fancy she will be more careful in future."

"And if they were stolen again—would the thief make much out of them? Am I right in supposing—well—that great things can be done with paste—and that your bank keeps not only documentary securities for you?"

Mr. Cresswell stopped, and, in his turn, grasped Bristow's arm. There was a twinkle in his eyes as he said, in a low tone of voice:

"I wondered if you had guessed—something you said the other day made me wonder—but, my dear fellow, for heaven's sake don't tell my wife!"

"Not I," replied Bristow. "Or anyone else, either. I think you're a wise man, Cresswell."

And they went in to luncheon.

THE END

A CATALOG OF SELECTED
DOVER BOOKS
IN ALL FIELDS OF INTEREST

A CATALOG OF SELECTED DOVER
BOOKS IN ALL FIELDS OF INTEREST

DRAWINGS OF REMBRANDT, edited by Seymour Slive. Updated Lippmann, Hofstede de Groot edition, with definitive scholarly apparatus. All portraits, biblical sketches, landscapes, nudes. Oriental figures, classical studies, together with selection of work by followers. 550 illustrations. Total of 630pp. 9⅛ × 12¼.
21485-0, 21486-9 Pa., Two-vol. set $25.00

GHOST AND HORROR STORIES OF AMBROSE BIERCE, Ambrose Bierce. 24 tales vividly imagined, strangely prophetic, and decades ahead of their time in technical skill: "The Damned Thing," "An Inhabitant of Carcosa," "The Eyes of the Panther," "Moxon's Master," and 20 more. 199pp. 5⅜ × 8½. 20767-6 Pa. $3.95

ETHICAL WRITINGS OF MAIMONIDES, Maimonides. Most significant ethical works of great medieval sage, newly translated for utmost precision, readability. Laws Concerning Character Traits, Eight Chapters, more. 192pp. 5⅜ × 8½.
24522-5 Pa. $4.50

THE EXPLORATION OF THE COLORADO RIVER AND ITS CANYONS, J. W. Powell. Full text of Powell's 1,000-mile expedition down the fabled Colorado in 1869. Superb account of terrain, geology, vegetation, Indians, famine, mutiny, treacherous rapids, mighty canyons, during exploration of last unknown part of continental U.S. 400pp. 5⅜ × 8½. 20094-9 Pa. $6.95

HISTORY OF PHILOSOPHY, Julián Marías. Clearest one-volume history on the market. Every major philosopher and dozens of others, to Existentialism and later. 505pp. 5⅜ × 8½. 21739-6 Pa. $8.50

ALL ABOUT LIGHTNING, Martin A. Uman. Highly readable non-technical survey of nature and causes of lightning, thunderstorms, ball lightning, St. Elmo's Fire, much more. Illustrated. 192pp. 5⅜ × 8½. 25237-X Pa. $5.95

SAILING ALONE AROUND THE WORLD, Captain Joshua Slocum. First man to sail around the world, alone, in small boat. One of great feats of seamanship told in delightful manner. 67 illustrations. 294pp. 5⅜ × 8½. 20326-3 Pa. $4.50

LETTERS AND NOTES ON THE MANNERS, CUSTOMS AND CONDITIONS OF THE NORTH AMERICAN INDIANS, George Catlin. Classic account of life among Plains Indians: ceremonies, hunt, warfare, etc. 312 plates. 572pp. of text. 6⅛ × 9¼. 22118-0, 22119-9 Pa. Two-vol. set $15.90

ALASKA: The Harriman Expedition, 1899, John Burroughs, John Muir, et al. Informative, engrossing accounts of two-month, 9,000-mile expedition. Native peoples, wildlife, forests, geography, salmon industry, glaciers, more. Profusely illustrated. 240 black-and-white line drawings. 124 black-and-white photographs. 3 maps. Index. 576pp. 5⅜ × 8½. 25109-8 Pa. $11.95

THE BOOK OF BEASTS: Being a Translation from a Latin Bestiary of the Twelfth Century, T. H. White. Wonderful catalog real and fanciful beasts: manticore, griffin, phoenix, amphivius, jaculus, many more. White's witty erudite commentary on scientific, historical aspects. Fascinating glimpse of medieval mind. Illustrated. 296pp. 5⅜ × 8¼. (Available in U.S. only) 24609-4 Pa. $5.95

FRANK LLOYD WRIGHT: ARCHITECTURE AND NATURE With 160 Illustrations, Donald Hoffmann. Profusely illustrated study of influence of nature—especially prairie—on Wright's designs for Fallingwater, Robie House, Guggenheim Museum, other masterpieces. 96pp. 9¼ × 10¾. 25098-9 Pa. $7.95

FRANK LLOYD WRIGHT'S FALLINGWATER, Donald Hoffmann. Wright's famous waterfall house: planning and construction of organic idea. History of site, owners, Wright's personal involvement. Photographs of various stages of building. Preface by Edgar Kaufmann, Jr. 100 illustrations. 112pp. 9¼ × 10.
23671-4 Pa. $7.95

YEARS WITH FRANK LLOYD WRIGHT: Apprentice to Genius, Edgar Tafel. Insightful memoir by a former apprentice presents a revealing portrait of Wright the man, the inspired teacher, the greatest American architect. 372 black-and-white illustrations. Preface. Index. vi + 228pp. 8¼ × 11. 24801-1 Pa. $9.95

THE STORY OF KING ARTHUR AND HIS KNIGHTS, Howard Pyle. Enchanting version of King Arthur fable has delighted generations with imaginative narratives of exciting adventures and unforgettable illustrations by the author. 41 illustrations. xviii + 313pp. 6⅛ × 9¼. 21445-1 Pa. $5.95

THE GODS OF THE EGYPTIANS, E. A. Wallis Budge. Thorough coverage of numerous gods of ancient Egypt by foremost Egyptologist. Information on evolution of cults, rites and gods; the cult of Osiris; the Book of the Dead and its rites; the sacred animals and birds; Heaven and Hell; and more. 956pp. 6⅛ × 9¼.
22055-9, 22056-7 Pa., Two-vol. set $20.00

A THEOLOGICO-POLITICAL TREATISE, Benedict Spinoza. Also contains unfinished *Political Treatise*. Great classic on religious liberty, theory of government on common consent. R. Elwes translation. Total of 421pp. 5⅜ × 8½.
20249-6 Pa. $6.95

INCIDENTS OF TRAVEL IN CENTRAL AMERICA, CHIAPAS, AND YUCATAN, John L. Stephens. Almost single-handed discovery of Maya culture; exploration of ruined cities, monuments, temples; customs of Indians. 115 drawings. 892pp. 5⅜ × 8½. 22404-X, 22405-8 Pa., Two-vol. set $15.90

LOS CAPRICHOS, Francisco Goya. 80 plates of wild, grotesque monsters and caricatures. Prado manuscript included. 183pp. 6⅝ × 9⅝. 22384-1 Pa. $4.95

AUTOBIOGRAPHY: The Story of My Experiments with Truth, Mohandas K. Gandhi. Not hagiography, but Gandhi in his own words. Boyhood, legal studies, purification, the growth of the Satyagraha (nonviolent protest) movement. Critical, inspiring work of the man who freed India. 480pp. 5⅜ × 8½. (Available in U.S. only)
24593-4 Pa. $6.95

ILLUSTRATED DICTIONARY OF HISTORIC ARCHITECTURE, edited by Cyril M. Harris. Extraordinary compendium of clear, concise definitions for over 5,000 important architectural terms complemented by over 2,000 line drawings. Covers full spectrum of architecture from ancient ruins to 20th-century Modernism. Preface. 592pp. 7½ × 9⅜. 24444-X Pa. $14.95

THE NIGHT BEFORE CHRISTMAS, Clement Moore. Full text, and woodcuts from original 1848 book. Also critical, historical material. 19 illustrations. 40pp. 4⅝ × 6. 22797-9 Pa. $2.25

THE LESSON OF JAPANESE ARCHITECTURE: 165 Photographs, Jiro Harada. Memorable gallery of 165 photographs taken in the 1930's of exquisite Japanese homes of the well-to-do and historic buildings. 13 line diagrams. 192pp. 8⅜ × 11¼. 24778-3 Pa. $8.95

THE AUTOBIOGRAPHY OF CHARLES DARWIN AND SELECTED LETTERS, edited by Francis Darwin. The fascinating life of eccentric genius composed of an intimate memoir by Darwin (intended for his children); commentary by his son, Francis; hundreds of fragments from notebooks, journals, papers; and letters to and from Lyell, Hooker, Huxley, Wallace and Henslow. xi + 365pp. 5⅜ × 8. 20479-0 Pa. $5.95

WONDERS OF THE SKY: Observing Rainbows, Comets, Eclipses, the Stars and Other Phenomena, Fred Schaaf. Charming, easy-to-read poetic guide to all manner of celestial events visible to the naked eye. Mock suns, glories, Belt of Venus, more. Illustrated. 299pp. 5¼ × 8¼. 24402-4 Pa. $7.95

BURNHAM'S CELESTIAL HANDBOOK, Robert Burnham, Jr. Thorough guide to the stars beyond our solar system. Exhaustive treatment. Alphabetical by constellation: Andromeda to Cetus in Vol. 1; Chamaeleon to Orion in Vol. 2; and Pavo to Vulpecula in Vol. 3. Hundreds of illustrations. Index in Vol. 3. 2,000pp. 6⅛ × 9¼. 23567-X, 23568-8, 23673-0 Pa., Three-vol. set $36.85

STAR NAMES: Their Lore and Meaning, Richard Hinckley Allen. Fascinating history of names various cultures have given to constellations and literary and folkloristic uses that have been made of stars. Indexes to subjects. Arabic and Greek names. Biblical references. Bibliography. 563pp. 5⅜ × 8½. 21079-0 Pa. $7.95

THIRTY YEARS THAT SHOOK PHYSICS: The Story of Quantum Theory, George Gamow. Lucid, accessible introduction to influential theory of energy and matter. Careful explanations of Dirac's anti-particles, Bohr's model of the atom, much more. 12 plates. Numerous drawings. 240pp. 5⅜ × 8½. 24895-X Pa. $4.95

CHINESE DOMESTIC FURNITURE IN PHOTOGRAPHS AND MEASURED DRAWINGS, Gustav Ecke. A rare volume, now affordably priced for antique collectors, furniture buffs and art historians. Detailed review of styles ranging from early Shang to late Ming. Unabridged republication. 161 black-and-white drawings, photos. Total of 224pp. 8⅜ × 11¼. (Available in U.S. only) 25171-3 Pa. $12.95

VINCENT VAN GOGH: A Biography, Julius Meier-Graefe. Dynamic, penetrating study of artist's life, relationship with brother, Theo, painting techniques, travels, more. Readable, engrossing. 160pp. 5⅜ × 8½. (Available in U.S. only) 25253-1 Pa. $3.95

HOW TO WRITE, Gertrude Stein. Gertrude Stein claimed anyone could understand her unconventional writing—here are clues to help. Fascinating improvisations, language experiments, explanations illuminate Stein's craft and the art of writing. Total of 414pp. 4⅝ × 6⅜. 23144-5 Pa. $5.95

ADVENTURES AT SEA IN THE GREAT AGE OF SAIL: Five Firsthand Narratives, edited by Elliot Snow. Rare true accounts of exploration, whaling, shipwreck, fierce natives, trade, shipboard life, more. 33 illustrations. Introduction. 353pp. 5⅜ × 8½. 25177-2 Pa. $7.95

THE HERBAL OR GENERAL HISTORY OF PLANTS, John Gerard. Classic descriptions of about 2,850 plants—with over 2,700 illustrations—includes Latin and English names, physical descriptions, varieties, time and place of growth, more. 2,706 illustrations. xlv + 1,678pp. 8½ × 12¼. 23147-X Cloth. $75.00

DOROTHY AND THE WIZARD IN OZ, L. Frank Baum. Dorothy and the Wizard visit the center of the Earth, where people are vegetables, glass houses grow and Oz characters reappear. Classic sequel to *Wizard of Oz*. 256pp. 5⅜ × 8.
24714-7 Pa. $4.95

SONGS OF EXPERIENCE: Facsimile Reproduction with 26 Plates in Full Color, William Blake. This facsimile of Blake's original "Illuminated Book" reproduces 26 full-color plates from a rare 1826 edition. Includes "The Tyger," "London," "Holy Thursday," and other immortal poems. 26 color plates. Printed text of poems. 48pp. 5¼ × 7. 24636-1 Pa. $3.50

SONGS OF INNOCENCE, William Blake. The first and most popular of Blake's famous "Illuminated Books," in a facsimile edition reproducing all 31 brightly colored plates. Additional printed text of each poem. 64pp. 5¼ × 7.
22764-2 Pa. $3.50

PRECIOUS STONES, Max Bauer. Classic, thorough study of diamonds, rubies, emeralds, garnets, etc.: physical character, occurrence, properties, use, similar topics. 20 plates, 8 in color. 94 figures. 659pp. 6⅛ × 9¼.
21910-0, 21911-9 Pa., Two-vol. set $14.90

ENCYCLOPEDIA OF VICTORIAN NEEDLEWORK, S. F. A. Caulfeild and Blanche Saward. Full, precise descriptions of stitches, techniques for dozens of needlecrafts—most exhaustive reference of its kind. Over 800 figures. Total of 679pp. 8⅛ × 11. Two volumes. Vol. 1 22800-2 Pa. $10.95
Vol. 2 22801-0 Pa. $10.95

THE MARVELOUS LAND OF OZ, L. Frank Baum. Second Oz book, the Scarecrow and Tin Woodman are back with hero named Tip, Oz magic. 136 illustrations. 287pp. 5⅜ × 8½. 20692-0 Pa. $5.95

WILD FOWL DECOYS, Joel Barber. Basic book on the subject, by foremost authority and collector. Reveals history of decoy making and rigging, place in American culture, different kinds of decoys, how to make them, and how to use them. 140 plates. 156pp. 7⅞ × 10¾. 20011-6 Pa. $7.95

HISTORY OF LACE, Mrs. Bury Palliser. Definitive, profusely illustrated chronicle of lace from earliest times to late 19th century. Laces of Italy, Greece, England, France, Belgium, etc. Landmark of needlework scholarship. 266 illustrations. 672pp. 6⅛ × 9¼. 24742-2 Pa. $14.95

ILLUSTRATED GUIDE TO SHAKER FURNITURE, Robert Meader. All furniture and appurtenances, with much on unknown local styles. 235 photos. 146pp. 9 × 12.   22819-3 Pa. $7.95

WHALE SHIPS AND WHALING: A Pictorial Survey, George Francis Dow. Over 200 vintage engravings, drawings, photographs of barks, brigs, cutters, other vessels. Also harpoons, lances, whaling guns, many other artifacts. Comprehensive text by foremost authority. 207 black-and-white illustrations. 288pp. 6 × 9.
24808-9 Pa. $8.95

THE BERTRAMS, Anthony Trollope. Powerful portrayal of blind self-will and thwarted ambition includes one of Trollope's most heartrending love stories. 497pp. 5⅜ × 8½.   25119-5 Pa. $8.95

ADVENTURES WITH A HAND LENS, Richard Headstrom. Clearly written guide to observing and studying flowers and grasses, fish scales, moth and insect wings, egg cases, buds, feathers, seeds, leaf scars, moss, molds, ferns, common crystals, etc.—all with an ordinary, inexpensive magnifying glass. 209 exact line drawings aid in your discoveries. 220pp. 5⅜ × 8½.   23330-8 Pa. $3.95

RODIN ON ART AND ARTISTS, Auguste Rodin. Great sculptor's candid, wide-ranging comments on meaning of art; great artists; relation of sculpture to poetry, painting, music; philosophy of life, more. 76 superb black-and-white illustrations of Rodin's sculpture, drawings and prints. 119pp. 8⅜ × 11¼.   24487-3 Pa. $6.95

FIFTY CLASSIC FRENCH FILMS, 1912–1982: A Pictorial Record, Anthony Slide. Memorable stills from Grand Illusion, Beauty and the Beast, Hiroshima, Mon Amour, many more. Credits, plot synopses, reviews, etc. 160pp. 8¼ × 11.
25256-6 Pa. $11.95

THE PRINCIPLES OF PSYCHOLOGY, William James. Famous long course complete, unabridged. Stream of thought, time perception, memory, experimental methods; great work decades ahead of its time. 94 figures. 1,391pp. 5⅜ × 8½.
20381-6, 20382-4 Pa., Two-vol. set $19.90

BODIES IN A BOOKSHOP, R. T. Campbell. Challenging mystery of blackmail and murder with ingenious plot and superbly drawn characters. In the best tradition of British suspense fiction. 192pp. 5⅜ × 8½.   24720-1 Pa. $3.95

CALLAS: PORTRAIT OF A PRIMA DONNA, George Jellinek. Renowned commentator on the musical scene chronicles incredible career and life of the most controversial, fascinating, influential operatic personality of our time. 64 black-and-white photographs. 416pp. 5⅜ × 8¼.   25047-4 Pa. $7.95

GEOMETRY, RELATIVITY AND THE FOURTH DIMENSION, Rudolph Rucker. Exposition of fourth dimension, concepts of relativity as Flatland characters continue adventures. Popular, easily followed yet accurate, profound. 141 illustrations. 133pp. 5⅜ × 8½.   23400-2 Pa. $3.50

HOUSEHOLD STORIES BY THE BROTHERS GRIMM, with pictures by Walter Crane. 53 classic stories—Rumpelstiltskin, Rapunzel, Hansel and Gretel, the Fisherman and his Wife, Snow White, Tom Thumb, Sleeping Beauty, Cinderella, and so much more—lavishly illustrated with original 19th century drawings. 114 illustrations. x + 269pp. 5⅜ × 8½.   21080-4 Pa. $4.50

SUNDIALS, Albert Waugh. Far and away the best, most thorough coverage of ideas, mathematics concerned, types, construction, adjusting anywhere. Over 100 illustrations. 230pp. 5⅜ × 8½. 22947-5 Pa. $4.00

PICTURE HISTORY OF THE NORMANDIE: With 190 Illustrations, Frank O. Braynard. Full story of legendary French ocean liner: Art Deco interiors, design innovations, furnishings, celebrities, maiden voyage, tragic fire, much more. Extensive text. 144pp. 8⅜ × 11¾. 25257-4 Pa. $9.95

THE FIRST AMERICAN COOKBOOK: A Facsimile of "American Cookery," 1796, Amelia Simmons. Facsimile of the first American-written cookbook published in the United States contains authentic recipes for colonial favorites— pumpkin pudding, winter squash pudding, spruce beer, Indian slapjacks, and more. Introductory Essay and Glossary of colonial cooking terms. 80pp. 5⅜ × 8½. 24710-4 Pa. $3.50

101 PUZZLES IN THOUGHT AND LOGIC, C. R. Wylie, Jr. Solve murders and robberies, find out which fishermen are liars, how a blind man could possibly identify a color—purely by your own reasoning! 107pp. 5⅜ × 8½. 20367-0 Pa. $2.00

THE BOOK OF WORLD-FAMOUS MUSIC—CLASSICAL, POPULAR AND FOLK, James J. Fuld. Revised and enlarged republication of landmark work in musico-bibliography. Full information about nearly 1,000 songs and compositions including first lines of music and lyrics. New supplement. Index. 800pp. 5⅜ × 8¼. 24857-7 Pa. $14.95

ANTHROPOLOGY AND MODERN LIFE, Franz Boas. Great anthropologist's classic treatise on race and culture. Introduction by Ruth Bunzel. Only inexpensive paperback edition. 255pp. 5⅜ × 8½. 25245-0 Pa. $5.95

THE TALE OF PETER RABBIT, Beatrix Potter. The inimitable Peter's terrifying adventure in Mr. McGregor's garden, with all 27 wonderful, full-color Potter illustrations. 55pp. 4¼ × 5½. (Available in U.S. only) 22827-4 Pa. $1.75

THREE PROPHETIC SCIENCE FICTION NOVELS, H. G. Wells. *When the Sleeper Wakes, A Story of the Days to Come* and *The Time Machine* (full version). 335pp. 5⅜ × 8½. (Available in U.S. only) 20605-X Pa. $5.95

APICIUS COOKERY AND DINING IN IMPERIAL ROME, edited and translated by Joseph Dommers Vehling. Oldest known cookbook in existence offers readers a clear picture of what foods Romans ate, how they prepared them, etc. 49 illustrations. 301pp. 6⅛ × 9¼. 23563-7 Pa. $6.00

SHAKESPEARE LEXICON AND QUOTATION DICTIONARY, Alexander Schmidt. Full definitions, locations, shades of meaning of every word in plays and poems. More than 50,000 exact quotations. 1,485pp. 6½ × 9¼. 22726-X, 22727-8 Pa., Two-vol. set $27.90

THE WORLD'S GREAT SPEECHES, edited by Lewis Copeland and Lawrence W. Lamm. Vast collection of 278 speeches from Greeks to 1970. Powerful and effective models; unique look at history. 842pp. 5⅜ × 8½. 20468-5 Pa. $10.95

THE BLUE FAIRY BOOK, Andrew Lang. The first, most famous collection, with many familiar tales: Little Red Riding Hood, Aladdin and the Wonderful Lamp, Puss in Boots, Sleeping Beauty, Hansel and Gretel, Rumpelstiltskin; 37 in all. 138 illustrations. 390pp. 5⅜ × 8½.   21437-0 Pa. $5.95

THE STORY OF THE CHAMPIONS OF THE ROUND TABLE, Howard Pyle. Sir Launcelot, Sir Tristram and Sir Percival in spirited adventures of love and triumph retold in Pyle's inimitable style. 50 drawings, 31 full-page. xviii + 329pp. 6½ × 9¼.   21883-X Pa. $6.95

AUDUBON AND HIS JOURNALS, Maria Audubon. Unmatched two-volume portrait of the great artist, naturalist and author contains his journals, an excellent biography by his granddaughter, expert annotations by the noted ornithologist, Dr. Elliott Coues, and 37 superb illustrations. Total of 1,200pp. 5⅜ × 8.
Vol. I 25143-8 Pa. $8.95
Vol. II 25144-6 Pa. $8.95

GREAT DINOSAUR HUNTERS AND THEIR DISCOVERIES, Edwin H. Colbert. Fascinating, lavishly illustrated chronicle of dinosaur research, 1820's to 1960. Achievements of Cope, Marsh, Brown, Buckland, Mantell, Huxley, many others. 384pp. 5¼ × 8¼.   24701-5 Pa. $6.95

THE TASTEMAKERS, Russell Lynes. Informal, illustrated social history of American taste 1850's–1950's. First popularized categories Highbrow, Lowbrow, Middlebrow. 129 illustrations. New (1979) afterword. 384pp. 6 × 9.
23993-4 Pa. $6.95

DOUBLE CROSS PURPOSES, Ronald A. Knox. A treasure hunt in the Scottish Highlands, an old map, unidentified corpse, surprise discoveries keep reader guessing in this cleverly intricate tale of financial skullduggery. 2 black-and-white maps. 320pp. 5⅜ × 8½. (Available in U.S. only)   25032-6 Pa. $5.95

AUTHENTIC VICTORIAN DECORATION AND ORNAMENTATION IN FULL COLOR: 46 Plates from "Studies in Design," Christopher Dresser. Superb full-color lithographs reproduced from rare original portfolio of a major Victorian designer. 48pp. 9¼ × 12¼.   25083-0 Pa. $7.95

PRIMITIVE ART, Franz Boas. Remains the best text ever prepared on subject, thoroughly discussing Indian, African, Asian, Australian, and, especially, Northern American primitive art. Over 950 illustrations show ceramics, masks, totem poles, weapons, textiles, paintings, much more. 376pp. 5⅜ × 8.   20025-6 Pa. $6.95

SIDELIGHTS ON RELATIVITY, Albert Einstein. Unabridged republication of two lectures delivered by the great physicist in 1920–21. *Ether and Relativity* and *Geometry and Experience.* Elegant ideas in non-mathematical form, accessible to intelligent layman. vi + 56pp. 5⅜ × 8½.   24511-X Pa. $2.95

THE WIT AND HUMOR OF OSCAR WILDE, edited by Alvin Redman. More than 1,000 ripostes, paradoxes, wisecracks: Work is the curse of the drinking classes, I can resist everything except temptation, etc. 258pp. 5⅜ × 8½.   20602-5 Pa. $3.95

ADVENTURES WITH A MICROSCOPE, Richard Headstrom. 59 adventures with clothing fibers, protozoa, ferns and lichens, roots and leaves, much more. 142 illustrations. 232pp. 5⅜ × 8½.   23471-1 Pa. $3.95

PLANTS OF THE BIBLE, Harold N. Moldenke and Alma L. Moldenke. Standard reference to all 230 plants mentioned in Scriptures. Latin name, biblical reference, uses, modern identity, much more. Unsurpassed encyclopedic resource for scholars, botanists, nature lovers, students of Bible. Bibliography. Indexes. 123 black-and-white illustrations. 384pp. 6 × 9. 25069-5 Pa. $8.95

FAMOUS AMERICAN WOMEN: A Biographical Dictionary from Colonial Times to the Present, Robert McHenry, ed. From Pocahontas to Rosa Parks, 1,035 distinguished American women documented in separate biographical entries. Accurate, up-to-date data, numerous categories, spans 400 years. Indices. 493pp. 6½ × 9¼. 24523-3 Pa. $9.95

THE FABULOUS INTERIORS OF THE GREAT OCEAN LINERS IN HISTORIC PHOTOGRAPHS, William H. Miller, Jr. Some 200 superb photographs capture exquisite interiors of world's great "floating palaces"—1890's to 1980's: *Titanic, Ile de France, Queen Elizabeth, United States, Europa,* more. Approx. 200 black-and-white photographs. Captions. Text. Introduction. 160pp. 8⅞ × 11¾. 24756-2 Pa. $9.95

THE GREAT LUXURY LINERS, 1927–1954: A Photographic Record, William H. Miller, Jr. Nostalgic tribute to heyday of ocean liners. 186 photos of Ile de France, Normandie, Leviathan, Queen Elizabeth, United States, many others. Interior and exterior views. Introduction. Captions. 160pp. 9 × 12. 24056-8 Pa. $9.95

A NATURAL HISTORY OF THE DUCKS, John Charles Phillips. Great landmark of ornithology offers complete detailed coverage of nearly 200 species and subspecies of ducks: gadwall, sheldrake, merganser, pintail, many more. 74 full-color plates, 102 black-and-white. Bibliography. Total of 1,920pp. 8⅝ × 11¼. 25141-1, 25142-X Cloth. Two-vol. set $100.00

THE SEAWEED HANDBOOK: An Illustrated Guide to Seaweeds from North Carolina to Canada, Thomas F. Lee. Concise reference covers 78 species. Scientific and common names, habitat, distribution, more. Finding keys for easy identification. 224pp. 5⅜ × 8½. 25215-9 Pa. $5.95

THE TEN BOOKS OF ARCHITECTURE: The 1755 Leoni Edition, Leon Battista Alberti. Rare classic helped introduce the glories of ancient architecture to the Renaissance. 68 black-and-white plates. 336pp. 8⅜ × 11¼. 25239-6 Pa. $14.95

MISS MACKENZIE, Anthony Trollope. Minor masterpieces by Victorian master unmasks many truths about life in 19th-century England. First inexpensive edition in years. 392pp. 5⅜ × 8½. 25201-9 Pa. $7.95

THE RIME OF THE ANCIENT MARINER, Gustave Doré, Samuel Taylor Coleridge. Dramatic engravings considered by many to be his greatest work. The terrifying space of the open sea, the storms and whirlpools of an unknown ocean, the ice of Antarctica, more—all rendered in a powerful, chilling manner. Full text. 38 plates. 77pp. 9¼ × 12. 22305-1 Pa. $4.95

THE EXPEDITIONS OF ZEBULON MONTGOMERY PIKE, Zebulon Montgomery Pike. Fascinating first-hand accounts (1805–6) of exploration of Mississippi River, Indian wars, capture by Spanish dragoons, much more. 1,088pp. 5⅜ × 8½. 25254-X, 25255-8 Pa. Two-vol. set $23.90

CATALOG OF DOVER BOOKS

A CONCISE HISTORY OF PHOTOGRAPHY: Third Revised Edition, Helmut Gernsheim. Best one-volume history—camera obscura, photochemistry, daguerreotypes, evolution of cameras, film, more. Also artistic aspects—landscape, portraits, fine art, etc. 281 black-and-white photographs. 26 in color. 176pp. 8⅜ × 11¼. 25128-4 Pa. $12.95

THE DORÉ BIBLE ILLUSTRATIONS, Gustave Doré. 241 detailed plates from the Bible: the Creation scenes, Adam and Eve, Flood, Babylon, battle sequences, life of Jesus, etc. Each plate is accompanied by the verses from the King James version of the Bible. 241pp. 9 × 12. 23004-X Pa. $8.95

HUGGER-MUGGER IN THE LOUVRE, Elliot Paul. Second Homer Evans mystery-comedy. Theft at the Louvre involves sleuth in hilarious, madcap caper. "A knockout."—Books. 336pp. 5⅜ × 8½. 25185-3 Pa. $5.95

FLATLAND, E. A. Abbott. Intriguing and enormously popular science-fiction classic explores the complexities of trying to survive as a two-dimensional being in a three-dimensional world. Amusingly illustrated by the author. 16 illustrations. 103pp. 5⅜ × 8½. 20001-9 Pa. $2.00

THE HISTORY OF THE LEWIS AND CLARK EXPEDITION, Meriwether Lewis and William Clark, edited by Elliott Coues. Classic edition of Lewis and Clark's day-by-day journals that later became the basis for U.S. claims to Oregon and the West. Accurate and invaluable geographical, botanical, biological, meteorological and anthropological material. Total of 1,508pp. 5⅜ × 8½.
21268-8, 21269-6, 21270-X Pa. Three-vol. set $25.50

LANGUAGE, TRUTH AND LOGIC, Alfred J. Ayer. Famous, clear introduction to Vienna, Cambridge schools of Logical Positivism. Role of philosophy, elimination of metaphysics, nature of analysis, etc. 160pp. 5⅜ × 8½. (Available in U.S. and Canada only) 20010-8 Pa. $2.95

MATHEMATICS FOR THE NONMATHEMATICIAN, Morris Kline. Detailed, college-level treatment of mathematics in cultural and historical context, with numerous exercises. For liberal arts students. Preface. Recommended Reading Lists. Tables. Index. Numerous black-and-white figures. xvi + 641pp. 5⅜ × 8½.
24823-2 Pa. $11.95

28 SCIENCE FICTION STORIES, H. G. Wells. Novels, *Star Begotten* and *Men Like Gods,* plus 26 short stories: "Empire of the Ants," "A Story of the Stone Age," "The Stolen Bacillus," "In the Abyss," etc. 915pp. 5⅜ × 8½. (Available in U.S. only)
20265-8 Cloth. $10.95

HANDBOOK OF PICTORIAL SYMBOLS, Rudolph Modley. 3,250 signs and symbols, many systems in full; official or heavy commercial use. Arranged by subject. Most in Pictorial Archive series. 143pp. 8⅛ × 11. 23357-X Pa. $5.95

INCIDENTS OF TRAVEL IN YUCATAN, John L. Stephens. Classic (1843) exploration of jungles of Yucatan, looking for evidences of Maya civilization. Travel adventures, Mexican and Indian culture, etc. Total of 669pp. 5⅜ × 8½.
20926-1, 20927-X Pa., Two-vol. set $9.90

DEGAS: An Intimate Portrait, Ambroise Vollard. Charming, anecdotal memoir by famous art dealer of one of the greatest 19th-century French painters. 14 black-and-white illustrations. Introduction by Harold L. Van Doren. 96pp. 5⅜ × 8½.
25131-4 Pa. $3.95

PERSONAL NARRATIVE OF A PILGRIMAGE TO ALMANDINAH AND MECCAH, Richard Burton. Great travel classic by remarkably colorful personality. Burton, disguised as a Moroccan, visited sacred shrines of Islam, narrowly escaping death. 47 illustrations. 959pp. 5⅜ × 8½. 21217-3, 21218-1 Pa., Two-vol. set $17.90

PHRASE AND WORD ORIGINS, A. H. Holt. Entertaining, reliable, modern study of more than 1,200 colorful words, phrases, origins and histories. Much unexpected information. 254pp. 5⅜ × 8½. 20758-7 Pa. $4.95

THE RED THUMB MARK, R. Austin Freeman. In this first Dr. Thorndyke case, the great scientific detective draws fascinating conclusions from the nature of a single fingerprint. Exciting story, authentic science. 320pp. 5⅜ × 8½. (Available in U.S. only)
25210-8 Pa. $5.95

AN EGYPTIAN HIEROGLYPHIC DICTIONARY, E. A. Wallis Budge. Monumental work containing about 25,000 words or terms that occur in texts ranging from 3000 B.C. to 600 A.D. Each entry consists of a transliteration of the word, the word in hieroglyphs, and the meaning in English. 1,314pp. 6⅜ × 10.
23615-3, 23616-1 Pa., Two-vol. set $27.90

THE COMPLEAT STRATEGYST: Being a Primer on the Theory of Games of Strategy, J. D. Williams. Highly entertaining classic describes, with many illustrated examples, how to select best strategies in conflict situations. Prefaces. Appendices. xvi + 268pp. 5⅜ × 8½. 25101-2 Pa. $5.95

THE ROAD TO OZ, L. Frank Baum. Dorothy meets the Shaggy Man, little Button-Bright and the Rainbow's beautiful daughter in this delightful trip to the magical Land of Oz. 272pp. 5⅜ × 8. 25208-6 Pa. $4.95

POINT AND LINE TO PLANE, Wassily Kandinsky. Seminal exposition of role of point, line, other elements in non-objective painting. Essential to understanding 20th-century art. 127 illustrations. 192pp. 6½ × 9¼. 23808-3 Pa. $4.50

LADY ANNA, Anthony Trollope. Moving chronicle of Countess Lovel's bitter struggle to win for herself and daughter Anna their rightful rank and fortune—perhaps at cost of sanity itself. 384pp. 5⅜ × 8½. 24669-8 Pa. $6.95

EGYPTIAN MAGIC, E. A. Wallis Budge. Sums up all that is known about magic in Ancient Egypt: the role of magic in controlling the gods, powerful amulets that warded off evil spirits, scarabs of immortality, use of wax images, formulas and spells, the secret name, much more. 253pp. 5⅜ × 8½. 22681-6 Pa. $4.00

THE DANCE OF SIVA, Ananda Coomaraswamy. Preeminent authority unfolds the vast metaphysic of India: the revelation of her art, conception of the universe, social organization, etc. 27 reproductions of art masterpieces. 192pp. 5⅜ × 8½.
24817-8 Pa. $5.95

CHRISTMAS CUSTOMS AND TRADITIONS, Clement A. Miles. Origin, evolution, significance of religious, secular practices. Caroling, gifts, yule logs, much more. Full, scholarly yet fascinating; non-sectarian. 400pp. 5⅜ × 8½.
23354-5 Pa. $6.50

THE HUMAN FIGURE IN MOTION, Eadweard Muybridge. More than 4,500 stopped-action photos, in action series, showing undraped men, women, children jumping, lying down, throwing, sitting, wrestling, carrying, etc. 390pp. 7⅞ × 10⅝.
20204-6 Cloth. $19.95

THE MAN WHO WAS THURSDAY, Gilbert Keith Chesterton. Witty, fast-paced novel about a club of anarchists in turn-of-the-century London. Brilliant social, religious, philosophical speculations. 128pp. 5⅜ × 8½. 25121-7 Pa. $3.95

A CEZANNE SKETCHBOOK: Figures, Portraits, Landscapes and Still Lifes, Paul Cezanne. Great artist experiments with tonal effects, light, mass, other qualities in over 100 drawings. A revealing view of developing master painter, precursor of Cubism. 102 black-and-white illustrations. 144pp. 8¾ × 6⅜. 24790-2 Pa. $5.95

AN ENCYCLOPEDIA OF BATTLES: Accounts of Over 1,560 Battles from 1479 B.C. to the Present, David Eggenberger. Presents essential details of every major battle in recorded history, from the first battle of Megiddo in 1479 B.C. to Grenada in 1984. List of Battle Maps. New Appendix covering the years 1967–1984. Index. 99 illustrations. 544pp. 6½ × 9¼. 24913-1 Pa. $14.95

AN ETYMOLOGICAL DICTIONARY OF MODERN ENGLISH, Ernest Weekley. Richest, fullest work, by foremost British lexicographer. Detailed word histories. Inexhaustible. Total of 856pp. 6½ × 9¼.
21873-2, 21874-0 Pa., Two-vol. set $17.00

WEBSTER'S AMERICAN MILITARY BIOGRAPHIES, edited by Robert McHenry. Over 1,000 figures who shaped 3 centuries of American military history. Detailed biographies of Nathan Hale, Douglas MacArthur, Mary Hallaren, others. Chronologies of engagements, more. Introduction. Addenda. 1,033 entries in alphabetical order. xi + 548pp. 6½ × 9¼. (Available in U.S. only)
24758-9 Pa. $11.95

LIFE IN ANCIENT EGYPT, Adolf Erman. Detailed older account, with much not in more recent books: domestic life, religion, magic, medicine, commerce, and whatever else needed for complete picture. Many illustrations. 597pp. 5⅜ × 8½.
22632-8 Pa. $8.50

HISTORIC COSTUME IN PICTURES, Braun & Schneider. Over 1,450 costumed figures shown, covering a wide variety of peoples: kings, emperors, nobles, priests, servants, soldiers, scholars, townsfolk, peasants, merchants, courtiers, cavaliers, and more. 256pp. 8⅜ × 11¼. 23150-X Pa. $7.95

THE NOTEBOOKS OF LEONARDO DA VINCI, edited by J. P. Richter. Extracts from manuscripts reveal great genius; on painting, sculpture, anatomy, sciences, geography, etc. Both Italian and English. 186 ms. pages reproduced, plus 500 additional drawings, including studies for *Last Supper, Sforza* monument, etc. 860pp. 7⅞ × 10¾. (Available in U.S. only) 22572-0, 22573-9 Pa., Two-vol. set $25.90

THE ART NOUVEAU STYLE BOOK OF ALPHONSE MUCHA: All 72 Plates from "Documents Decoratifs" in Original Color, Alphonse Mucha. Rare copyright-free design portfolio by high priest of Art Nouveau. Jewelry, wallpaper, stained glass, furniture, figure studies, plant and animal motifs, etc. Only complete one-volume edition. 80pp. 9⅜ × 12¼. 24044-4 Pa. $8.95

ANIMALS: 1,419 COPYRIGHT-FREE ILLUSTRATIONS OF MAMMALS, BIRDS, FISH, INSECTS, ETC., edited by Jim Harter. Clear wood engravings present, in extremely lifelike poses, over 1,000 species of animals. One of the most extensive pictorial sourcebooks of its kind. Captions. Index. 284pp. 9 × 12. 23766-4 Pa. $9.95

OBELISTS FLY HIGH, C. Daly King. Masterpiece of American detective fiction, long out of print, involves murder on a 1935 transcontinental flight—"a very thrilling story"—NY Times. Unabridged and unaltered republication of the edition published by William Collins Sons & Co. Ltd., London, 1935. 288pp. 5⅜ × 8½. (Available in U.S. only) 25036-9 Pa. $4.95

VICTORIAN AND EDWARDIAN FASHION: A Photographic Survey, Alison Gernsheim. First fashion history completely illustrated by contemporary photographs. Full text plus 235 photos, 1840-1914, in which many celebrities appear. 240pp. 6½ × 9¼. 24205-6 Pa. $6.00

THE ART OF THE FRENCH ILLUSTRATED BOOK, 1700-1914, Gordon N. Ray. Over 630 superb book illustrations by Fragonard, Delacroix, Daumier, Doré, Grandville, Manet, Mucha, Steinlen, Toulouse-Lautrec and many others. Preface. Introduction. 633 halftones. Indices of artists, authors & titles, binders and provenances. Appendices. Bibliography. 608pp. 8⅜ × 11¼. 25086-5 Pa. $24.95

THE WONDERFUL WIZARD OF OZ, L. Frank Baum. Facsimile in full color of America's finest children's classic. 143 illustrations by W. W. Denslow. 267pp. 5⅜ × 8½. 20691-2 Pa. $5.95

FRONTIERS OF MODERN PHYSICS: New Perspectives on Cosmology, Relativity, Black Holes and Extraterrestrial Intelligence, Tony Rothman, et al. For the intelligent layman. Subjects include: cosmological models of the universe; black holes; the neutrino; the search for extraterrestrial intelligence. Introduction. 46 black-and-white illustrations. 192pp. 5⅜ × 8½. 24587-X Pa. $6.95

THE FRIENDLY STARS, Martha Evans Martin & Donald Howard Menzel. Classic text marshalls the stars together in an engaging, non-technical survey, presenting them as sources of beauty in night sky. 23 illustrations. Foreword. 2 star charts. Index. 147pp. 5⅜ × 8½. 21099-5 Pa. $3.50

FADS AND FALLACIES IN THE NAME OF SCIENCE, Martin Gardner. Fair, witty appraisal of cranks, quacks, and quackeries of science and pseudoscience: hollow earth, Velikovsky, orgone energy, Dianetics, flying saucers, Bridey Murphy, food and medical fads, etc. Revised, expanded In the Name of Science. "A very able and even-tempered presentation."—The New Yorker. 363pp. 5⅜ × 8. 20394-8 Pa. $5.95

ANCIENT EGYPT: ITS CULTURE AND HISTORY, J. E Manchip White. From pre-dynastics through Ptolemies: society, history, political structure, religion, daily life, literature, cultural heritage. 48 plates. 217pp. 5⅜ × 8½. 22548-8 Pa. $4.95

SIR HARRY HOTSPUR OF HUMBLETHWAITE, Anthony Trollope. Incisive, unconventional psychological study of a conflict between a wealthy baronet, his idealistic daughter, and their scapegrace cousin. The 1870 novel in its first inexpensive edition in years. 250pp. 5⅜ × 8½.   24953-0 Pa. $4.95

LASERS AND HOLOGRAPHY, Winston E. Kock. Sound introduction to burgeoning field, expanded (1981) for second edition. Wave patterns, coherence, lasers, diffraction, zone plates, properties of holograms, recent advances. 84 illustrations. 160pp. 5⅜ × 8¼. (Except in United Kingdom)   24041-X Pa. $3.50

INTRODUCTION TO ARTIFICIAL INTELLIGENCE: SECOND, EN-LARGED EDITION, Philip C. Jackson, Jr. Comprehensive survey of artificial intelligence—the study of how machines (computers) can be made to act intelligently. Includes introductory and advanced material. Extensive notes updating the main text. 132 black-and-white illustrations. 512pp. 5⅜ × 8½.   24864-X Pa. $8.95

HISTORY OF INDIAN AND INDONESIAN ART, Ananda K. Coomaraswamy. Over 400 illustrations illuminate classic study of Indian art from earliest Harappa finds to early 20th century. Provides philosophical, religious and social insights. 304pp. 6⅜ × 9⅜.   25005-9 Pa. $8.95

THE GOLEM, Gustav Meyrink. Most famous supernatural novel in modern European literature, set in Ghetto of Old Prague around 1890. Compelling story of mystical experiences, strange transformations, profound terror. 13 black-and-white illustrations. 224pp. 5⅜ × 8½. (Available in U.S. only)   25025-3 Pa. $5.95

ARMADALE, Wilkie Collins. Third great mystery novel by the author of *The Woman in White* and *The Moonstone*. Original magazine version with 40 illustrations. 597pp. 5⅜ × 8½.   23429-0 Pa. $7.95

PICTORIAL ENCYCLOPEDIA OF HISTORIC ARCHITECTURAL PLANS, DETAILS AND ELEMENTS: With 1,880 Line Drawings of Arches, Domes, Doorways, Facades, Gables, Windows, etc., John Theodore Haneman. Sourcebook of inspiration for architects, designers, others. Bibliography. Captions. 141pp. 9 × 12.   24605-1 Pa. $6.95

BENCHLEY LOST AND FOUND, Robert Benchley. Finest humor from early 30's, about pet peeves, child psychologists, post office and others. Mostly unavailable elsewhere. 73 illustrations by Peter Arno and others. 183pp. 5⅜ × 8½.
                                                      22410-4 Pa. $3.95

ERTÉ GRAPHICS, Erté. Collection of striking color graphics: *Seasons, Alphabet, Numerals, Aces* and *Precious Stones*. 50 plates, including 4 on covers. 48pp. 9⅜ × 12¼.   23580-7 Pa. $6.95

THE JOURNAL OF HENRY D. THOREAU, edited by Bradford Torrey, F. H. Allen. Complete reprinting of 14 volumes, 1837–61, over two million words; the sourcebooks for *Walden*, etc. Definitive. All original sketches, plus 75 photographs. 1,804pp. 8½ × 12¼.   20312-3, 20313-1 Cloth., Two-vol. set $80.00

CASTLES: THEIR CONSTRUCTION AND HISTORY, Sidney Toy. Traces castle development from ancient roots. Nearly 200 photographs and drawings illustrate moats, keeps, baileys, many other features. Caernarvon, Dover Castles, Hadrian's Wall, Tower of London, dozens more. 256pp. 5⅜ × 8¼.
                                                      24898-4 Pa. $5.95

AMERICAN CLIPPER SHIPS: 1833–1858, Octavius T. Howe & Frederick C. Matthews. Fully-illustrated, encyclopedic review of 352 clipper ships from the period of America's greatest maritime supremacy. Introduction. 109 halftones. 5 black-and-white line illustrations. Index. Total of 928pp. 5⅜ × 8½.
25115-2, 25116-0 Pa., Two-vol. set $17.90

TOWARDS A NEW ARCHITECTURE, Le Corbusier. Pioneering manifesto by great architect, near legendary founder of "International School." Technical and aesthetic theories, views on industry, economics, relation of form to function, "mass-production spirit," much more. Profusely illustrated. Unabridged translation of 13th French edition. Introduction by Frederick Etchells. 320pp. 6⅛ × 9¼. (Available in U.S. only)
25023-7 Pa. $8.95

THE BOOK OF KELLS, edited by Blanche Cirker. Inexpensive collection of 32 full-color, full-page plates from the greatest illuminated manuscript of the Middle Ages, painstakingly reproduced from rare facsimile edition. Publisher's Note. Captions. 32pp. 9⅜ × 12¼.
24345-1 Pa. $4.50

BEST SCIENCE FICTION STORIES OF H. G. WELLS, H. G. Wells. Full novel *The Invisible Man*, plus 17 short stories: "The Crystal Egg," "Aepyornis Island," "The Strange Orchid," etc. 303pp. 5⅜ × 8½. (Available in U.S. only)
21531-8 Pa. $4.95

AMERICAN SAILING SHIPS: Their Plans and History, Charles G. Davis. Photos, construction details of schooners, frigates, clippers, other sailcraft of 18th to early 20th centuries—plus entertaining discourse on design, rigging, nautical lore, much more. 137 black-and-white illustrations. 240pp. 6⅛ × 9¼.
24658-2 Pa. $5.95

ENTERTAINING MATHEMATICAL PUZZLES, Martin Gardner. Selection of author's favorite conundrums involving arithmetic, money, speed, etc., with lively commentary. Complete solutions. 112pp. 5⅜ × 8½.
25211-6 Pa. $2.95

THE WILL TO BELIEVE, HUMAN IMMORTALITY, William James. Two books bound together. Effect of irrational on logical, and arguments for human immortality. 402pp. 5⅜ × 8½.
20291-7 Pa. $7.50

THE HAUNTED MONASTERY and THE CHINESE MAZE MURDERS, Robert Van Gulik. 2 full novels by Van Gulik continue adventures of Judge Dee and his companions. An evil Taoist monastery, seemingly supernatural events; overgrown topiary maze that hides strange crimes. Set in 7th-century China. 27 illustrations. 328pp. 5⅜ × 8½.
23502-5 Pa. $5.00

CELEBRATED CASES OF JUDGE DEE (DEE GOONG AN), translated by Robert Van Gulik. Authentic 18th-century Chinese detective novel; Dee and associates solve three interlocked cases. Led to Van Gulik's own stories with same characters. Extensive introduction. 9 illustrations. 237pp. 5⅜ × 8½.
23337-5 Pa. $4.95

Prices subject to change without notice.

Available at your book dealer or write for free catalog to Dept. GI, Dover Publications, Inc., 31 East 2nd St., Mineola, N.Y. 11501. Dover publishes more than 175 books each year on science, elementary and advanced mathematics, biology, music, art, literary history, social sciences and other areas.